NEW AMERICA

D. Ann Kelley
James G. Kelley

Lypton Publishing

New America

This book is a work of fiction. All incidents and dialogue, and all characters, with the exception of some well known historical and public figures, are products of the authors' imaginations and are not to be thought of as real. Where real-life historical and public figures appear, the situations, incidents, and dialogues concerning those persons are entirely fictional and are not intended to describe actual events or to change the entirely fictional nature of the work. In all other respects, any resemblance to persons living or dead is entirely coincidental.

Although the location Drummond Island exists, this book is a complete work of fiction. Institutions, and organizations mentioned in this novel are either a product of the authors' imaginations, or if real, used fictitiously without any intent to describe actual content.

First Edition, May 2007
Copyright 2007 Lypton Publishing
Printed and bound in the United States of America.

Library of Congress Cataloging-in-Publication Data

Kelley, D. Ann & James G. Kelley
New America
1. Fiction 2. Mystery 3. Great Lakes 4. Jill Traynor

ISBN 978-0-9752780-3-1
LCCN 2006903529
SAN 256-0143

10 9 8 7 6 5 4 3 2 1

With All Our Love
this book is dedicated to
Lorna E. Kelley

Also by

D. Ann Kelley and James G. Kelley

Lighthouse Paradox

Legacy

Stowaway

Acknowledgements

Shikha Lopez, Guest Relations Officer for Celebrity Cruises answered questions concerning the world of cruising and cruise ships.

Ken Hayward provided information on the Grand Hotel and allowed us to use pictures of the Grand Hotel on our cover.

Mark Bak and Carrie Noren shared the scrapbook of Emma Johnson's cruise on the S.S. Noronic, and other historical information on the history of the Noronic including the fire of 1949.

Gwen Patterson and Pam Tessier, Research Coordinators of the Genealogy Research Center Penetanguishene Centennial Museum and Archives in Penetanguishene, Ontario.

Mickey Stadler and Derek White (both esteemed chefs).

Steve Walker aided with developing political content within the novel.

Terry Phipps Photography (terrywphipps@charter.net) provided pictures of the Grand Hotel for the cover.

Author and diver Patrick Folks of Tobermory, Canada helped in locating what is believed to be the Alice Hackett in Indian Harbor at Fitzwilliams (Horse) Island off the southeast corner of Manitoulin Island.

Bowling Green State University, Historical Collections of the Great Lakes, proved the Alice Hackett once sailed the Great Lakes, and specifically Robert Graham, the Archivist.

Melanie Cotter edited the novel with a keen eye and insightful feedback. Thanks.

Once again, Sue Kelley edited, advised, and offered her guidance at nearly every stage of the novel with unfailing grace and patience that only she could possess. Thank you.

Last but not least, to those that have written us from far off places as well as from close to home, to those who have walked into North Haven and visited us, or supported us at book signings, provided encouragement and asked when the next book will be done, we are deeply appreciative. We enjoy meeting you and sharing correspondence. Thank you for your continued support.

Prologue

May 3rd, 2007

4:08am

There are cities that never sleep; streets that know little peace. If anyone looked out a window or walked along the sidewalk of Dearborn Street at 4:08 AM, the morning of May 3rd, he might not know the difference, might not realize he was present the night a stone fell from the sky and caused an unbelievable ripple. And of course, there are those who could argue that the ripple began earlier.

It could have began in 1987 when a small child was saved from a plane crash, or 1949 when a fire burned fascinating directions for fate, or even earlier, in 1828 when a woman climbed a schooner's mast to save her daughter's life. Perhaps the ripple goes even further back, but like so much unwritten history it has been lost in the sands of time. It matters less when the ripple began, or which points were crucial to the unraveling of this web, than simply the fact that it happened, that there are forces at work fighting for the future and for their own evolution.

It isn't fitting to know why, precisely, a black van drove slowly tonight. What is more important is that the van never stopped as the side door slid open, as a long black clothed arm appeared in the shadows holding onto something that looked like a bowling ball. The ball sailed through air, touched down on the pavement and rolled until it came to a complete stop at the massive metal framed doors of 219 South Dearborn Street: a perfect strike. The van didn't wait to make sure the projectile had found its target; it rolled forward, the door slid closed and it was gone.

The "package" dripped as it flew through the air, smacked hard on the pavement and smeared as it rolled toward the doors, creating a sickly artistic pathway to the building that housed the Federal Bureau of Investigation. The severed head bled out and stained the concrete, the face of the victim almost unrecognizable as human.

*   *   *

Hour One

"Can anyone tell me how this happened?" The man in charge yelled as soon as he reached the third floor conference room of agents. His voice carried authority, but his face was pale, drawn together with worry and outrage. "I've got sicko's throwing heads at the damned building? Do we know what happened?"

"Sir, we believe we know what happened." Special Agent Seth Sampson, a man in his late forties, stood from his chair, and looked through some of his paperwork quickly to get his bearings. His sport coat was thrown off, tie loosened and sleeves rolled up. He took a long swig of coffee before he spoke. "The victim has been identified as Agent Mitch Lowell."

The room gained a peculiar silence. Those who had just been called in, who weren't aware of the details, felt the injustice as if they had each been personally wounded. When one of their own was taken down, it reminded them of their mortality, the less-than-superpower protection of their badges.

"I spoke with Agent Moroni, Lowell's partner. He's on holiday this week in California. His son's getting married."

"What are they working on?"

"They were tracking a long known assassin who recently blipped across O'Hare's security monitoring system's facial recognition program. There have been some bugs in the program, so by the time anyone realized the target should be held, she was gone. Lowell told Moroni last night that he had followed a thin lead but found an address that was somehow connected. Moroni told him not to go without back-up, but Lowell was a bit of a loner. Moroni didn't give him details, but he said..." He paused.

The leader urged him forward. "Sampson?"

"He said, 'They're going to ignite a war'."

"A bomb?"

"Moroni didn't think so. He did say that Lowell was edgy."

"How can we be sure that this is connected?"

"We can't be at this time. We're going to look at everything. It may have been personal. Old cases, someone in Lowell's life. It may be random--some group trying to make a statement to us. The head is being studied by our medical examiner. I have agents already gathering information downstairs."

"Put together as large of a team as you need. I want updates every thirty minutes. And move on the address. We don't know it's connected, but we do know

Lowell was disturbed about it."

"Yes, Sir."

"And bring Moroni back."

"His son's wedding, Sir?"

"Bring him back, Seth."

"Yes, Sir."

*　　*　　*　　*　　*

Hour Thirty-Seven

Sampson walked back into the main office, gripping a manila folder. He was waved into his superior's office without a word.

The leader stood hunched behind his desk, straightened when the other man walked in. "What do you have for me?"

"The place has obviously been scrubbed. I could smell bleach," Sampson commented.

"Bleach?"

"Yes. It struck me too, sir. It was extremely low tech, obvious even. Why use it, unless it was all they had there? Wiping the place down would have been as efficient. Yet, there was a strong odor throughout the house--the kind that comes from wiping walls with it. They didn't think everything through, though. The place was absolutely vacant. Not only did we find no usable prints, but there was very little in the way of furniture to leave prints on. The carpet was vacuumed with something commercial grade, and they took that.

"The apartment was clean, but I think we may

have caught a break." Sampson continued when his boss sat down and listened. "There was a small trash can in the hall outside the apartment. I looked inside for the contents and noticed a very faint odor of bleach again. By this point, I believed it was on me or in my nose somehow. I changed gloves and dumped the trash can onto a sheet of plastic. I looked at the items one by one. I picked up each piece of trash with tweezers and smelled it." His face reddened a bit. The current trend was to use more advanced technology for detecting, but he followed his instinct on this one. "I thought if it smelled like bleach, then it was probably put there by someone who cleaned the apartment."

"Go on."

"I came across these two pieces." Sampson opened the manila folder and laid out two small clear plastic evidence bags. The man leaned closer. One was a ticket stub with time and date on it, but he wasn't sure what the ticket pertained to. The second was a book of matches. Inside the cover appeared to be some scribbling.

"What is this?"

Sampson explained, "The book of matches came from a restaurant down on the pier. The ticket is from a ferris wheel ride in the same location. It took some digging to tie the ticket to the wheel, but we did. The date and time on the ticket is important, sir. At the time shown, the cruise ship *New America* was sitting at a dock visible from that location, being loaded for its maiden voyage on the Great Lakes. I went down, took a ride on the wheel myself to gain some perspective. It stopped me at the very top. From there I had a great view of the whole area."

Sampson's boss looked at him blankly. "You're

telling me that you think this cruise ship is being targeted, because on the day a ferris wheel took a ride, the boat was parked there? That is awfully damned thin."

"Anorexic, yes Sir."

"I don't understand what the cruise ship New America has to do with our dead agent?"

Sampson leaned over and pointed to the symbols on the book of matches. "These symbols... mean target in Korean. I think Lowell got onto these letters, WW. Moroni told me Lowell thought someone was starting a war. He must have gotten onto these letters some other way."

"What do they really mean?"

"Hold on. I'm getting to that. The is owned by the Magellan line. Magellan is owned by a group of Americans who have far right and protectionist views. They are old money, one language, one color, one church, one party sort of people... but I don't know why that would make them a target. That political slant isn't all that well known. It doesn't make sense for any Korean groups that I know of to get involved. Besides, I cannot see why the New America would be a target... but I believe that it is."

Sampson pulled one more item from his manila folder. He handed a brochure of the *New America* to his boss and flipped it over. On the reverse side was a list of summer special events and themed cruises. One event, more than the rest, jumped off the page. Campaign Launch Cruise: Candidate Wayne Walker & Party. August 10th-17th.

"Oh, shit."

Day Nine

"What is wrong with the Walker people?"

"The Walker campaign does not find this threat likely. There are many more public events, and if someone wanted to take him out, there are easier ways to do it than on board a ship," Sampson reported.

"You tried everything?"

"Sir, I used every logical and emotional appeal I could think of to sway Walker's team. They will not cancel this trip. They will update security, and they've got a plan for that, but they will not cancel. Apparently, the upper echelon of support--the Walker faithful--will be the only vacationers during the week. It's one massive floating fund raiser with stops at Great Lakes destinations along the way."

"What is your plan?"

"I think we should place an agent on board the ship."

"Are you serious?"

"Yes, Sir. Let me hand pick someone to go undercover. Protection and investigation. Let's keep it between us."

"You want me to send an undercover agent without anyone's knowledge."

"Sir, have you listened to any of the Walker speeches? He has some radical ideas. I think what has been made public so far is just the tip of this man's real message. We have no idea how far his connections spread, but I would take this threat seriously."

"Sampson, the truth is that we still can't connect Lowell's death directly to this apartment."

"We can connect the matchbook and the ticket stub to the apartment. Even if the people behind Lowell's death are unrelated, this is what he was working on. Don't we owe it to him to do everything possible to make sure this lead isn't for nothing?"

"No, we don't owe it to Lowell, Sampson. We owe it to Walker. It's possible that this man will be our next president. Even if he's not, he's still an American citizen who might be too stupid to protect himself. And in that case, it is our job. Put the agent in play, Sampson. Close the file on this. No one knows but us."

"Yes, Sir."

Chapter 1

August, 1987

Tina Schapetta glanced up from the tall, standard grey steel airport desk and grinned widely. "Sherri! I didn't know I was working with you tonight."

Sherri tugged on the tunic of her uniform and smiled. "You know me, always looking for an extra shift. No... actually, something just happened with Jon. I don't know why, but he wasn't able to fly, or he got pulled or something. Anyway, better news for you, since I actually pull my weight."

Tina laughed, enjoying the humor.

"Looks like it's going to be a long one, hey?" The flight attendant murmured between passengers.

Tina glanced out the window, squinting up at the sky. "And it's sprinkling. At least the weather will be nice in California."

"I know. But there's another whole flight between now and then."

"Excuse me, Miss?"

Tina glanced up and smiled warmly at the passenger. "How can I help you?"

"Hi. My husband and I are traveling with our daughter. We have three seats together, but I wondered if there might be an empty seat or two on board that we could sit near. This has been the longest week of my life, and my little girl is so tired. I would feel better if she could stretch out." The late twenties woman pointed toward a man who held a small brown haired child in his arms.

"I'm sorry. We're capped with this one... 143 passengers and the crew. In fact, there are a few people on stand-by who aren't going to make it onto the flight."

"Okay. Thanks anyway."

"Isn't she a cutie?" Tina mumbled after the woman had turned away. "Someday, I am going to have one of those."

Her co-worker giggled. "The man or the child?"

"Both," Tina said firmly.

"Alright, time to call the first class cabin."

"We're never going to leave on time."

"I know. I just hope we make up for it between Phoenix and Orange County. Rudy says there is one helluva shindig going on tonight, and since I have tomorrow morning off..."

Tina grinned. "I know what you mean." She picked up the phone and pressed in the code to link her to the local P.A. system. "Flight 357 with service to Phoenix, Arizona will now be boarding passengers in our first class cabin."

      *   *   *

"Mumma..." The four year old brunette's whimper was enough for her mother to unclasp her from the airplane seat and haul the child into her arms, defying regulations and the cheerful light beacon from

15

above their chairs reminding them to remain buckled.

"Laura, wait till after take-off. What kind of an example..."

The woman rolled her eyes at her husband and wrapped her arms around her daughter. The plane rumbled as it gathered speed, escalating to incline off the runway. The little girl smiled sleepily and rested her head on her mother's chest. "There now, baby girl. I love you," she whispered. "I've got her, Tom." As soon as she snapped, she felt bad. She smiled, apologizing with her eyes. "I'm sorry. For everything."

He sighed beside her. "I know."

The man leaned back against the force of the plane, finally rising off the tarmac, over twenty minutes behind schedule. He ruffled his daughter's hair and tried not to think, tried to calm his rattled nerves with her image. He hadn't closed his eyes for more than a second when they were startled open.

A passenger across the aisle shrieked as an ungodly roar came from the plane itself. The plane wobbled from side to side radically, groaning a bit as it clipped a telephone pole. Orange light beamed forward through the windows from the engines as the temperature rose and the fuel tanks erupted.

Passengers screamed as the belly of the plane skimmed the top of a building and then exploded as it slammed against the ground. Fire leapt through the cabin and into the sky.

*   *   *

In minutes, the intersection of Wick and Middlebelt was surrounded by ambulances and paramedics. The sirens overwhelmed the noise of the plane burning, but no one lost focus of the mission as firefighters wielded hoses over the wreckage.

Civilians cried, gawked and pointed from sidewalks--some tried to help but could do nothing as flames rolled upward into the sky, into black smoke met by the falling water of fire trucks.

A team of rescue workers moved in, hoping for some sign of survivors. "I can't even tell what part of the plane this is."

"Oh Jesus, there's an arm."

"Do you hear that?"

"What?"

"It sounds like... moaning." The man rushed forward. "I think I hear someone! I need those hoses over here. Bob!" He yelled. "We've got a survivor. Your hose!"

Hoses were redirected before the rescuers could get close enough to pull the woman from the debris. "She's stuck between these seats."

"Careful guys. Pull it back easy."

"Hold on. Guys, she's dead." The rescuer who announced this had a good look at her face and felt for a pulse.

"I can still hear..."

"There's a child! Pull her body back. There's a child underneath her."

They worked to separate the small moaning girl from the woman's body. "She's burned bad." The paramedics took over, carefully rushing the girl onto the gurney and into the ambulance. They worked on her carefully as she was transported to the hospital.

Those rescuers left behind continued searching for survivors for a long while, but none were found. The child was named the "Miracle Girl." Doctors later reasoned through the impossibilities of surviving the plane crash. She was found sandwiched between her mother's body and plane seat. Her body was utterly surrounded by layers of protection with her face pressed against her mother's abdomen. Debate existed for some time whether she was the product of complicated and fortunate circumstance, or if her mother's love saved her life.

Chapter 2

Early August, 2007: Monday Afternoon

"Tell me about the dreams."

Jill swallowed audibly, fidgeted in her chair. She gave herself a moment to look away to collect her thoughts. Through the open blinds, she watched cars roll by on Ashmun Street and a couple walked hand-in-hand down the sidewalk. Once they strolled out of view, she concentrated on the nearby plant perched on the window-sill. The green leaf petals were shiny, as if they'd recently been dusted. It was a different kind of cleanliness than Jill was used to lately, living with two men and a dog. She should be used to it by now, Jill thought. After all, it had been well over a year since Quinn, Chase and the golden retriever, Ridge had moved to her home on Cream City Point.

"Jill?" Dr. Letters prompted.

Jill folded her hands together in her lap and smiled sheepishly. "I'm sorry, Dr. Letters. I was thinking about how different life is today than it was a year ago."

She raised an eyebrow, allowing Jill to continue. "When Quinn brought me here that first time, I was so afraid of being left alone."

"You've made remarkable progress."

"I still don't feel like me. I feel like there's something missing inside," Jill admitted.

"Healing takes time. This isn't drive-thru therapy, Jill. In the last year, we've excavated your assault and torture, as well as your near death. There aren't many people who just wake from a coma and don't need to process what has happened to them."

Jill nodded, feeling encouraged. "That's true. Even before the assault, I would have been an excellent candidate for therapy. From my parents being killed when I was six, to seeing both my grandparents die..." Her voice trailed off.

"Let's not forget that you moved to Drummond to find peace. You were making good choices."

"But then Joe was murdered... and ever since, I've been part of one trauma or another." Jill allowed herself to think backwards to remember meeting Joe when she first moved to Drummond. He had made her recognize for the first time that she was an islander in her soul. And he had loved her. She hadn't known him long, but her world had tipped on its end when he was killed.

"I think that might be minimizing your experiences, but yes. Your life has certainly been chaotic." She paused, then said gently, "You are healing, Jill. You're coming back into a sense of self-confidence. Don't you think so?"

"Thanks largely to you, yes."

"You've done the critical work here, Jill, not me." Dr. Letters allowed a moment to pass before she spoke. "Let's talk about the dreams."

"It's my parents," Jill said.

"What about them?"

"When I dream at night, I watch them die all over again."

"And you didn't dream about them before the incident?"

The incident. It had been nearly two years since Jill was tortured for information and beaten to death-- if death was that space when one's heart stopped, when breathing stopped. Jill wasn't sure if she had died or not. She supposed it didn't matter. Her grandfather left her a letter asking her to track down a truth--and in doing so, Jill was nearly killed. She could recall the pain of that experience back into her body on command. She shuddered in her chair. She didn't want to think about it now, didn't want to live within that day any longer.

She refocused on the question. "I have always dreamed of them, but this is different," she finally answered.

"How is it different?"

"I remember nightmares from my childhood, but they were vague and blurry. I stopped dreaming of their deaths somewhere in my early teen years. They were still in my dreams then, but alive. Lately, when I dream about them..." Jill paused, still confused about the dreams, unsure of the relevance. "My parents were killed in a car accident. I was in the back seat. I remember my mother's face. I remember crying out with no answer. And now, it's different."

"Explain it to me."

"Well, we're not in a car anymore. I watch them die, but we're not in a car. There is fire in the dream."

"Fire?" Dr. Letters asked. "You have never

mentioned fire before."

Jill looked puzzled and didn't reply.

"Where are you?"

"I'm not sure. There are walls and seats."

"A car?"

Jill did not reply and just stared out the window.

"A room?"

"Yes. No. I'm not sure. I feel like we're moving, but I don't know."

"And the car is on fire?"

Jill shrugged noncommittally but remained quiet.

The therapist tried another tactic. "Why do you think you're dreaming about your parents?"

Jill turned her head slowly to look directly at Dr. Letters for the first time in several minutes. "I think my mind is trying to expunge and heal. I read somewhere that memory is connected with sleep, that short term memories are processed into deeper memory holding... maybe... maybe, I... I don't know."

"No, stay with that for a moment, you're getting somewhere."

Encouraged, Jill focused. "I guess what I'm saying is that I don't have any clear memories of my parents' death. I have images in my mind, but I'm not sure if I remember them or..." Jill's voice trailed off.

"Or?" Dr. Letters questioned.

"Do I remember my parents' death, or am I remembering the stories of how they died? I was told the story. Maybe I don't remember at all." Jill paused. "I know what my parents look like because I have pictures of them. I can fill in blank spaces of memory with images captured of the three of us." Jill bit her lip, concentrating.

"What about the fire?"

"Fire?" Jill asked.

"You mentioned dreaming about a fire."

"I did?" Jill frowned.

"Sometimes a fire can be a metaphor for a new beginning. Fire destroys and purifies, Jill. I think your soul is trying to tell you something."

Jill nodded slowly. "I keep going back to my assault."

"Okay. Go on."

"In my mind, I can see what happened to me. I can envision a white light at the end of a tunnel, and Kate and Quinn watching over me at the hospital. I can feel my beaten and hurting body. I can look down at my scars and watch a bullet rip through this flesh," Jill said as she hugged herself tightly and shivered. "And I can't trust any of it, because I don't remember. I don't trust myself anymore. I just listened to what people told me and recreated the scene."

"Which is a gift, isn't it? Isn't that the way you find solutions that other people can't seem to find?"

Jill considered that and shook her head. "It's not a gift if it has enabled me to deceive myself."

"Why do you think you've deceived yourself?"

"The images I'm dreaming about my parents are

unknown to me."

"But they are based on the event as it was explained to you, right?" Dr. Letters urged.

Jill leaned back in the chair, releasing a long breath. She hadn't thought of it that way before. "You're saying that I might not have been told the truth?"

The therapist's eyes widened. "No, not at all. I just meant that your dreams might be reflecting an internal state of confusion and healing."

Jill deflated, sinking lower in her chair. "I do feel confused."

Dr. Letters studied her client for a moment and leaned forward. "What are you not telling me?"

"What?" Jill asked, startled.

"I think you've dealt with and have mostly healed from a substantial knot of complicated events during the past months. But there is something blocking you from moving on, from going forward with your life. Do you know what it is?" Dr. Letters studied the young woman's blank face, her flat green eyes, and her tense forehead.

"What's blocking me?" Jill asked for clarification, receiving a nod. "I don't know where to go from here. I'm not really working much. I'm not helping Quinn with the business at all. I feel stagnate, and I hate that. I just want to scrape all of this off of me and move on. I loved my life."

"Did you?" Dr. Letters pressed.

Jill raised an eyebrow at the challenge.

"Before the incident, you quit your job. And I don't think it had anything to do with the business."

"I quit my job working construction so I could focus on photography."

"Are you sure?"

Jill looked straight into the other woman's eyes and lied, "Yes."

"Then what's stopping you?"

Jill couldn't tell her the truth. About one year earlier, Jill confronted a friend who was complicit in two bank robberies and murder. Rather than turn Kate Dombrowski over to the authorities, Jill aided in the cover-up and swore an oath to protect the truth from being discovered. Looking back, she wouldn't have changed her actions--but her guilt often haunted her. One of the young men involved in the robbery as well as a police officer were both killed. For Jill, their deaths were now also on her shoulders.

The therapist allowed a few moments to pass before she spoke. "This is what it feels like, Jill. Your memories are surfacing. You're going to have to go through them, not around them, to heal. You're going to have to fight the ugly fights with yourself. Listen to your body when it needs to calm, to heal. You can't just scrape this all off of you, because it's your life we're talking about. Even though much has been taken from you, there is bounty undiscovered. We will get there. Do you want to heal?"

"You know I do."

"Something is blocking you from exploring your whole life fully with me, and I think it's trapped in your subconscious."

Steadying herself, Jill took a sip of bottled water as she listened.

"I have an idea on how to access it."

"How?" Jill asked.

"What do you think about trying hypnosis?"

Jill didn't say no at first, but she knew she'd have to.

"I see hesitation, but I think it might be necessary. I think there's something at the childhood level blocking your healing process. Your mind is trying to work through it, which is why you're experiencing the dreams. Hypnosis might help."

Jill smiled. "Maybe we'll go that route--but I think I'm getting somewhere on my own. I mean, I think these sessions are working. I feel better inside, more today than before."

"I'm glad you're feeling better, Jill."

"And I think I just need to immerse myself in the things I love. I've already started becoming more active, but I need to take more jobs, more pictures, and get out more. I could work with Quinn and do some traveling, maybe."

"These are all good steps you're suggesting, but please consider hypnosis. I've seen very good results from the technique."

"I will consider it," Jill lied.

"In the meantime, try talking about your dreams with someone, like I suggested last week. Have you made any progress with that?"

"I called Uncle Dave a few days ago, but he hasn't called me back."

"Keep trying. Or try someone else. It really will

help to talk about them; explain them fully and in detail." She looked at her watch. "Unfortunately, our time is up. I think we've made great progress today." Dr. Letters smiled softly. "I also suggest keeping a dream diary or a voice recorder. Either one would be a great tool to help process what you're seeing at night."

"Okay."

"I'll see you next week at the regular time?"

"Thank you, Dr. Letters."

"Take care, Jill."

Chapter 3

Monday, August 6th, 2007

The relative peace of Jill Traynor's Cream City Point home was obliterated by Chase McCord, who came home for the summer between semesters at Schoolcraft College, down state. Each window and door was wide open, allowing the summer breeze to ripple in through the French door, back through the breezeway and into the garage. Even though the rhythmic sound of waves rolling over the rocky south shore was less than seventy feet away, Chase couldn't hear a whisper. Metallica, with a little extra bass, pounded at the floor boards under his feet as he chopped vegetables.

Ridge, the bounding Golden Retriever, ran in and out of the house, chasing butterflies, bugs, and who knows what else around the yard. Chase didn't pay any attention to the dog as he was in the kitchen, his zone, where everything made sense as ingredients came together in his hands.

In the past year, he had studied with master chefs and had become the protégé and teacher's pet of a number of professors. There were only a few short weeks of summer left before he'd be back there, learning and studying culinary masterpieces. Tonight, he was doing his brother a favor--Quinn had asked him to create something so tasty that he might just weep at experiencing it. Chase lived for challenge.

"Ridge, down!" Quinn yelled, walking to the

dining table. He set down wrapped flowers and pulled a new large bone from a grocery bag, tossing it to the dog.

"Damn! Did you go overboard or what?" Chase exclaimed.

"We really don't buy him new bones all that often."

Chase rolled his eyes and turned down the music and left his vegetables for the moment as he eyed the flowers. At least three dozen long stemmed roses were now on the table, ready to be arranged.

Quinn laughed. "Well, I was going to just get two dozen--but the vase I bought is quite large, and I thought I might as well fill it. Hold on, let me go grab it."

Chase shook his head, amused. Quinn had taken the morning off work to clean house, an unprecedented event since Jill began regaining health. He scrubbed floors, walls, windows, watered plants, vacuumed, washed dishes, and took the few loads of laundry to the laundromat to get it all done at once. He now returned carting a large pottery vase glazed in blues and browns that Jill would love. "Do you know anything about arranging flowers?"

Chase laughed. "You're on your own with that one, man."

"Shit."

"Why didn't you have the flower shop do it?"

"I was out of time."

"When's Jill going to be home?"

"5:40 ferry."

"It's only a little after four," Chase retorted.

"I have to get cleaned up. Can you please do this for me?"

"Not on a bet. I'm making dinner, and I'm finding some place else to crash for the night." Chase grinned. "I'm going to be the best man at the wedding. Honestly, I've done enough."

"She hasn't said yes, yet."

"Only because you haven't asked."

Quinn smiled shakily. "I'm nervous."

Chase eyed him. "No shit."

"Where are you staying tonight?" Quinn asked, moving back to the bedroom he and Jill shared.

"Wherever," he shrugged. Chase lived in the bunk room in Jill's attached garage. It had been transformed into his personal suite for the months, holidays, and weekends he needed to use it.

"Thanks, little brother." Quinn called, as he stopped and looked at him and glanced at the heavy preparations taking place in the kitchen. His brother had grown in the last year or so. His jaw line was now chiseled, his arms thick with muscles, his chest taut. In no way was Chase a "little brother," but he didn't seem to mind being called that occasionally. Quinn emptied his pockets onto the table, but couldn't resist inspecting the diamond engagement ring one last time.

"Quinn, stop worrying. Your rep is in danger of being seriously damaged from this point forward. Just think what some of the bar folk would say if they could see big ass-kicking Quinn McCord sweating blood over proposing to Jill. Ha!"

"Thanks for understanding," Quinn said sarcastically. "When it's your turn, I'm going to remember this day."

Chase ignored that, but beamed. "Call Mrs. Eby. Maybe she'll put the roses together for you."

Quinn scoffed. "Last time I let that woman near roses for Jill, she stole them. I'm going to get cleaned up."

Chase rolled his eyes and returned to the kitchen, remembering stories of the incident. "She did not steal them," he muttered, resuming the preparations. Hearing the shower turn on, Chase picked up the phone and dialed their neighbor's number.

*   *   *

Arlene clasped her hands together excitedly. "Oh my goodness, look at these flowers! Some of the prettiest roses I've ever seen, never mind me sayin' it. Except I remember one time when Clark had the damnedest bouquet of lilies and daffodils that put every other flower to shame. 'Course, I suppose it could have just been the night. Oh, the stars were bright, glittery diamonds in the sky and the way he smiled... melt a woman's heart. 'Course, had I known he was going to be an old slug of a man that he is today, I'd have turned right around and waltzed out with that other fine young man, whatever was his name? I'm sure he turned out to be a stalwart gentleman. You know, Chase, you'd do well to remember the code of good gentlemanly conduct. I could walk you through some of the..."

"I'd appreciate that, Mrs. Eby, but right now we need to get these roses in the vase."

"Oh, sure, sure." She sniffed the air. "What is

that you're making, child?" She headed right over to the stove, grabbing a spoon along the way and stuck the spoon into the sauce giving it a good taste. "Mmm... wow, dear boy, that melts my heart. You know what I'd do is add a bit of pepper..."

Chase dove between Arlene and the pepper, grabbing it just as she did. Arlene's grip was stronger than he would have guessed. "No, no, Mrs. Eby. I'll add the pepper later, I promise--just not right now. Thank you, though..."

"Just hand it over. I know you boys just don't have the knack that some of us women do..."

Chase gripped the pepper tightly, giving it a strong yank that sent Mrs. Eby flying with it, straight on top of him and against the counter. Mrs. Eby was fine, but Chase groaned loudly as he caught the force of her weight and his own against the counter's edge.

Bewildered, and unaware of Arlene's presence, Quinn entered the kitchen wrapped in a towel, unsure of how to proceed and ended up giving in to laughter, which earned him scowls from both Arlene and Chase before they joined in. Quinn offered his assistance.

Arlene shook her head and inhaled sharply. "Dear heavens look at you. Been a long time since Clark looked like that. My, my, what a handsome devil. No wonder what Jill sees in you, is it?"

Having no idea how to respond, Quinn stared dumbly.

"It's indecent to be standing around with no clothes on, young man. Get along. Chase, I need a real sharp knife and the sink if I'm going to cut these roses proper. Three dozen, my, my. Man must be completely head over heels for our Jill," she said.

Chase helped her move them and slid the seasonings out of sight, still inwardly traumatized by someone attempting to adjust one of his dishes. No one altered his dishes. He couldn't even remember the last time, outside of class, that someone dared to critique one of his works of cuisine art.

"Don't think these thick glasses mean I can't see you slide the pepper out of sight, young man," Arlene advised. "A gentleman would have known when to take advice from a kind matronly sort. It's not too late to learn some manners, you know. To find a woman as kind and lovely as our Jill, you'll need some manners. I would think about introducing you to my granddaughter, but I can't be trusting someone who lives in a kitchen and won't allow for a smidgen of pepper. No, sir. You can judge a soul by ingredients in the pot, you surely can. Why, now that I think about it, maybe my granddaughter would be just the right influence on you. Just right. My granddaughter knows how to use pepper."

Giving up, Chase bit his tongue and held the pepper out so she could reach it.

Arlene snorted, but her eyes were twinkling. "Won't be helping you now, Chase. But that's a good start on improving those devilish manners." She finished cutting the roses and arranged them in the new vase. "I best be getting home now."

"Thanks, Mrs. Eby," Chase said.

She smiled, winked. "Good luck, Quinn!" Arlene called, listening for his thanks before she left.

Quinn returned from the bedroom with his wet, dark hair combed behind his ears. "I should have gotten my hair cut."

Chase groaned. "I don't think Jill is going to care."

"What if she says no, Chase?"

"She won't."

"But what if she does? What if it's still too soon? What if..."

"We could do this all night," Chase muttered. "She'll say yes."

"But if she says no, how will we go on?" Quinn's forehead was creased, his eyes shadowed with concern. "Seriously."

"Quinn, we're survivors. We'll always go on, but she'll say yes. She loves you." Chase wheeled around, hearing a car pull into the drive.

Quinn's gaze followed. "What the..."

Chase stared out the window, connecting wild dots in his mind as a silver car came to a complete stop. The man inside the car was probably approaching fifty with graying hair and familiar features. He looked at his brother. "That's not..."

"Uncle Dave. Talk about timing," Quinn whispered as he rushed past Chase.

"Dave!"

"Hi Quinn!" Dave called out, rising from the silver rental car. He reached out, hugged the younger man warmly.

"What the hell are you doing here?" Quinn greeted him, grinning.

"Oh, I was in the neighborhood."

"Liar," Quinn joked as Chase came up behind him. "You've met my brother, right?"

"Chase," Dave greeted, nodding. "How the hell are ya?"

"Real good. Nice to see you, Uncle Dave."

"Where's my girl?"

"Off island. She'll be back on the next ferry," Quinn explained. "Come on in. Let's get your bags."

Dave opened the trunk and retrieved a small carry-on sized suitcase and a briefcase. He paused for a moment, fully taking in the home. "Holy shit. Jill wasn't kidding when she said she'd made some changes. I was expecting a coat of paint."

"She didn't tell you about the garage? Or the office? The bunk room?"

Dave looked sheepish. "Yes, she did but still... it looks bigger than I thought it would."

"We're about to make more of them, too. I'll show you."

"When were you last on the island?" Chase asked.

Dave whistled. "Not since before Mom and Dad passed."

Chase shot a look at his brother, behind Dave's turned back. There was no way in hell the man was just in the neighborhood. Quinn's glance told Chase he was well aware of the fact, and hell's bells--Jill would be thrilled to see the man, but did it have to be today?

Dave Kinney stepped into the breezeway, setting his luggage down and followed Quinn into the kitchen.

He looked from the stovetop to the three dozen roses and then back at Quinn. "Oh, I've got a shit sense of timing, don't I?" He muttered.

Quinn laughed and pulled the velvet box out of his pocket. "Take a look."

Dave cracked open the box and groaned. "Wow. Talk about a rock. God, that's a beauty." He turned to Quinn and scowled. "And why the hell didn't you call me? You're supposed to ask for permission, get a blessing, whatnot."

Quinn grinned. "I knew you were coming, so I thought I'd get it in person."

Dave gave him a second look then grinned. "Yeah, right."

Chase slugged his brother. "There's a step you missed, Quinn! Ha!" He moved past the men, checking on the kitchen. He draped a towel over his shoulder, leaned against the counter, enjoying the interaction.

Dave grinned. "Never mind. Welcome to the family, son." He offered his hand and Quinn shook it. "Assuming she says yes, right?"

"Right," Quinn swallowed.

Dave's attention was captured by the framed photographs decorating the living room wall. The collection included at least a dozen prints matted in a variety of colors, but all were framed identically. "She is really getting good."

Quinn agreed. "She changes that wall two or three times every year." Currently, the photographs were all character shots of people Jill had lost--not snapshots or portraits--but something in the middle ground that managed to capture slices of soul. Some of them she had taken, some she had not. To Quinn's eye, it was a good collection, if not terribly sad. He hoped she would change it soon.

"Did you take this one?" Dave asked, pointing to a black and white of Jill at Arlington National Cemetery, taken the year before. In it, she knelt by a plain white grave marker, her long dark hair hiding her face, her hand clenched into a fist, her body surrounded by the stark beauty of a resting ground honoring the nation's courageous and brave.

"Yes." Quinn cleared his throat, wondering at last if he spent so much time at work because he simply couldn't handle being near that collection. Amongst the prints was the only picture Quinn and Chase had of their birth parents. There was one of Joe Barber who had been killed a few years before as well as a variety of Jill's family members. There was a family photo of Pete and Kate Dombrowski and their children. Years ago, Jill had been very close to her then employer and friend. Even though they were still alive, they weren't a part of Jill's life anymore and she missed them. This wall was a memorial, but it required a keen eye to recognize it, and visitors were a rare thing these days.

"You should show him the rest of the place. And the plans outside, Quinn. He'd appreciate that," Chase suggested.

"Sounds good." Quinn showed Dave through the original house first, and then explained how Jill had added on to it with the addition of a garage, office space and dark room as well as a bunk room and bathroom that had become Chase's home. Quinn tried to point out the construction elements that Jill had built herself, which impressed Dave at various points. Afterward, they walked out onto the deck where a segment of land was staked out.

"She really has done a lot with the place. Well, you both have, right?"

"No," Quinn corrected. "Jill has done everything herself up to this point. We're going to do the next stage together. This here is going to be a six-sided, two-storied room. A space to showcase her work with an artistic space designed to bring the natural beauty in through walls of glass." Quinn walked a bit, pointing to another set of stakes. "And that will be the new master bedroom with a wall of windows looking out at the water and a fireplace right over here."

Dave looked at the stakes in the ground, at then back at Quinn. "I remember this." Dave pointed at the stakes. "I got a call from Jill. She was all excited about her plans for this addition to the cottage. Next thing I know, she is in business with two brothers and making barbecue sauce. I told my girlfriend at the time that I thought she had made such a mistake. You know Jill," Dave mumbled, shaking his head. "She doesn't even cook." Dave shrugged his shoulders. "About a year later, I was in my local grocery store and there on the shelf was Three Bobbers Barbecue Sauce. I had to check the label to prove to myself it was made on Drummond." He finally shifted his gaze out to Lake Huron. "How did this all come about, Quinn? How did Jill get involved with you and Three Bobbers?"

Quinn smiled. "I was a bartender at the Northwood when I met Jill, but I wanted more out of life. I have been good in the kitchen since I was a kid. I started messing around with ingredients and loved it... the creativity of it." He smirked, lost in a memory perhaps. "I played with barbecue sauces and tried hundreds of different recipes until I came up with what is now known as Three Bobbers Original Sauce. I took samples to over sixty specialty shops as far south as Lansing and Grand Rapids. It caught on like wildfire. Soon I was in barbecue sauce up to my neck." Quinn rocked back on his heels, grinning at the stress he lived with then. "I was four months behind in my orders. I had made my personal life and those around me a mess. About this time I got my first large contract to supply a grocery chain. It meant that I would have to triple production. I couldn't handle it. I was making the stuff in my garage when I wasn't working at the bar. Sixteen and eighteen hour days were usual. I was burning out hard. I received an offer to buy me out. I was all set to take it when Jill and Chase offered to loan me their money. Actually, they offered to give me the money originally-but we worked out a deal."

"They had that kind of money?"

"Chase had a modest chunk set aside for college. Giving it up meant he wouldn't be able to afford culinary school. Jill had cash and this house and the land. We pooled all of our money and collateral and borrowed everything we could to build the factory." Quinn looked Dave in the eye. "I promised them, the day we formed the partnership that Chase would go to school and I would help him get his own restaurant. I promised Jill that Three Bobbers' first goal was to pay off the lean against this property. One day Three Bobbers would build her this addition. I am proud to say that the loan has been paid, Chase is in school and we are building this addition with cash."

Dave's eyes widened, before he chuckled. "So it's going well, I take it?"

"Amazingly well, yes. It's almost growing too fast. I can barely keep up with some of it. We've got the factory here plus the one in Indiana. And we're shopping on the west coast for a third location."

"You must be damned near everywhere, hey?"

"Without missing a beat, Quinn answered, "Forty-two states, five provinces of Canada and four Central American countries." He quieted when Dave didn't say anything. "It was my dream to do this. Chase and Jill made it happen, so you can see why I cannot let them down. That's what you really want to know, isn't it? If I can take care of her?"

Uncle Dave nodded his head, smiling. "Son, I know you can take care of her. But thanks for filling in the gaps."

Quinn smiled. "So, how is your work?"

"Oh, let's not talk about that. We'll fall asleep from the drudgery of it in no time. Where's that beer you promised me?"

Quinn chuckled. "Right this way."

Chapter 4

Jill pulled her black Pontiac Vibe, a recently purchased car, onto the ferry boat per the deck hand's directions. She parked the car and shut the engine off, leaving the windows down. She gazed ahead, clenching her ferry ticket to be punched for her passage. An ocean freighter was mid-river charging forward north-bound through the ferry path, cutting off her view of Drummond. The ship would be long clear by the time the Drummond Islander IV was ready to return to the island. Her cell phone rang from its position on the seat next to her. She flipped it open, saw that it was Dean and closed it. She wasn't in the right mood for her agent's energy-high.

She looked down at her hands, her chewed fingernails, her long arms. She ran her fingers over the scar on her arm, the only evidence on her body that the car accident had taken place. She had more scars now. Sometimes she felt her body was covered in them. Dr. Letters once told her that people who have experienced personal violence sometimes never recover their former selves--they never quite become the same people they once were.

Her gaze drifted off through the window past the miles of deep blue water to the DeTour Reef Light. In so many ways, the lighthouse anchored her life here. She inclined her head toward it, just a bit, and smiled. Her phone rang again. She flipped it open; Dean again. She flipped it shut. "Leave me a voice mail," she muttered to no one in particular.

She relaxed back into her seat, but couldn't stop thinking about her therapist's suggestion. A Frito Lay truck pulled into the space next to hers. The driver waved and she waved back, her mind preoccupied by today's therapy session. What would happen if she was hypnotized? Was it worth the risk? What would Dr. Letters uncover from her past? She didn't trust her memory anymore, and she hated that. It felt like a weakness. Dr. Letters told her to talk to someone, but who was left from her past besides Uncle Dave?

Her intensely busy uncle was more devoted to work than anyone she had ever known, but he had carved time out of his schedule to come when she needed him, sitting with her during her coma. Of course, she didn't remember seeing him. In the time before she awoke, he had bonded with Quinn. Intense situations made easy friends sometimes, she guessed.

She flipped her phone back open and handed the ferry ticket through the window, receiving it back with the hole punched through the last number left. Next week, she'd have to buy another one, she thought as she dialed her uncle's phone number.

Four rings, no answer. At the beep, Jill left a message. "Uncle Dave, it's Jill. I don't mean to be filling up your voicemail, but if you have time, give me a call. I am still having dreams about when Mom and Dad died. Something's not right with what I remember, and I..." Jill paused, unsure of how to explain. "Well, I don't know what's wrong. I just need to talk to someone who remembers. It would be good to hear your voice. Bye." She clicked the phone off. She wasn't going to call her uncle again until he called her.

She closed her eyes and attempted to go back, to

relive the dream. In the image, there was something wrong with the walls. They weren't normal walls, but identifying what was wrong with them wasn't easy or clear. She couldn't get there, couldn't see her parents or herself. She opened her eyes, frustrated. Hypnosis was simply not an option. She couldn't afford to relinquish control of what she said. Jill trusted her therapist with her own secrets, but she wouldn't risk divulging those she swore she'd protect.

Kate Dombrowski had been involved with bank robbery, murder, and a premeditated intention to physically harm Jill, but in the end she chose to save Jill's life. Jill and Kate had come to an agreement to let the past, for the most part, live in the past. Kate turned over her share of the cash stolen from the banks, and Jill arranged for it to be discovered, thereby letting Kate off the hook.

Quinn came up with the plan for its return. He hid it in an old out-building that Jill wanted emptied and destroyed. Quinn asked Deedee and her husband, Billy, over one Saturday to help. Less than an hour after starting, Billy found the bag of cash. The cash was turned over to the police and the foursome was issued a reward check. Quinn and Jill donated their half to the other couple for their down payment on their first home.

Jill justified her decision by considering Kate's children. She couldn't let them grow up without a mother. Jill had lived that life, and she didn't wish it on anyone. Jill, Quinn, and Kate made the deal to protect Kate's secrets together. No one else would know. So, when Jill told Dr. Letters she'd consider hypnosis, she knew she was lying. If Jill couldn't heal without hypnosis, she simply wouldn't heal.

Chapter 5

"Long time no see, Jilly."

She was just wondering who the silver car belonged to when she heard his voice. She hesitated, overwhelmed and sort of afraid to look up from her car seat. When she did, Uncle Dave opened his arms and she dove into them like she did when she was a little girl, like she did the night her grandparents brought her home from the hospital and she was scared and alone.

"Ohmygod, what are you doing here?" She exclaimed against his chest.

He backed up a bit, grinning. "Oh, I had a few hours to kill..."

"And you flew up here?"

"To Kincheloe and rented a car."

"Are you staying a week or two?"

"More like forty-eight hours."

Knowing the man didn't like to travel if he couldn't get away for a good chunk of time, Jill was puzzled. "You've got to stay longer than that. It'll take that long just to show you around. You haven't been to the island in years."

Uncle Dave raised his hand to slow Jill down, "I can't. It's a long story. I will tell you all about it a little later."

She narrowed her eyes at him, then grinned and hugged him again. "It is so good to see you."

"It's great to see you not in a hospital gown. Last time I saw you, you looked considerably worse, my dear." Dave had flown up after getting the call from Quinn two years ago. He had to leave before she broke through the coma. "Are you feeling well?"

"My body feels great, save for a few annoying scars."

"And your heart?" He asked.

"Better everyday. Can I get you a beverage? Are you hungry?"

"Quinn and Chase have taken good care of me."

"They're both here?" She asked, surprised. She wondered when the last time was that Quinn had been home before her.

"Yes. I'm afraid I might have interrupted something," he mumbled, as they walked through the breezeway together.

Jill's mouth watered as she smelled the meal Chase cooked. "Wow. Chase, let me weep for a moment--that smells amazing." She looked down at the freshly mopped floor, polished furniture in the living room, and the tidiness of the space. Quinn stood behind them. She walked around the table. "Hi, Babe. You cleaned?"

Quinn shrugged. "Seemed like a good thing to do."

"Did you know Uncle Dave was coming?" She asked.

"No clue." He leaned down and hugged her, pleased to see her smile. "Good day?"

"Better now," she sighed. "How did I get so lucky?" She touched one of the rose petals.

"Those aren't for you," Chase piped in. "They are for Arlene."

"Everybody's a comedian," Quinn grumbled.

Jill turned around in Quinn's arms. She kissed him quickly and asked, "What is the occasion?"

Quinn shrugged his shoulders. She twisted her body back to face her uncle and smiled. "How long have you been here?"

"I beat you by one boat."

"I showed him the house and the plans for the addition already," Quinn said.

"You haven't taken him out to Three Bobbers?"

"No, not yet. I thought about it, but I wanted to be here when you got home," Quinn mumbled against her hair, his arms still wrapped around her.

"You didn't see it when you were here last, did you?" Jill asked.

"Never left the Soo." Dave admitted. "You've done quite a bit. It looks great. I love these pictures," he gestured to the collection of pictures hanging on the wall and sitting atop bookshelves and end tables.

Jill wrinkled her nose. "Actually, I was brainstorming a bit on my way down about a new collection. I'm thinking seasons of sunrise and big sky shots. What do you think, Hon?"

"I like it."

Dave gazed out the French door window, grinning. "I forgot how beautiful it is here."

"Quit your job and move here then. We've got an extra room."

He winked at her. "Sounds good to me," he sighed. "Let's call a moving truck and have my stuff shipped."

Jill brought her hands to her face in mock horror. "Oh no! I said you could move in. I said nothing about your stuff. I seem to remember life sized ewoks and the green dude."

"Yoda. Say it, Jill. Yo-da."

"Yoda." She laughed, took a seat on the couch, and pulled Quinn down next to her. "You should at least visit more."

Dave sat as well. "Kind of like when you and Quinn went to Arlington in D.C. and didn't come see me?"

"D.C. is a ways from Florida, Uncle Dave."

"It's not far at all by plane. I could have even met you there. It's been a while since you came to Florida. You should drop by."

"I have a hard time believing you came for a spontaneous visit."

"Didn't you call me a few days ago? I thought you wanted to talk."

"So you flew here?"

"I have been meaning to anyway." He looked like he was going to speak and then nothing came out. "You keep raving about how well these guys can cook, and I haven't had a good meal in a while."

Chase chortled. "Exactly! I have a reputation. I cannot believe that woman tried to add pepper to my..."

"Chase, let's be adults and let it go," Quinn instructed.

"Uh-huh," Chase muttered as he plated servings of food for everyone. "Dinner's ready. Now, guys, I know this is going to look like I haven't been slaving in the kitchen all day..."

"Which he has, trust me. I had to bribe him out of there, mid-day, to clean," Quinn grumbled.

Jill laughed at him, poking him in the ribs to quiet him.

Chase finished prepping the table as they took their seats. "This is a bib salad with a wide variety of vegetables and fruits depending on each person's taste. The lasagna is my own special recipe. Both the sauce and noodles were made from scratch, as well as some of the layered components and my own blend of packaged cheeses. The garlic bread is also homemade. You'll find nothing out of a box tonight. And for dessert, well... we have a lovely apple torte that I think everyone will find pleasing."

Jill beamed at him, skipping past the salad to stick her fork right into the lasagna. She took a bite and moaned. "Oh, God."

They kept up simple chatter during dinner, with each of them filling each other in on their lives and plans for the future. At points, Dave regaled them with stories of Jill's childhood, which were amusing and often focused around some dangerous spot she got into when trying to find a perfect angle for a photograph.

After dinner, when everyone was too stuffed to move, Dave asked Chase to take him out to the factory and show him around. Quinn merely raised an eyebrow at the scheming look in the man's eye, how he deftly talked Jill into staying home and helping Quinn wash dishes. She still seemed a bit perplexed when they left, but attempted to shrug it off when she caught Quinn looking at her.

"What are you thinking about?" she asked him.

"How beautiful you are," he said, meaning it. She was still the most remarkable looking woman he knew or had ever known. Her trademark t-shirt and jeans hugged her body comfortably and her dark hair wisped out from the gathering at the back of her neck. A small key pendant he purchased for her on their trip to D.C. last year gleamed a bit against her skin.

Her green eyes sparkled. She stood up from her chair and came to his and sat down on his lap. "I missed you, today."

"Me too."

"Therapy went well?"

Jill shrugged. "She wants me to try hypnosis. She says something is blocking me from moving forward."

Quinn's eyes widened as he considered the ramifications.

"I know. I'm not going to do it. I can't risk revealing something about Kate."

"Don't blow it off just yet, Jill. Ask some questions. Do some research. Maybe she can stay out of current events."

"Do you think it works that way?" she asked.

"I haven't got a clue how it works," he admitted. The velvet box was still in his pocket and his mind. It was now or never, Quinn thought. "Let's go outside for a few minutes, okay?"

"That sounds lovely. The dishes won't be offended." She rose from his lap and grabbed his hand. They walked down the steps from the deck to the shore. The sun was still more than an hour from touchdown, with the sky painted in streaks of orange and red. She squeezed his hand, sharing the solitude. A few more moments passed before she spoke. "I love that we do this, that we come out here together."

Many evenings Quinn and Jill found themselves sitting on rocks by the shore, talking about life. It was their spot long before he moved in, and her spot long before she knew Quinn, but it felt right to have him here. She hoped she never forgot to appreciate him. She shook her head at the strange track her mind was on, smiled, and looked at him. He smiled shakily, and it occurred to Jill that he was nervous. It was such a rare event that she'd missed it at first, and now she paid even closer attention. The scrutiny wasn't helping, she decided.

"Thank you for cleaning, and for dinner, the flowers--what a beautiful evening. It would have been lovely with or without Uncle Dave's impromptu visit. What inspired it, Babe?"

Quinn swallowed air abruptly and coughed. "I spend too much time working and not enough time with you."

"You've got a massive business to run. I'm not upset with you for taking care of our future. God knows

I haven't helped."

"You do help," he countered. "I want you to know it's not always going to be this way."

Alarmed, Jill stared into his eyes. "What way?"

"I'm not always going to be so busy, especially when Chase is totally finished with school. I will hire enough people so I don't have to live at the factory and just visit home. I know it has been hard for you."

Jill brought her finger to his lips, leaned in and kissed him. "Babe, you have taken care of me so well. It's time for me to take care of myself."

"You have been."

"No... what I'm trying to say is that you don't need to be so worried anymore. I am okay, better everyday. I'm going to start acting like it. If you're going to be home more, that's awesome. I love spending time with you. Maybe we could go on a trip somewhere or something, but I want you to do what needs to be done for Quinn. You've spent too much time making me your only priority, and I can do it myself now. Okay?"

Quinn smiled, brushed her hair back from her face. "I love you, too. We've been through a lot together, right?"

It was such an understatement that Jill couldn't help but laugh, which made Quinn laugh. The tension in his throat broke free. He visibly calmed, knowing this was the right moment. He reached into his pocket and pulled out the box. He placed it into the palm of her hand, shocked when he saw tears fill her eyes and spill onto her cheeks. He held it there because he wanted her attention; he wanted to say everything he had practiced. He knew precisely what would be enough.

"The thing is, Jill--I want you to be my priority. From the moment you walked into the Northwood, when I was nothing more than a bartender jealous of his best friend's girl, I knew you were the one. I knew you were the woman who would understand me, who would really know me someday, and you do. We have been through a lifetime these past few years, and I want to do it all over again. Every moment of it that makes me love you more today then I did yesterday." He paused, searching for words he hadn't prepared. "I know you are still healing. We may always be healing, in one way or another. Inside this box is a symbol of our connection, our history--place, time, hardship, and the element that can't be harvested from the ground. Love me, Jill. Marry me. Spend the rest of your life being the challenge that makes my life worth living."

She opened the box and gasped. Inside was the most exquisite, flawless, princess cut diamond she'd ever seen. She pulled the ring from the box, examined it, and blinked through her tear filled eyes.

"Look," Quinn brought her attention to an inscription on the inside of the band. "These are the coordinates where the diamond came from."

"Oh, Quinn," she cried, recognizing the numbers.

"It is from Lac de Gras," he said, referring to a lake in Canada where the richest diamond strike on the planet was discovered.

Undone, Jill gave into the tears. Quinn picked her up and nestled her onto his lap, holding her until the tide passed. She kissed him, remembering the first time. Just days after Joe had died, she needed him to make her feel alive, to convince her that she wasn't cursed, that everyone around her wouldn't die like they had all her life. She had never loved another person the way she loved Quinn, with her whole soul, with everything she was. This was the man who brought her life daily, who knew her dark places and stayed, who understood why she chose to protect Kate. How could she not marry him? She kissed him hungrily, the ring clenched in her hand.

"Quinn..." She paused, taking a breath.

Quinn looked into her large green eyes that sparkled gold and waited for her to go on. With her heart stuck in her throat, all she could say was, "Yes."

Chapter 6

Tuesday morning

Jill padded out to the kitchen in her bathrobe and pajamas and waved to Uncle Dave. She poured herself a cup of coffee and saw the note from Quinn. Apparently, he ran out to Wazz's, was going to stop by work, and be back for some visiting. Uncle Dave let her gather her thoughts for a few moments, remembering how she was a bit of a bear in the morning without caffeine.

Finally, she brought her mug into the living room and sat down.

"Good morning."

"Same," she spoke softly.

"Okay, I can't believe you haven't told me yet," Dave muttered, bringing her hand closer for inspection.

"I've been awake for five minutes."

"Not a word last night, either."

"I was already in bed by the time the two of you got back. What took you guys so long?"

"Chase decided to give me the extra-special tour of Three Bobbers."

"He showed you the broom closet and everything, didn't he?"

Dave grinned. "Do you know how many brooms and mops are in that place?"

Jill groaned. "He still gets so excited about it."

"Well, hell yes, and he should. Intelligent, accomplished young man. It was good to get to know him."

"And then he took you to the bar, didn't he?"

"We might have stopped by. I met someone with crazy red hair..."

"That would be Deedee. She works at Three Bobbers."

"That's right. Tell me about this," he said, gesturing to her ring.

She narrowed her eyes at him. "Don't think I didn't see through your clever ploy to go exploring last night. You knew Quinn was going to propose."

"Yeah, when I got here yesterday, I realized my timing couldn't have been worse."

"Not true. You're always welcome. And he still asked, so no harm done." Jill sipped the coffee, glancing at her hand from time to time. She never would have thought she would like a big diamond, but the rock on her hand was perfect.

"When is the wedding?"

"Soon. Sooner the better, if you ask me. Next month?"

"Seriously?" Dave asked, surprised.

Jill nodded. "Quinn and I lived through our friends, Billy and DeeDee, the woman you met at the factory... anyway, we lived through them getting married. It was an absolute nightmare. She's the sweetest woman, but she was a bit of a shrew before the wedding. Everyone went a little crazy trying to make the day just right." She shook her head. "Last summer, Quinn had this lovely mini-park of sorts built near the factory. I bet Chase didn't show it to you, did he?"

Dave shook his head, amused.

"I can't believe he showed you the closets and not the park. Men," she muttered. "Anyway, it is really nice. It has a gazebo and lots of planted flowers. He wanted a nice space for workers to lunch in. We'll just bring in some big white tents, throw a barbecue and invite the island. You have to fly back for it. You need to walk me down the aisle, you know." She smiled, eyes twinkling.

When he didn't immediately agree, she set her cup down and looked at him. Something changed in his eyes.

"That might be a bit difficult."

"Why are you here, Uncle Dave?"

"We all make mistakes," Dave started. "I've always thought I'd live forever. There comes a point when you just know that's not the case. For me, I never found the type of partner who would give up everything and sit with me day after day through sickness and health. I wish I would have taken the chance. I spent most of my life looking for an ideal. I should have just found someone who would love me."

He took a sip of water and bought time. "Next week I am scheduled to have bypass surgery."

Jill shook her head. "They don't do that anymore unless..."

"I've been through all the other steps, stints and everything. I've survived a major heart attack. I'm not sure I'd survive another. Well, they're not sure--that's why I'm doing the surgery."

"Why didn't you tell me?" Jill asked, worried.

"I didn't think it was a big deal. And I didn't want to worry you."

"How could you not think it was a big deal? Major heart attack, stints, surgery, and you didn't think it was a big deal? I'm family. It's my job to worry," Jill answered fervently. "Did your doctor say it was okay to fly up here?"

"I didn't ask."

"Damn it, Uncle Dave! When are you going to take some precautions for yourself?" Jill stated, raising her voice.

"I'm not having this operation for fun, Jill."

"I'm sorry. I'm out of line and yelling at a heart patient. I am so sorry." Jill hung her head.

Looking to change the subject, Uncle Dave jumped in before Jill could go on. "I needed to come see you. When you called the other day, I knew it was time, that I couldn't put this off any longer."

"Put what off?" He wasn't talking about a leisure trip to the island. Something else was going on here, and she needed to get to the bottom of it. "Uncle Dave... put what off?"

"The truth. There are things you need to know." He looked away, collecting his thoughts.

She hesitated, a bit afraid. "I'm listening."

"Mom, ah, sorry, your grandma that is, decided that your life would be better if you didn't know certain things."

"What things?"

"Oh, things about Dad's side of the family, his mother, others further back on the family tree. A few more current things..."

"Could you be any more vague?"

"I know." He shook his head. "Sorry. I just don't know how to tell you all this. If I tell you chronologically, it'll get messed up."

"I have some experience breaking news to people. Let me give you a few tips," Jill said, smiling softly. "Start with what's most important. Don't sugar coat the details: just get it out there. And don't hold anything back. If you came to speak the truth, then speak it. Okay?"

He nodded. "Your parents didn't die in a car accident."

Jill's eyes widened, startled. After a moment of quiet, she shook her head. "No. I remember. I can see..." But lately, her memories had seemed muddy. Details were out of place, inconsistent with what she remembered being told.

Dave was quiet for another moment as Jill considered this first sentence, this beginning of unraveling. "Memories lie, Jill."

"How did they die?" she asked, her eyes closed.

"They were killed in a plane crash in Detroit. August 16th, 1987. The same day of the car accident you were told about. 155 people died."

She looked at her uncle and shook her head again. "But I know I saw them..."

"You did see them. You were the lone survivor on the flight." Dave reached into the bag by his feet and pulled out a manila folder. He opened it and withdrew a few yellowed newspaper clippings. He handed them to her. Jill read the headline of the one on top: "Girl may be sole survivor of flight." She set it aside and read the next headline, "The Final Moments of Flight 357."

Jill stared into the eyes of her younger self. There she was, pictured beside an article headline that read "Miracle Girl on Flight 357." She read through it quickly, the details of the crash, the miracle of her survival. It didn't make sense to her. Jill sat the newspaper clipping down and picked up the next one. In a picture, she saw a much younger version of herself beside her grandfather. The headline read, "Grandfather identifies girl who survived."

"I don't understand. Why did Gram and Grandpa lie to me?"

Dave swallowed another large drink of water. "That's where it gets complicated. Your grandma believed you were following a long tradition afflicting the Kinney line of women. She thought lying to you might save you. She didn't believe in the pride the Kinney family felt about its women's bravery."

Utterly confused, Jill leaned back against the couch and stared at him. "Uncle Dave, what are you talking about?"

Uncle Dave sat for a moment not sure where to start. He looked for the words to give his niece. "I'm not sure. I need to tell you a story about a woman that lived on Drummond a long time ago."

Chapter 7

Late Fall, 1828

The Decline of an Empire

Angelique struggled to wake from a nightmare, tried to believe the encompassing horror was not real. She couldn't have been abandoned by her husband, with her daughter tied and bound to her chest, and the schooner she had made her home these last few days sunken beneath her feet. The storm raged as every fourth or fifth wave was so monstrous that she needed to hold her breath as it rolled over her soaked body. She prayed that her daughter was somehow still alive.

Therise, Angelique's ten-year-old daughter, had stopped sobbing and trying to communicate with her over half an hour ago. She knew their chances to live were minimal, at best. If her daughter didn't die in her arms, she lived only by the miracle of God. Angelique tipped her head back and let her wail fill the night's sky. Oh, to go back, she cried.

*   *   *

The Treaty of Ghent signed the official end of the War of 1812. Fort Michilimackinac on Mackinac Island had been turned over to the U.S. for the second time. Peace had finally come to the Northwest. The British needed a new location close to the Straights of Mackinaw to control the fur trade, so they fell back to Drummond Island. Its deep and well protected harbor in the southwest corner attracted them, but the fact that it was on the border and in question to ownership was even more appealing.

As the Crown's choice in 1815, Fort Drummond was settled and plans were made for a great installation. A large star-shaped fort measuring 580 feet by 350 feet was planned to be built. Since there were already strong ties to Indian nations there, they believed they could continue to control the much coveted fur trade. However, with the fur trade waning and the British government having troubles at home, their interest in Drummond and the Northwest changed. The fort would never be built and what started in 1815 with three full companies, and a Lieutenant Colonel in command was reduced to a half company under the command of a Lieutenant.

The final blow came in 1822 when the border commission, including both English and U.S. representatives, decided that Drummond Island was within U.S. territorial waters. There was only a matter of time before Fort Drummond and Port Collier would be vacated by the British.

In Fort Drummond, the rumor that started several weeks earlier had finally been confirmed as fact. Fort Drummond's commanding officer, Lieutenant Carson held a meeting with his officers, top sergeants, the local head of the Northwest Company, and other leading members of Port Collier. He explained that the British had to leave Drummond on or before 14 November 1828. They had been on U.S. soil without invitation for the past six years.

The U.S. Schooner, the Cincenata and the British warship, the Duke of Wellington, were chartered from Fort Erie. The Alice Hackett, among others, were also brought from surrounding areas to remove the garrison and anyone else wishing to leave the island before the 14th. Some British stores would be ferried to Fort St. Joseph, but the main armament, garrison, livestock, and civilians would travel east to Penetanguishene in southern Georgian Bay.

The Alice Hackett was captained by owner and sailing master, James Hackett. The "Alice," as her crew lovingly called her, was a much smaller ship than the Cincenata. The decision concerning who left on this ship was a difficult one, since the Alice was only a little over fifty feet in length, and less than half the tonnage of the Cincenata.

With orders in hand, all property owned by the British government went first, including cannons, shot, powder, livestock, tack and all other items of value; Lieutenant Carson had little room to accommodate passenger's belongings.

The word went out to military personnel before civilians. The British stores armament, livestock, and personal property followed in importance. By late afternoon on the second day of loading the ships, civilians realized most, if not all they owned, was going to be left behind. Of the eighty-nine people leaving Fort Drummond, seven were officers, forty men, fifteen women, twenty-six children and three servants. Lt. Carson assigned seventeen to board the schooner, Alice Hackett, and sail as soon as the ship was loaded.

*   *   *

An hour before first light

"Get up, Pierre! It is an hour till dawn and we will be leaving. We need to get the last of our personal items to the ship before there is no room left," his wife coaxed.

With a modest hang-over, Pierre sank back into his bed, pulling the wool blankets up around his neck. He grumbled through his heavy French accent, "There is no room now, wife. That cagey tavern keeper, Fraser, had drinks last night with Captain Hackett. They were laughing as the Captain guzzled down the free whiskey. Late last night, on my way home, I saw men loading barrels of whiskey on his ship."

Mrs. Lepine, known to her friends as Angelique, was a small woman who was the daughter of a First Nation Mother and a father who died while she was in her teens. Angelique had long brown hair, dark eyes, and stood just a few inches over five feet. She was a proud woman. Her father told her as a child that if she had been born a man, she would have been a leader.

She stood in the small doorway in her white washed hand hewn log home and said goodbye. It wasn't large, but it was built well and had a good fireplace. Her husband, even though he liked to drink and was a little lazy at times, was a good provider. He could speak English, French and three native dialects which gave him work with the Northwest Company. He was one of their best traders and sometimes would be gone for weeks buying fur. During those times, she found good company in her neighbors.

On this day, she glared at her husband, urging him to get up while moving quickly back to the main room of the house going through the items she planned to take. She spared them down to the essentials. In minutes she had a large bundle ready for her husband to take to the schooner. As soon as he returned, they would all go. She had a second large bundle made up for her husband and one for herself as well as a smaller bundle for her ten-year-old daughter to carry.

Hours later, aboard the Alice, Angelique realized what her husband said was true. She counted thirteen barrels of whiskey, two span of horses, four cows, twelve sheep, eight hogs, harnesses and other tack for the horses, two cannons, and several barrels of pork besides the seventeen men and women (women meaning herself and her daughter) from Port Collier or Fort Drummond and the crew of the Alice. There was also some personal property mainly owned by soldiers.

With the sun shining and an easterly breeze, Alice Hackett pulled anchor to set sail to Penetanguishene, or as the locals called it Penetang. Penetanguishene was named by the Abinaki tribe of the Algonquin and meant "place of the white rolling sands." Angelique was nervous about moving and hated to leave Drummond. Pierre told her that they must.

The British chose this location the same way they had chosen Drummond. Penetanguishene Bay had steep sides, deep water, and was defendable. It was at this location on the far southeastern corner of Georgian Bay that the British first built a naval base, then a shipyard for repairs, a supply center for other Forts, and out post and trading centers. In the late twenties it also became a military garrison, and over twenty supply ships sailed from her docks.

The first day of sail, the Alice headed south, clearing the harbor at Port Collier. Once they had traveled a mile south of Drummond, the schooner turned east and ran the length of Drummond. The Alice sailed the full length of Cockburn Island on the west end. On the south side of Cockburn was a large bay, which Captain Hackett steered the schooner into and anchored.

The next morning the ship again headed first south then east, traveling the length of Cockburn, before running down the length of the Manitoulin Island. Several times, Indians came out to meet the schooner and some trading took place.

Angelique tried to spend as many hours on deck as possible. She realized the men needed to do their jobs, so she found several spots that, for the most part, were out of the way and yet offered her and Therise a good view forward or to the port. As much as she hated to leave her home, she was excited to go to Penetang. Her husband told her stories of the place he'd visited on his fur trading trips. It was much larger than Port Collier and more populated. There was even a school for the children and several stores with a wider choice of goods. There would be ships arriving daily from around the Great Lakes bringing news and opportunities for her and her family. Therise would probably have a better life there.

Early on the fourth day, the ship anchored in the last main harbor on the southeast corner of the Manitoulin Island. Several of the soldiers and fur traders had been to this area before and knew there was a large Indian encampment nearby. After some discussion, they decided to see if they could do some trading and try to catch some fresh fish. After three or four hours of trading, the men tapped one of the kegs of whiskey to celebrate the business.

The weather had been unseasonably warm and calm for November, so the captain reluctantly allowed it. In another day they would be inside Georgian Bay. By mid-afternoon, however, the weather had freshened and the wind had shifted to the northwest. Captain Hackett gave the order to pull anchor. Soon, the schooner was under sail and on the deck a drunken party had broken out. The idea was to run down the remaining coast of the Manitoulin, turn south by southeast, bypassing a large island off the southeast corner of Manitoulin. It was the captain's intention to travel between it and a much smaller island, then turn east and sail well east of Bruce Peninsula.

A few minor mistakes by his drunken crew altered his plans. Hackett was off the mouth of Indian Harbor when he noticed a woman and a small child at the bow of the ship waving their hands frantically and yelling. He strained through the noise of the men's talk and the wind snapping at the sails. The Captain, now drunk, didn't seem to care, and yet there was something about her that got his attention. There was a sense of urgency in her movements. What was she saying? Why was she so excited?

At once, through the foggy haze of whiskey, he sobered at the reality of the one word that drifted to his ears: rocks!

*   *   *

It started with a loud scraping sound just forward of mid-ship before the whole ship rocked. Crew and passengers were thrown to the deck violently and air was filled with the sound of breaking timbers. In seconds, the once fast moving schooner sat still and silent. Angelique was one of the first to recover, since she was not drunk like the men. She had seen it coming. At the last second, she braced herself in the bow, putting her back to the ship, holding Therise in a tight bear hug. Therise, even with her mother's loving arms around her, did not fair as well. When the schooner finally stopped its forward motion, she flew backwards with her mother, landing hard on the deck with her mother on top of her.

If Therise hadn't been seasick and needed to watch the waves to calm her stomach, Angelique didn't know how they would have faired. Her daughter was scraped and cut, and she would definitely bruise, but she was mostly okay.

Chaos ballooned on the deck in the next few hours, as whiskey fueled arguments added to disorganization. The men decided to off load the livestock, passengers and personal stores. The captain and crew examined the hull. The ship was badly damaged. And, still drinking, the men off loaded the barrels of whiskey first. They also moved hogs and one horse. With a sick daughter, Angelique chose to wait on the ship for the men to return.

Angelique was disgusted with her husband, the captain, and the whole mess. She took Therise below into the bow where there was still a dry area to bandage her hand and knee from the fall. With her sea sickness, Therise had not slept well the night before. As soon as the bandages were in place, with the boat moving minimally against the rocks, the girl had drifted off atop a large pile of hemp rope. Angelique stayed with her daughter, deciding that the best thing for her and Therise was to stay in this spot and wait for their turn to clear the ship. It would take hours, if not days, in the crew's state of drunkenness to get all the livestock and other items off the schooner. As uncomfortable as sleeping on the ship was, finding comfort on an uninhabited desolate island in late fall, in the northwest, would be worse.

Angelique awoke with a start. She did not mean to fall asleep but somehow she had. And now, the ship was much too quiet. The animals still cried out occasionally, but Angelique was used to that. Something was wrong.

Angelique Lepine didn't dare to move as she listened to the world of noise around her. The ship rocked and ground on the shoal. Waves slapped the walls of the schooner. Wind snapped a loose piece of sail slack and then taut. Animals whinnied and screeched. They sounded panicked and possessed. The absence of noisy men moving across the deck above horrified her. There were no barrels, no drunken men, no one shouting out orders.

She glanced at the sleeping face of her ten-year-old daughter, Therise. She moved quietly, sloshing in water that splashed down the stairs. She gathered her shawl around her shoulders and made her way to the main deck. Leaning into the wind, concentrating to stay upright, she trudged through water covering the ship's surface. One of the two cannons had broken loose from its lashing and now moved as much as two feet with every wave. Angelique looked all over for a sign of life, but found none. She squinted toward the shore but couldn't see any sign of her husband or the crew.

A wave reared up against the side of the schooner, knocking her to the deck. She rose slowly, now soaked to the skin in water, and skirted out of the way as the canon slid down through the open hatch cover and landed on the outer edge of the broken timbers, which was the deep end of the shoal. The canon didn't slow as it crashed through the bottom of the broken schooner. In seconds the ship began to shift. Angelique watched as the storm grew into a monster.

She couldn't panic. She would wait until later to panic, but right now she needed to concentrate. She looked hard over the deck in what little light was available, realizing that the ship would continue to settle downward even amongst the rocks. Soon, the entire deck would be totally under water. She glanced

68

up to offer God a prayer for her daughter's life when she spotted the mast.

Angelique made her way below deck quickly, trying to stay out of the water as much as possible. The animals frantically stomped and cried as water rose around them. A few had broken free somehow and now tried to make it above decks. Her heart broke for them, but she had no time to help. She waded through the water and found her daughter shivering and afraid, but still right where Angelique had left her. She grabbed two wool blankets from a neighbor's sack, found an axe, and grabbed that as well. She wrapped her daughter in the blanket and hugged her tightly.

Angelique used the axe to cut a good size piece of the hemp rope they had been sleeping on. She fashioned the rope around her daughter, tying it over the blanket before she did the same thing to herself. Hand in hand, they climbed up to the open deck. The schooner rocked less, but there was now two or three feet of green water splashing above the deck's surface. Angelique tugged her daughter along, paying close attention to waves and the rolling motion of the ship.

So far, the blankets seemed to hold in their body heat. By the time they made it to the forward mast, the deck was underwater by over a foot and sinking fast. Angelique climbed the mast, making sure each step and hand hold was secure before moving on. She kept Therise ahead of her, yelling encouragement above the fury of the storm. In time they both climbed to the fore topmast.

At the top, there was a small T built so a crew member could stand to work on sails or ropes or be used as a place for a lookout. Angelique wrapped the blankets around herself and Therise together. She hugged her daughter close to her to give her body warmth and secured them both to the mast. She looked to the stern. The Mizzen topmast was just a few feet out of water. Panic threatened her, but Angelique closed her eyes and calmed down for her daughter's sake. She listened for sound, but could no longer hear the livestock. In the morning, her husband would find her dead body. If her daughter lived, Angelique prayed that she would learn from this event. She could give her daughter one last lesson--there were moments worth risking everything for. If her daughter lived, she would know this extraordinary measure that her plain, simple mother could provide her. Therise could know she had the strength to save another's life, to face fear and still act with courage and faith.

Faith, Angelique thought, was all she had now. Please baby, just live through this night. I'll keep you safe.

Chapter 8

"What happened to the daughter? To Angelique? They didn't make it, did they?" Jill's voice cracked with emotion.

"Jill, they survived."

"Oh, thank goodness." She wiped tears from her eyes. "And we're related to these women?"

"Yes. Angelique saved her daughter's life. We are related to both of them. Angelique was like a great-great... well, I don't know how many generations precisely, but she's a direct patrilineal link."

"That's incredible."

"No more than being the Miracle girl, surviving a plane crash when no one else did. No more than being pronounced dead and having your boyfriend put a gun to the side of the EMT's head and demand that he try again. And really, no more unbelievable that the damned machine actually worked the way it does in the movies. What the hell is the name of that thing?"

"A cardiac defibrillator," Jill smiled.

"It's strange that he didn't go to jail for that, isn't it?" Dave asked.

Jill shrugged. "Small towns have a way of working things out. Quinn wouldn't have hurt anyone."

"That's not how I heard the story," Dave said

softly. "Just think. Someone loves you enough to kill for you."

"Uncle Dave, that's creepy."

"But true," he supplied.

Sitting on the edge of the sofa, Jill put her head in her hands and sighed deeply. She used to be able to connect the dots and see the whole picture easily, quickly. Today, her legs trembled and she had to force herself to relax. "Okay, so it's believable, but I still don't see how this relates to me, or my parents. I mean--it is amazing that I'm connected to Drummond deep in my history. And the story is incredible. It explains some things."

"Oh?"

"Well, at least it explains why Grandpa and Grandma came here. They always told me it was because the Ebys were here."

"That still might be partially true." Dave stood and looked out at Lake Huron. "Do you realize that the Alice Hackett sailed right by this location on the way to Penetanguishene. Dad and I sat out on those rocks once, and he told me the story about Angelique and Therise. He was sad for them, but proud." Dave shook his head and smiled.

Jill joined him at the glass door and leaned against his side. Dave put his arm around her, enjoying the quiet.

After a few moments of silence, Jill added, "It doesn't make a whole lot of difference that there's a heroine in our family."

"Jill, she's not the hero of the family. She was simply the first we know about. It was a different time back then, and yet she was able to stand in the face of death and survive. She taught her daughter how to be courageous. Generation after generation, the Kinney women have been extraordinary individuals. I could tell you dozens of stories that we know of women risking their lives for others, sometimes complete strangers."

"And you think this is passed down?"

"Who really knows about nature and nurture, but ultimately, yes. They were women caught up in major crisis situations, women who gave themselves over for a larger purpose. Unusual circumstances have plagued the Kinney women for a very long time. Your grandmother didn't tell you about your parent's death, because your mom was one of them. And worse, Jill, she knew that you were one of them, too."

"Just because my mom died in a plane crash it makes her one of these cursed women? Uncle Dave, people die everyday," Jill said, pointing out the obvious.

"She didn't simply die in a plane crash."

"What?"

"Dad believed your parents were murdered."

The floor felt shaky to her feet once again, as if her history was about to implode upon itself, replacing things she might have called facts with hodge-podge stories heard second-hand. Why had Uncle Dave taken so long to trod through these other stories when he knew her parents had been murdered? Murdered? No, it wasn't possible. Jill's life had only known chaos in the last few years, as she inadvertently intertwined herself with danger. She looked back on her early childhood as a place of relative peace. Jill paced the living room floor, looking for answers but none came. Her mind filled with just one fact: her parents were murdered.

She turned back, needing answers. "Why? How?"

Dave brought another article from the folder. The date read August 25th, 1984. "Ship carrying uranium sinks off Belgium," she mumbled. "Containers of uranium hexafluoride, a product that could be used to make nuclear bombs or fuel were stolen from a downed ship." Jill read further. Before her mother died, Jill knew she was employed by a shipping company, but she couldn't make any other connection. She looked up, expectant.

"We believe your mother discovered that the company she worked for was involved with the theft of the nuclear material."

"What?" Jill asked, needing clarification. Dave understood.

"Before she was killed, she told a little of this to your grandpa. She was scared out of her mind, Jill, but she had to make the right choice. After she died, we were visited by an off-the-clock agent who explained his theory. Your mom had been working with the FBI to bring her company down, but someone found out. Officially, we weren't supposed to be told anything. The agent couldn't stand us not knowing, so he told us what they thought happened."

"155 people died because my mother knew about stolen nuclear cargo," Jill muttered. "These people took down a whole plane just to kill my mother?"

"Yes."

"But I survived?"

"Yes."

"How?"

"You were held in your mother's arms and pinned between her and the seat in front of you. It created a wall of protection."

Jill's hands shook. She clenched them together. "And Gram lied?"

"Because she thought she could save you, yes."

"I can't believe Grandpa went along with it."

"He didn't want to, Jill. He fought her at every step. I think Mom was planning on telling you at some point, but she had already buried her child. Not being able to protect you scared the hell out of her, and when she saw you develop the same personality traits she had seen in her own daughter, in her husband for that matter, she couldn't risk it. It was actually Dad who gave me the articles. He made me promise to tell you someday, knowing Mom never would."

"If Grandpa had this thing, whatever it is, then why are the women alone credited?" Jill asked.

"Dad was nosy and interested in everything, but he never really finished anything. Like that picture from the Fitz, for example. He found the life ring, picture, and locket from the Edmund Fitzgerald, but he didn't know what any of it meant. I remember that, Jill. He was a man possessed, but he made no progress. Thirty years later you connected it to a diamond mine in Canada."

"And nearly died for it," Jill said. She paced a bit. "So... I really am cursed. All these years I kept insisting to anyone who would listen that I am cursed. First my parents died, then my grandparents. Joe was killed. My best friend got involved with some very bad folk. I almost died. I am doomed."

Dave studied her, not caring for her pale color and haunted eyes. He stood up and forced her to look at him. "Jill, you're not cursed. All of this just means you've had a crazy life. You're unlike your mother and yet the same."

She shook her head. "What?"

"You lived. When the probability was damned close to zero, you walked away from a plane crash that killed everyone else on board. And a couple of years ago, when they beat you and shot you--you survived. Hell, Jill. Clinically, you died... and yet, here you are. I think," he paused, "you survived for a reason. Most of the women have lived long lives. You're not doomed."

She sat down again, feeling overwhelmed by everything he told her. "My God... everything was a lie, wasn't it?"

Dave didn't know what to say, so he kept silent. Jill's face was pale and her eyes had lost the extra-sharp edge that characterized them. She forced her muscles to relax and leaned back against the couch. After a few moments she said, "I always felt cursed." She took a breath. "Like people couldn't live very long around me, like being near me shortened their life spans."

Dave considered that and understood it. "I think it's less that you are cursed and more that you are destined to be involved in moments of chaos."

"I'm not sure that's uplifting, if you were trying to be." Jill cracked a smile, teasing her uncle.

Dave laughed, throwing his hands over his head in mock defeat. "I am only the messenger. Don't shoot."

"Why didn't you tell me earlier? Years ago."

"Part of me was concerned that you'd try to go

after the shipping company your mom worked for."

Jill crooked her head to the side, surprised.

"And the other part... I wanted to tell you quite a few times but something would happen. I was going to tell you right after mom passed, but you moved up here. You needed to settle, and I gripped that. The timing was off, but Drummond would be right for you. But then your friend was killed and you were caught up in finding the killer and in mourning your friend. Life got in the way for me, too. I've been too busy with work and everything. Honestly, I just didn't want to tell you. You've been through so much, Jill."

"My parents were murdered," she whispered, feeling tears fill her eyes.

"We can't prove it, Jill. I know they died in a plane crash that you survived. The rest is all intelligent conjecture."

Another moment passed, Jill's mind blank rather than racing. "I'm kind of on borrowed time, aren't I? I mean," she hurried, "I shouldn't have lived through that crash or the assault. Instead of being cursed, maybe I'm simply lucky to be here."

"Don't forget the woman who tied herself to the mast of the sinking ship to save her daughter. She showed her daughter how to live."

Jill nodded her head.

"They both lived very long lives after that night."

Jill wiped tears from her eyes and moved to sit next to her uncle. Dave hugged her tightly. He began to tell her stories of some of the other women from the family she came from. The longer Dave talked and the more stories he told, the more Jill realized her life was just one more branch of the bizarre Kinney family tree. As he shared stories and details with her, she could almost visibly see him relax. She put on another pot of coffee and tried to be open minded, as she learned more about her heritage. Hours slipped by unnoticed.

Chapter 9

Quinn pulled into the driveway behind Dave's car and sprung from the Jeep like a seventeen year old on prom night. Work had taken too long, as usual. He fielded four phone calls, brought Chase up to speed on a few decisions, and cleared his calendar for the rest of the day.

He shuffled the groceries around so he could open the door and was surprised to find Jill still in her bathrobe. She liked to be productive. Wearing a bathrobe for hours was not her idea of being constructive.

"Good morning!" He called.

"Well, there's the man of the hour. Congratulations, Quinn. Welcome to the family!" Dave stood up and shook Quinn's hand once again, now that it was official. "I'm blinded by this rock here. Did you think she'd say no unless you dazzled her?"

Quinn grinned, taking the comment in stride. If Jill had wanted to explain the diamond, she would have, so he let it go. "I meant to be back a little earlier," he mumbled to Jill.

Her smile filled her face. "Don't worry about it."

"I'm going to take a shower. Are there towels and everything in this bathroom, Jill?" Dave asked.

"Yep. Just look in the cabinet. Everything you

need should be there." Jill walked to Quinn and eyed the groceries. "Are you going to cook breakfast?"

"How does pancakes, fried eggs and toast made from that homemade bread of Chase's, sound? Maybe a little of the flower thief's strawberry jam?"

"Perfect," Jill said. "But don't you think it's time that you left Arlene alone?"

"Ha, Jill. Funny. That's a story destined to live on."

Jill let him go, watching him make breakfast preparations. She considered how stories changed over time, how some of them were passed down for generations. The Kinney women were like that, she supposed. She couldn't help but wonder what stories might be shared about her someday.

Jill glanced at the clock. "It's 11:20 already? You really are late." She poked Quinn's side. "It's nearly lunch time."

Quinn studied her for a moment. "Are you okay? You look like you've been crying."

"All morning," she admitted, biting her lip.

"Talk to me. What's wrong?"

Jill placed her hand on Quinn's arm. "Uncle Dave is having bypass surgery a few days after he gets home."

"He came up here to tell you in person," Quinn realized, rubbing her back. "I'm so sorry, Hon."

"He came here to tell me the truth about my parents, about myself really."

"What's that?"

"Quinn... I don't think I can marry you," she blurted.

"What?!" Quinn pulled away from her. "Stop."

"No, it's..."

"Stop right there, Jill. You love me."

"Yes."

"And I love you and that's just it. It doesn't matter what you've learned that you didn't know last night. Does it change your feelings? What could possibly change your feelings over night?"

"Baby, I didn't mean it that way. Of course, I'm going to marry you. I just might need some time. Uncle Dave is having surgery next week. I need to be there with him. He won't be ready to come back for the wedding, so we should postpone it. I want him to walk me down the aisle, Quinn."

"Postpone it?"

"Yes. And, I might need some time."

"Time for what?"

"To heal."

"I thought you said you were doing better. I rushed it, didn't I?" Quinn asked, blaming himself.

"No, it's not your fault, Quinn. Uncle Dave told me that my parents were murdered."

He began to speak and then stopped. She could see his mind turning over that, which seemed impossible.

"Speak slowly. Tell me everything." She began talking, and while she did, he cooked, because he needed to do something with his hands. He needed to give his brain time to process everything she said, to ease the panic that had exploded in his chest the minute she said she couldn't marry him.

While she spoke, she took moments of pause, fit pieces that didn't make sense an hour or so ago into the whole again, and saw how they connected. She fought the feelings of anger toward her grandmother. Her grandma couldn't change it now, and she might have been right. Even just a couple of years ago, before the assault, Jill might have tried to go after the company, to find her parents' killers. She wouldn't think of it now, or she would try not to. That part of her life was behind her.

Dave returned from the bathroom, showered and dressed. He had taken some time to use the internet, check email and touch base with his doctor by leaving her a message about his spur of the moment trip to Michigan. When he came back into the dining room, he found Jill and Quinn at the kitchen table waiting for him.

"We're coming home with you," Quinn announced. "We're family, Dave. No arguments. We'll be there at the hospital with you."

Jill squeezed Quinn's hand, touched by his thoughtfulness. They talked about the family history over brunch, and through the hours of conversation, Quinn's worry for Jill grew with every unfolded layer. He had always been more superstitious than she had. If there was a curse, or a legend, or whatever he could call it, Jill was definitely afflicted. She tried to accept it without focusing, knowing the hard hours of introspection would come later. Perhaps by paying attention to the deep historical ties, she could avoid facing her parents' murder. Quinn wondered if it was right for Dave to be telling her all of this now. If not now, he realized there might not be a chance to tell her.

The timing was more than unfortunate, Quinn thought, but understood. Jill was just beginning to regain her total health. He worried that this vindication for her proclivity to get into dangerous situations might give her even more courage to help solve problems, to seek answers no matter the cost. He hoped not.

The hours slipped by. It was the longest time Jill had ever seen Quinn sit in one spot. They drained another pot of coffee and listened while Dave retold many stories of the Kinney women. They reread the newspaper clippings, and this time Jill made copies.

Quinn called the office and had Noel make reservations for them to go back on the same flight with Dave. He left a message for Chase to call or come home as soon as possible. Less than twenty minutes passed before Chase drove in.

Quinn excused himself from the conversation and went outside to meet his brother.

"What's up?" Chase asked.

"What's going on at the office?" Quinn returned.

"Let me get this straight. Noel tracked me down mid-recipe and told me to come home ASAP, and you want to know what's going on at the plant?" Before Quinn could reply, Chase shook his head and grinned. "Ass!" He exclaimed and shoved his brother lightly. "Brenda has called a couple of times. She has two locations lined up for you to go see. There is one in Oregon that is her favorite. Do they have the soil to grow good tomatoes in Oregon?"

Quinn chuckled.

"Can't we just add on to the one in Indiana?" Chase asked.

"We'd have to double the size of it," Quinn replied. "It's doable, but a plant on the west coast would cut shipping costs. It would give us a presence over there for expansion."

"Makes sense," Chase agreed.

Quinn smiled. He studied his brother for a moment. "Listen. I need you to go and look at these plants. Look at the area. Check the soil. Talk to the farmers. "

"Go with you, you mean?"

"No. I need you to just take this one. I trust your judgment."

Chase hesitated. "I love the whole equal partnership thing we've got going here, bud, but ah... I don't know what to look for. I'm going to be in the yard looking at the soil, hanging out at the area farms, and checking out the tomatoes. I don't know the first thing about factories or labor costs or anything like that really."

"First, you know more than you think. You manage this one just as much as I do. Second, I want you to think about those things. Find a good tomato and a good plant, and we can put it together. Listen to Brenda's opinions. Bring back a few cases of tomatoes from each place. You can test them out here. Will you go?"

"When? Because I've got school soon."

"We'll work that out. It'll be the next few days or

early next week at the latest."

"You're sure about this? Why don't you want to go?"

"I have to go to Florida with Jill. Uncle Dave has to have bypass surgery."

Chase swallowed hard. "Damn man, that sucks. Why didn't you just say so instead of letting me carry on about school? Set it up. I'll go."

"You're going to need to take the digital camera. I want pictures and full reports on each location, blue prints, electrical, plumbing prints, land surveys. I'm going to run the locations against our customer base and see where there's opportunity for expansion."

"Is there a price range in mind? Do we have funding immediately?"

Quinn grinned at that. "Brenda will only show you places we can afford. We've paid both loans--the one here and the one in Indiana-- forward for four years. We've got about four hundred thousand in the bank and another four hundred plus in accounts receivable. We're doing well, partner."

"Sounds good. Certainly enough for tuition."

"Shit. Is that due already?"

Chase laughed. "Nice try."

As Quinn and Chase entered the house, Uncle Dave spoke loudly. "Man, am I glad to see you! Chase, it seems all your brother can do is fry eggs and make coffee. Somewhere into today's mix, I missed lunch."

"In honor of your visit my brother just informed me that we're all going to Bayside for dinner tonight," Chase lied, winking in his brother's direction.

Quinn didn't miss a beat, "I thought it was a good idea, but only if you all want to go."

*   *   *

Dinner at Bayside was wonderful. The group of Quinn, Jill, Dave and Chase were joined by Chase's sometimes girlfriend Noel. Per usual, Chase regaled the group with entertaining antics. When they returned home, Quinn needed a moment to himself to process and relax, so he walked out to the mailbox and loaded his arms with the contents that were jammed inside. With three people living in the home, they often each assumed someone else had taken care of things, like mail. As a result, the box was usually stuffed full before they got to it.

He pulled his key from his pocket to re-open the door, surprised to find it unlocked. Jill must not have gone to bed yet. Since the attack, she locked and checked every door and window throughout the house before sleeping. He locked the door behind him. The lights were turned off, but the French door was open. He tossed the mail on the dining table, and moved to the bedroom. Jill lay in bed, staring up at the ceiling.

"I wish we had a skylight," she said.

It was the first night in over a year that the house wasn't locked down. Quinn was thrilled, but didn't comment. They had enough to talk about. When he crawled into bed next to Jill, he couldn't hide his worry, couldn't stop the scowl that crossed his face. She turned to face him, unsure how to start. "Quinn, I know you're worried about me."

He didn't say anything, waiting for her to continue.

"I called Uncle Dave because I was beginning to

question my parents' death. Dr. Letters suggested I find someone to talk about it with. I remembered things through therapy that didn't make sense. It makes sense now."

"Do you feel better?"

"No," she said slowly. "My parents were probably murdered. I survived a plane crash that should have killed me, and apparently this trouble I get into is in my genes." She paused, considering. "It's a lot to take in, but it feels more like the truth. And I understand why Gram didn't tell me. I don't agree with her decision, but I get it." She sighed. "I just feel... exhausted. Like all of my emotions have been sucked right out of me by a giant vacuum."

She smiled through it and reached out to hold his hand.

"What about the wedding?"

"I want to marry you, Quinn. I just want to give it some time. I don't want to set a date yet."

"That sounds like you're taking back your yes." He hated the way he sounded, but he couldn't help it. He felt for her ring finger, surprised when he didn't feel a ring.

"It's not that I don't want to marry you, Quinn. I just need to take some time for myself first. I need some space to make sense of everything."

"So you took the ring off? That's a real good way to support your claim, Jill. Nice."

"I feel like I don't know who I am right now."

He leaned upward, supporting himself with a crooked arm. "You're planning on leaving, aren't you?"

She hadn't worked out the details in her mind. "I think I'll stay with Uncle Dave for a while after the surgery. That way I'll get some space, and I can help take care of him."

He sighed. "On a logical level, it makes sense," he admitted.

"I do want to marry you. Yes, Quinn, I will become your wife. I just need some time. Trust me, okay?" She looked hopeful. She didn't want him to be angry with her. Of course, there was no stopping his disappointment. She'd have to live with that.

"I understand." Quinn rolled over, feeling selfish and miserable and alone.

Chapter 10

Wednesday, August 8th

Whatever it was, it smelled amazing. Jill opened her eyes slowly, squinting at the sheer volume of light in the room. She was naturally an early riser, waking with dawn easily as long as she had her coffee. The light suggested this was hours past, but she felt wonderful. Her whole body was rested and relaxed in a way that it hadn't been in a long time. She grinned at how light she felt, how wonderful it was to have it all out there in the open with no more secrets. She tossed Quinn's robe over her pajamas and opened the bedroom door.

Uncle Dave sat at the kitchen table looking through one of Jill's picture albums sipping coffee. Jill glanced worriedly toward the coffee maker, but saw the decaf container on the countertop and relaxed. Quinn stood over the stove, amidst a flurry of pans, pots, and mixing bowls. Dave noticed her first. "Good morning, Jilly."

Quinn turned, smiled fully, and watched her stretch her arms over her head. He hugged her. "I'm sorry about last night," he whispered.

She smiled fully and moved away from him. "I don't remember the last time I slept in so late, but I feel wonderful." She sat down next to Dave in front of the pile of mail from the night before. "What's for breakfast?"

"Stuffed French toast, American fries, sliced cantaloupe and strawberries, scrambled eggs with Chase's cream herb sauce... and decaf coffee and orange juice."

She gaped at him while her uncle chuckled. "Oh, is that all?"

"From the look on your face, I take it that Quinn doesn't treat you quite this well every morning. Since he cooked for us yesterday, I thought this might be the rule rather than the exception."

"Quinn doesn't cook for me all that often, but Chase does. He spends a few days each week experimenting on new dishes, and I am always the first to sample with him." The house phone rang, and Quinn picked it up. After a moment, he handed it over to Jill. "It's Dean."

Jill frowned but took the phone. "Hey."

"Are you avoiding me on purpose or what?"

"No, Dean..."

"Because I've left four voice mails and two messages on your answering machine--all of them urgent--and I haven't heard a word."

Dean actually sounded upset, a quality Jill was only vaguely familiar with in him. Jill glanced over at the machine and grimaced at the blinking light. "I'm sorry, Dean. Uncle Dave flew in for a surprise visit and..."

"He's there now?"

"Yes."

"Oh. Damn. Sorry, Jill."

She listened to him shuffle around, the odd ambient noises always in the background of his speaker phone calls.

"Well, at least you've had time to see the package. I would have liked to talk you through some of it, but you must be packed by now. You are packed, right? I know how you put these things off. I can't believe you haven't called me. With something this big going down, I would have thought you'd like a little help prepping."

"What are you talking about?"

"The cruise."

"Dean, start back at the beginning and speak slowly."

"Did you fall off the earth or what? Don't you open your mail?"

Jill pulled the pile in front of her and spotted a large manila package immediately. She ripped it open and slid out a folder, a few photographs, a glossy magazine, and a typed note from Dean's office. "I'm seeing it now. Hold on."

She skimmed through the note and itinerary of a week long cruise through the Great Lakes. "This is some kind of job?"

"A whole bunch of big wigs are getting together for a fund raiser or something like that, and they need a photographer. They had one set up months ago, but the deal fell through just last week. You're their first choice to replace him. And better yet, someone way up the food chain requested you by name. Jill,this is the gig we've been dreaming about, the one that separates you from the flock."

Uncle Dave pulled the magazine from the pile and started glancing through it. Jill stood away from the table and paced the living room.

"When is the trip?"

"You'll need to be in Traverse City tomorrow."

"Tomorrow? Dean, are you crazy?! I can't go tomorrow."

"Jill, it's triple your standard pay for a destination shoot. I've already booked you. You have to go."

"No, Dean. It's complicated. Uncle Dave's having bypass surgery, and I'm going to Florida to be with him."

Dean quieted. "Shit. I didn't know."

"You couldn't have. It's okay. But I can't go, Dean. He's all the family I have."

Dean didn't say anything for a moment. "I understand, Jill, but I need you to do something for me. Just look through the information. I'll call you back in half an hour. If you still need to turn it down, okay. If you do this, you can fly from the trip to Uncle Dave's. Spend a month if you want. I'll give you a whole month off with no phone calls or jobs from me."

"Yeah, right."

"I'm dead serious, Jill. No calls."

He was lying, even if he didn't mean to be--but that wasn't the issue. Jill wanted to be there for her uncle.

"I don't know when we'll get an opportunity like

this one again. Just think about it."

Jill knew he wouldn't let her off the phone until he had his way. "Okay, I'll look at the package. Call me in an hour, and I'll let you know."

"One hour. Good."

She clicked off the phone, caught off guard. Both Quinn and Dave were hovered over the materials, talking quietly.

When they didn't stop talking, she cleared her throat. "What's up, guys?"

Dave shook his head, not taking his eyes from the page. "Jill, you cannot come to Florida with me. You have to go on this boat."

"What?"

"You have to take this job. That's what your agent was referring to, right? There's a job on this boat?"

"I'd have to leave tomorrow. I'm not taking the job, Uncle Dave. I'm going to Florida with you."

Dave stared her down. He slid the magazine across the table. "Just look at those pictures. It's unreal."

"I don't need to look at the pictures. I am going to Florida."

Quinn placed a hand on her uncle's shoulder. "Dave and I just talked about it, Jill. This isn't a bad idea. I'll go to Florida with Uncle Dave as planned. You can fly down when the job is finished." Quinn gave her a lascivious wink. "Maybe, if this guy isn't a pain in the ass, we can even get an afternoon or two at the beach," he offered, winking at Dave.

Dave enjoyed the joke. "Look at these numbers, would ya? That's a helluva paycheck to turn down."

Jill nodded. "Dean said it was about triple the rate."

"Yeah, but triple the rate with no costs to you. They're paying for your transportation, your lodging, food, and giving you all that money. They're even supplying an assistant."

"It's not about the money, Uncle Dave."

"Listen, Jill. I know you love me. I know you want to be supportive. It's not like I'll be alone. Karen will be there too, you know."

"Who?"

"My new girlfriend. I've been seeing her for a few months. Quinn will come down, too."

Quinn nodded as he moved back into the kitchen. "Besides, you don't do well in hospitals," he called over his shoulder.

"It's not like we need the money," she said, shaking her head.

Dave smiled. "Jilly, it's like you said, it's not about the money. Look at this ship."

Reluctantly, Jill pulled some of the materials toward her. The magazine sized brochure was crisp, showcasing a full cover photograph of a bright white ship with stars and stripes emblazoned across the bow and hull. The *New America*, according to the article, was a brilliant combination of state of the art technology and design that placed the guest first, even within the architecture, in a way that cruise lines hadn't truly done in decades.

The state rooms were considerably larger than the typical fare on other ships, and the entertainment included less of the hokey let's-play-trivia variety and focused more on maximizing space with attractive interests. For example, the ship was the first to have a convertible IMAX on board that transitioned into a planetarium.

At 628 feet in length, the *New America* was as long as possible to sail through the St. Lawrence Lock system in the transition between seasons. While the *New America* would sail exclusively throughout the Great Lakes in the summer months, the winter would bring the ship to southern destinations. Jill read on, quickly intrigued by the floating palace.

"Have you read the part about the beds yet?" Dave asked.

Quinn laughed. "Do you mean the California Balinese Dream beds?"

Jill rolled her eyes at their tactics, but she was definitely intrigued. "I wonder who requested me," she mumbled.

"What?"

"Dean said that their first choice fell through, but I was requested by name. There's some big event happening. Lots of really rich and important people, I guess." She continued to look through the flyer. Quinn brought out plates of food for them.

Not more than fifteen minutes had passed when the phone rang again. Jill frowned. "It hasn't been an hour."

Quinn reached back over the counter edge to grab the phone. He answered it, "Hello, oh hey, Dean."

Rather than hand Jill the phone, he clicked on the speaker button and set it in front of her.

"Jill?"

"Hey, Dean. You're on speaker. Say hi to Uncle Dave."

"Hi, Uncle Dave. I'm sorry about your health concerns."

"Thanks," Dave mumbled.

"I know it's early to be calling you back, Traynor, but if you're going to cancel, I've got to go to work on this."

"She's not canceling," Dave said.

"Great! Good decision..."

"Uncle Dave, no!" Jill interrupted. "I said I'd go to Florida with you, and I'm going."

"I'll go with him, Jill. I am completely capable."

"Babe, I know you're capable."

"Jill, this is the chance of a lifetime. You know what your mother would say, don't you?" Uncle Dave asked.

Jill paused. "No. What would she say?"

"You only live once."

Quinn leaned back in his chair and smiled but said nothing.

"If you don't go, I'll be stressed that you're blowing this major career move on some dumb hospital procedure. It will increase my blood pressure substantially, adding more risk to the surgery. You don't want me to be aggravated before my bypass surgery, do you?"

Jill sighed. "No, I guess not."

Dean pounced. "So, you're going to be there?"

"I'll be there."

"Great. Then we need to go over some details." Jill picked up the phone, took Dean off speaker, and walked back to her office.

After she had left the room, Quinn smiled at Jill's uncle. "Nicely done," he said and resumed eating.

"Being in a hospital again wouldn't have been good for her. I'll be out of it, most of the time. No sense making her come down for that. Hell, if I hadn't decided to come up here, I wouldn't have even told her I was having the operation until it was over."

Quinn hesitated. "There's a difference between protecting her and sheltering her," he said gently.

Dave paused between bites. "Yeah. You're right, Quinn."

Chase chose that moment to scuffle into the kitchen. "Uncle Dave! I didn't know you were still here." The men shook hands.

"I didn't know you were here," Quinn said in response. "I thought maybe you'd stayed out for the night."

"No, I got back late. Closed the bar."

"Do I have to remind you that you're not yet twenty-one?" Quinn groaned.

"No, I literally closed the bar. They're a little short handed, and I stepped in to help out for a few minutes and next thing you know, I'm being handed keys and shit."

"You have a job."

Chase heaped a plate with food and sat down with the men. "I know, I know. I have a demanding job. I didn't pick up a second occupation, I swear. I just helped out a friend."

"It's a woman, isn't it?" Uncle Dave asked.

Chase smirked. "She's a honey. Six feet tall and all legs. She's the new manager." To his brother he said, "They have gone through quite a few of them since you left, you know. This one's a keeper."

"For the bar or for you?" Quinn asked.

"The bar, jackass. But I have to say, I wouldn't mind her interest."

They shared a laugh as Jill came back.
"G'morning." She patted Chase's arm as she sat down next to him. "Well, I leave for Traverse City in the morning."

"Yeah?" Chase asked. "What for?"

"I'm going on a cruise of the Great Lakes."

"Sweet... but what about Florida?"

Quinn piped in before Jill could go through a list of objections again. "I'm going to Florida in the morning. Which leaves you with two things--are you ready?"

"Yeah."

"You're in operational control of Three Bobbers. And second, I need you to take those meetings with Brenda. I'll call her and tell her you'll fly out tomorrow."

"Which means I really don't have operational control of Three Bobbers until I get back?"

"DeeDee can handle it for a few days."

"Okay. I'll give her a call."

From breakfast forward, neither Jill nor Quinn had a moment to spare as they each hurried to make arrangements in separate directions. Thankfully, Quinn had caught up on the laundry recently, but packing was still a chore. Chase was also leaving soon, but he made his plans the easy way by calling Noel to set up both sets of travel plans and the meeting with Brenda. Uncle Dave borrowed a novel and vegged out on the sofa in a calm self-sanctuary of peace that belied the outer chaos.

By mid-afternoon, Quinn and Jill began to close their projects and finish packing. Chase had made two trips back and forth to the office, cutting into Quinn's packing time with questions and details. The younger McCord finally settled in the living room with paperwork.

Dave sat down his book. "Tell me something."

Chase picked up his head. "Sure. What do you want to know?"

"I was under the impression that the young woman... what was her name?"

"From last night? That was Noel."

"I thought the two of you were together. Am I wrong?"

"On and off for about three years... or shit, more than that. On and off since I've been here. Since high school."

"Is it a May through September thing?"

"No, not really. Noel goes to Central Michigan University, uhm that's mid-state. About three and a half hours from here."

Dave groaned. "Chase, I grew up in Michigan, remember?"

"Right. My mistake, sorry. She's in a nursing program. We see each other quite a bit. I usually stop on my way up north when she's free, and she rides home with me."

"On now or off?"

"Well, I thought she was pissed off at me, but last night she was wearing the necklace I bought her. So, I think I'm off the hook."

"I noticed that," Dave sat up, interested. "Unusual piece. I meant to ask her about it. What kind of a stone was that?"

Chase grinned. "No stone. Believe it or not, it was made from the wing of a butterfly."

"No shit?"

"Yeah, it's a blue something. I don't remember the name. I bought it at a place with all kinds of kick ass jewelry just down the road from the plant . I use it to get me out of trouble quite a bit. Are you in trouble with Karen?" Chase asked, raising an eyebrow.

"It wouldn't hurt to bring her back something nice."

"Well, come with me then. I need to stop by the plant anyway."

Dave rose from the sofa and headed toward the

door to find his shoes.

"Hey guys," Chase called, peeking his head into the bedroom. "Uncle Dave and I are going out for a while. We'll be back in an hour or so. Do you need anything?"

"Nope," Quinn said. "If I do, I'll call the office."

"Sounds good. See ya later."

As soon as the men had left, Jill turned to Quinn. "Did you put them up to this?"

Quinn moved the suitcase off the bed. "No, but I wish I had," he said. He brought her body toward his and kissed her, pulling her with him toward the bed.

Chapter 11

The drive from Drummond to Traverse City was largely uneventful, but Jill always enjoyed passing through Petoskey. A little over two years ago she was hired to photograph a selection of historic homes and the downtown area for a magazine article. Jill fell in love with the old charm and color of the place. She liked the hills and shops and homes that were pristinely kept with attention paid to every detail. Moreover, she loved the flowers that seemed to be everywhere and the people. At some point, Jill would find time to spend there.

She parked in a lot near the Traverse City airport, following the instructions in her packet precisely. A long black car, engine running, was parked at the edge of the lot. As Jill stepped out of her vehicle, a man stepped out of the limo. "Ms. Traynor?" He called.

Jill smiled and nodded her head. "That's me."

"I'd be happy to gather your luggage. I'll be taking you to the heli-port."

Jill shrugged. "Well, you can help if you want, but I'm not going to stand here and watch you carry my luggage."

"It's really no problem, miss."

Jill sensed a twinkle lurking in the man's eyes somewhere just out of sight. "Great." She chose to carry her camera equipment, leaving him the suitcase of clothing. They loaded the trunk together, with the man opening the door in the back for Jill to enter after they finished. When they started off, Jill lowered the partition between them by pressing a button. "Do you work for the cruise company?"

"No, miss."

Well, isn't he a chatty one, Jill thought, smiling. Minutes later they parked, and Jill was escorted through a lobby into another room followed closely by her cart of luggage. "I don't mean to be a pain. I would just feel more comfortable if I could push the cart," she argued quietly to the bellman beside her, who rolled his eyes and maintained control.

Inside the room, a tall dark-haired heavy man was waving his arms abruptly, his face drawn into a tight scowl directed at a petite blonde. "This just isn't right!" He yelled. "A chef is not separated from his knives. It's insulting."

The woman smiled calmly and spoke in a volume just out of Jill's earshot. Jill looked away, not wanting to stare. There were others in the room including three men dressed in black, whom Jill suspected were security agents.

At the bellman's direction, Jill moved closer to the woman but declined an offered chair.

"Listen, Chef. Your knives will be perfectly safe. This man," she gestured to a bulky man with security in yellow letters across the sleeve of his upper arm, "will not let them out of his sight until they are locked in the kitchen. You cannot take them personally on board."

"Then I'll wait for them."

"We need you to be on board today. If you want to wait, you might as well fly back home. I have alternate chefs waiting in the wings. No hard feelings." Her voice was firm and direct. Something in the way she squared her shoulders made Jill believe she was bluffing.

"They will not know how to make my Northland Surf and Turf," the chef rambled on. Jill listened to them carry on, feeling at home. Eventually realizing he had lost the battle he added, "Fine. If you must, then take them."

The late thirties brunette turned toward Jill, never losing a beat. "Ms. Traynor?"

"Yes, that's me. But please call me Jill."

"Very well. I'm Debi White," she extended her hand. "I'm the Special Events Coordinator for the *New America*. I'll be your contact and go-between for everything and anything you need assistance or direction with. I will also be your roommate."

"Great," Jill said, liking her instantly. "Where do I go from here?"

"First, I need you to sign some forms." Debi opened a brown leather briefcase on the nearest table and pulled out a thick file folder. "These are pretty standard," she began, flipping through them. "This is the one I want to draw your attention to." She pulled out a legal-sized, stapled document. "Each place that is highlighted in yellow needs to be signed and dated. It goes through some of the rules and expectations of this job, but one piece is crucial. You cannot take any of the pictures with you. All rolls of film and all digital pictures must be turned over with your cards wiped clean before you leave. Do you understand?"

"Yes." Jill frowned.

"Is this a problem?"

It just meant that she wouldn't be able to expand her personal collection. "So... even pictures without people... like one of a lighthouse, or a bird--I can't keep any of it?"

Debi considered. "If you keep a separate file of non-human shots, I can have someone go through them. It's possible that they'll let you keep those, but they'll have to decide on an individual basis. I can't make any promises. Good enough?"

"Yes, that's fine." Jill nodded her acceptance. It was a little late to say no anyway, she thought.

Debi smiled. "Good. Now, you can have a seat at this table and fill out these papers. The security detail will search your bags over there." She pointed to the large tables, standard x-ray equipment, and a big machine that Jill didn't recognize. "The security force is outstanding. They'll go through each piece of luggage, but they'll be kind about it."

"Is this typical of cruise ships?" Jill asked. "Do they always check your luggage right in front of you?"

"No. If you were arriving via port, you wouldn't see any of this. And it isn't typical to check this thoroughly. Of course, the *New America* has a security team, but an external team has been brought in for this week. I'll tell you more about it later. I'm sure we'll have time to talk. Okay?"

"Sounds good," Jill said. She moved to the table, sat down, and began filling out the forms.

"Ms. White!" Another young man rolled a luggage rack into the terminal. "Your luggage has arrived. And the ice man is on his way in."

Jill wondered what the "ice man" looked like and followed her entourage to one of the security tables while Debi's luggage was brought to the next station. She glanced up between pages, checking the progress. Carefully, case by case, each item was inspected. She tried not to intervene when they began looking through her equipment but felt some sympathy for the chef. During the check, a tall, thin man with long white-blond hair was escorted to Debi.

She was about to greet him when he started talking. "My ice is a special concoction. It must be guaranteed that it is treated as I specified. I am not comfortable boarding the ship days ahead of my ice. My sculptures cannot be guaranteed if the ice care is not maintained. The cases have generators, but they only perform at optimal conditions for six hours. If someone forgets to plug them back in, or there's a delay..."

Debi opened a file and pulled out a type written document that Jill couldn't see. "Mr. Volkov, I have a signed and dated guarantee from the Captain of the *New America* that your ice will be handled as you instructed during the Chicago boarding. Please, sir, the staff is competent at following directions, I assure you."

Volkov scanned the agreement and nodded curtly. "My luggage has already been checked, yes?"

"Yes. You are free to board the helicopter once you've passed the security scan. He will show you where to go." She motioned for her assistant to come forward.

Jill brought her attention back to the luggage check. Although they checked through everything, they also placed it all quite nicely back into the bags. The guard took an extra moment to zip the awkward toiletry bag from Debi's case that not only housed make up and self care products, but insulin, needles, and other medications. Several more minutes passed before her luggage passed their scrutiny.

"Jill?"

Jill turned.

"We can board the helicopter now. I'll try to answer any questions you have along the way."

Debi led the way from the terminal to the helipad. "Jill, this Ian Volkov and Chef Ramon Guillermo. Mr. Volkov is a master ice carver. Chef LeFranc is a world renowned chef of haute cuisine. Jill is a national award winning photographer."

"Bonjour mademoiselle."

"Good day."

"Hi." Jill smiled and shook their hands.

She followed Debi to the helicopter, a medium sized bird with a white body and marine blue striping. She climbed in and sat next to the window. When they were boarded and buckled in, Debi gave them a brief orientation to helicopters, signaled the pilot, and handed out headphones. Even through the headphones, Jill was surprised at the sheer volume surrounding her. She felt as if she sat inside a speaker, her body vibrating against the quick whir of blades overhead.

The bird rose, darting quickly over Traverse City, the buildings progressively smaller, until Jill could only see miles of the dark blue Lake Michigan waters. She closed her eyes against a wave of motion sickness and attempted to put life into the perspective of the moment. Right now, she was on her way to a cruise ship where she had been requested to do that which she loved above all else-compose living works of art through photographs.

At home, a man loved her enough to want to spend the rest of his life with her, enough to fly across the country to sit with her uncle before and after surgery. She might only have one relative, but Uncle Dave had finally told her the truth. Jill knew that some people lived entire lives without knowing their history. She might have been through a great deal in her life, but things were looking up. All she needed was for her Uncle Dave to be well again. She glanced into the endless blue down at the point where the sky kissed the horizon line--one shade of blue leaning down to love another--and grinned, feeling sappy. When she got home, she'd marry Quinn McCord because she loved him, because life was short. As Uncle Dave reminded her throughout the years, there is only enough time to really do what we love, so why not get started?

Lost in her thoughts, Jill was startled when Debi tapped her shoulder. Debi leaned over and swiveled a microphone down and flipped a switch on Jill's headset. "How are you doing?" Debi asked, her voice soothing and clear in Jill's ears.

"That's amazing," Jill said, touching the headphones at her ears. She could no longer hear the roar of the helicopter but for a soft distant rumble.

"State of the art," Debi laughed. "They cancel out background noise. I keep wanting to sneak a pair to take home with me."

"No kidding." Jill smiled. "How long will the flight be?"

"We should actually be standing on the boat in

about forty-five minutes. It takes a few to disembark the chopper. You might think the *New America* looks small when we get closer to it, and in some respects that's true. It has to be smaller than typical cruise ships because of the St. Lawrence Seaway Locks. They made up for it by compacting a lot of cool features and transformative spaces into less square footage.

"It's really a remarkable ship. Two sections along the side of the ship fold down using a huge hydraulic system. From this location they launch canoes, kayaks, jet skis and tour boats besides the water taxis used to ferry guests to ports of call that do not have docking," Debi explained.

"Have you worked on the ship long?"

"This is the *New America*'s first season, so no one's worked on her very long. I've been with Magellan Adventure for about six months. Before that, I come from a long background of event management. Have you ever been on a cruise boat?"

"No. This is a first for me," Jill admitted.

"You'll probably love it. Of course, working on a cruise ship is different than vacationing on one."

"I understand that."

"You'll begin to understand the marvel of *New America* when we land. Take some time today and tomorrow to look around. Once the people arrive, you'll be pretty slammed, but the *New America* is a gift to cruise ships."

"It would have been good to have my camera with me. I'd like to take some aerial shots."

"Magellan has a collection of aerials. Jill, I'm not sure your agent filled you in on your purpose here,"

Debi said, not unkindly.

Jill leaned back. She had assumed she was taking a collection of shots of the ship, but she hadn't stopped to consider that. Of course, the cruise line already had a broad collection; the *New America* had been sailing all summer. It would be a bit late to put together an ad campaign. Then why was she here? "Good point. I guess I have no idea what I'm doing here." Everything is happening so fast, she thought, feeling unsettled.

"Are you familiar with the name Wayne Walker?"

Jill's eyes widened. "He's running for president. Yes, I'm familiar." Familiar might not be the right word, she thought. She knew he was a collage of radical, republican, and very popular to the far right wing of the party. She didn't know much about his politics, and she hadn't spent much time watching the news lately.

"This week aboard the *New America* is a special event cruise. It's a fund raiser for Wayne Walker's campaign. You're not here to take pictures of the ship as much as you are here to capture the individuals on board partaking in the week's events--on and off the ship. Walker's campaign is built on the idea of... well, of a *New America*. The primary shareholders of Magellan Adventures, the company that owns this ship, are personal friends and substantial contributors to the Walker campaign."

"Was this ship named after the campaign?"

"No. They were both named after their shared ideology, so to speak. It's a bit confusing and really beside the point." Debi shrugged it off. "When we land on board, you'll meet your assistant for the week."

"I get an assistant?"

"Yes. Erin is in training to be a cruise photographer, but she just started and I see no reason not to let her help you." Debi paused, glancing out the window. "So you'll meet Erin, and she'll show you to your work space, and then the room you'll share with me. I apologize for the shared accommodations. With so many extra security staffers on board, we had to make some adjustments."

"I don't mind sharing a room."

"Good. I won't be there much, but I'm betting that you won't be there much, either. You'll have a daily itinerary. Events you'll be expected to attend, clothing requirements, etc. Erin will be a great resource. I've been able to work with her for a while now, and I find her invaluable. I'd like to steal her as my own personal assistant."

"Ooh, Jill, look." Debi pointed out the window. In the distance, Jill could see a small line against the water.

Jill watched out the window as the ship became closer. The helipad was on the fantail of the ship about a half-mile out. It looked so small that Jill barely believed they could land on it. It was round and blue in color with a white star in the center. As Debi said earlier, it was astounding. The helicopter landed with little fuss in the center of the white star. It must have been difficult but appeared simple from a bystander's view. Once the rotary blades stopped, a guard rail raised mechanically around the edges of the deck. A team approached the copter, opened the doors, and escorted the passengers through the connected dock system into the ship. When they reached an open space near the fourth floor elevators, they were met by a group of employees. Debi made introductions and headed off.

Erin Nettles was a mid-twenties, attractive plus-sized woman with shoulder length blond hair and perfectly applied make-up. She was dressed in a sharp black suit and red blouse, black heels that gave her a bit more height and possibly a bit more confidence. Her smile was infectious, and Jill found herself grinning back.

"I'm Erin Nettles," she greeted, holding out her hand.

Jill shook it warmly. "Jill Traynor."

"I know Debi said our names, but it always seems more personal to say it myself," she offered. "Your work is exquisite. As soon as I found out who I'd be working with, I Googled you. I love that piece with the cardinal on the grave site."

Not being a real fan of the internet, Jill was often surprised by the people who commented on liking her work. The piece Erin referred to had won a few national competitions. Jill took it when she was just a little girl, right after her parents passed. No, Jill corrected, her parents were murdered, she thought. It was best to remember the truth. She realized Erin was waiting for her to respond. "Sorry. I didn't mean to space out just then. Thank you, Erin. The cardinal piece is one of my favorites also."

Erin smiled. "Let me show you our workspace. It's on deck six. Actually," she paused to flip through papers on her clipboard, "let me show you to your quarters first. It is one deck up then we'll walk up to six. Or would you rather take the elevator?"

"I'll just follow however you want to lead, but I don't mind stairs," Jill said looking around. The hallways were narrow, but the stairwells were beautifully finished with mirrored walls and dark stained wooden molding. After years of being out of the construction business, Jill still paid attention to carpentry details. A small part of her missed the work. "Have you ever been on a cruise ship before?" Jill asked.

"Absolutely. I've traveled on three cruises as a tourist before I came to work for Magellan. When I started the training program here, I also spent a week on another one of their ships, the Daybreak. It's much bigger than this one but not nearly as fancy or modern," Erin explained. "And this one is so much more... American. Have you ever been on one?"

"Nope. This is my first."

"Oh, well, welcome then."

"What do you mean, more American?"

"First of all, most cruise ships are registered to other countries. They sail international waters, but other countries have more lenient standards. Magellan cruises are registered to the United States. Secondly, the staff is predominantly American or Canadian on this ship. On other ships, you'd be pressed to find many Americans. All of the waiters in the Grand Palace and Lighthouse Room are Jamaican, of course, and some of the hotel staff is more internationally based--but the rest of us are almost totally American."

"All the waiters are Jamaican?"

"If they're not Jamaican born, they're Jamaican

trained. The best waiters in the world come from Jamaica, or so they say."

Erin, Jill quickly realized, was a fountain of information. Who knew this sort of trivia? Of course, most people probably didn't know the inner working of a culinary factory, Jill told herself silently. "Where are you from?"

"Born and raised until my late teenage years in Kalamazoo, Michigan. My family lives in Sandusky, Ohio now, though. They own a little restaurant there. I am looking to move to Chicago eventually. You're in northern Michigan right?"

"Yep. Drummond Island."

"We sail past there, I think. I've never been there, but the small towns we've toured with the cruise are amazing." Erin stopped in front of a door and handed Jill a plastic card key. "E517."

Jill moved the card in and out of the slip, waiting for the green light before she twisted the handle. She was expecting to walk into something like a dorm room and couldn't contain her grin as she went in. "Wow!"

Erin laughed pleasantly at Jill's expression. "This is an Erie Suite. You're sharing it with Debi White, but the room is designed for three. It's approximately 350 square feet." They walked through a small sitting room into the master bedroom that held two beds. The room was creatively designed, featuring closets and storage spaces in every conceivable hideaway. For example, the ottoman next to the love seat opened for storage. The vanity mirror built over the desk opened to a hideaway safe and storage shelves. There were deep dresser drawers and well built cabinets. Further, the decor of the rooms was impressive. The fabrics combined shades of blue in an elegant and somehow understated manner. Erin took several moments showing Jill some of the smaller features of the room. "And of course, an Erie suite would not be complete without the forty inch television and set-top-box kiosk."

"Huh?" Jill asked, dumbfounded.

Erin found the remote control and turned on the television. She opened a cabinet beneath the television to reveal a wireless keyboard and other remote devices. "From this one menu system, you can check out menus, make reservations for dinner, look for entertainment options, send e-mail, surf the web, view any number of scenes around the ship through live feed, see the course of the ship plotted continuously along a map, listen to any band or group that has been or is on the planet, and watch any one of sixteen thousand movies."

"The coolest part of the machine is this," Erin explained, unable to keep her excitement from her voice. She held up a small device that had a tube shaped hole in it. Jill looked on puzzled, wondering what could possibly be so important about this item. "You see, this kiosk system is known as a smart set-top box, and the device here is a prototype being tested aboard this ship. If it runs successfully, it will be a household item one day. By pressing in this code, we're linked to a medical services system." She pressed it to show Jill exactly how it worked, and Jill watched instructions pop onto the screen.

The monitor directed her to place her right index finger over the hole. "This machine can take your blood pressure, pulse and temperature and, believe it or not, they can even examine your blood without poking you." Erin showed Jill another device that was connected to the screen. It folded down from a place on the wall and contained a headrest and a box with eye holes. "Sometimes, depending on your ailment, the computer will ask you to place your forehead here and look into the goggle. In here," Erin opened a drawer, "are disposable tips for this thing. Instead of a doctor using this instrument to look into your nose or throat, for example, it takes a picture and readings, transmitting the information through the system."

"You're telling me that there's basically a doctor in every room?"

"So to speak, yes. Of course, it can only handle a set number of ailments, but in time... Sorry, I must sound like such a geek. I have been so jazzed about the deal to test this technology that I forget others aren't quite as excited about it as I am."

Jill smiled. "It sounds interesting."

"This system really is incredible. Beyond all the medical stuff, you can watch much of the surveillance feed from the room as well. This channel flips through the decks in four second flashes, or you change the setting and just people watch for a while."

"The video feed is piped into the rooms?" Jill asked, stunned.

"Yes." Erin clicked over to reservations. "Also, because of the diverse options on board, there isn't one main seating for dinner. You can literally eat whenever and wherever you want to." Some require reservations while others are available for walk-in if you just can't make it to a terminal. For example, Debi has you scheduled to meet her for dinner in the Lighthouse Room." Erin smiled appreciatively. She glanced at her watch, then up at Jill. "Most of the time, I'm sure we'll be eating at the events we work."

Jill looked around, feeling overwhelmed. "I thought I'd be staying in a dorm or something."

"If you had staff status, your accommodations would be different. You have guest status because you're a contract employee. I'm assuming that you have a blue pass. Am I right?"

"I don't have any idea what you're talking about," Jill admitted.

Erin flicked the television back to the menu and quickly maneuvered to Jill's account. She pointed to the words "Blue Status" across the screen. "That means that any type of charges accrued from food and beverage are automatically deducted from your bill. Gift shop or miscellaneous charges up to one hundred dollars are deducted from your bill as well."

"One hundred dollars?"

"The cruise line philosophy is that contract guests are potentially future clientele. They want you to pick up some souvenirs to take with you. It's a helluva advertising plug if you ask me." Erin smirked. "Okay, I'll admit it--I came up with that one."

"I thought you were a photographer in training."

Erin nodded. "I am. I transferred from home office. I worked there for two years as an administrative assistant to an advertising executive. Really great boss, but to move up in Magellan you have to work on a ship for a few years in whatever capacity. I got my B.S. at Ohio State in Business and Advertising. Magellan recruited me. They wanted me to do something administrative, but I've always liked taking pictures, so here I am. Eventually, I'll move to something more like what Debi does."

"She mentioned that she wanted to steal you as her assistant."

Erin's eyes twinkled. "Debi's pretty new to Magellan. She was trained in a branch program, so I'm not sure she's aware of my background."

Jill saw something there, but let it pass.

"Anyway, let's get moving. I need to show you the work space and give you a tour. The itinerary should be there by now, and you'll want to prep. I can help you with any of that kind of stuff too. I want to learn all that I can, so just tell me when I could be doing something better, okay?" Erin requested.

"Just keep talking. You are a fountain of information."

"Chatter box is more like it," Erin blushed.

"Useful," Jill countered. She stuck the card key in her pocket and followed Erin up the stairs.

"Just so you know, the Lighthouse Room is on the top of the ship toward the bow. The Grand Palace is directly beneath it. Right now, we're at midship level 6 where the office is. The gift shops are on this level. So are several bars and clubs. Here we are." Erin stopped at a wall designed to house photographs. In the middle of two wall sections were touch screen kiosks, similar to the ones in the suites but smaller.

Jill understood, soaking in everything Erin said. She hoped she'd have some time to explore. The sheer luxury was startling. Jill had always been told that cruise boats were posh, but she had no idea. She braced her legs against a roll, feeling slightly out of balance. "Where is the office?" Jill asked, hoping she hadn't missed that part.

Erin smiled. "Another thing about cruise ships:what looks like a wall, sometimes isn't a wall." She felt at the edge of a wall section and pressed a button.

"You've got to be kidding me," Jill whispered. She hadn't noticed as much as a seam in the wall, not that she had been paying close attention. Revealed behind the wall was a very small, but efficient looking office system. The space was maybe six by four feet total, but it maximized the walls with built in shelves holding office equipment like a fax machine, printers, whatnot, and another section loaded with supplies.

"This is a special guest-staffers office. They re-equip it, depending on the need. All the shelves are interchangeable. For example, this," Erin tapped the side of a large box shaped printer, "is a photo printer. It's not one that produces pictures for the masses. It is simply for our use for the week. You've got an inter-ship phone and small kiosk. The directions to make ship to shore phone calls are on all of them, and you need a credit card. These drawers lock." Erin took a moment to go through her keys, which were color coded with rubber attachments. She stopped at a lime green one and opened the largest lock drawer.

Inside, Jill's cameras had been carefully packed in a foam lined drawer. The drawer above it included her external flash guns, memory cards, battery packs and other related items. It also contained Jill's set of keys, which were a much smaller collection than Erin's. Erin swept her hair over her shoulder. "Feel free to explore and get comfortable. If there is anything you need that isn't on the list, mention it to me and I'll track it down for you. Or, if I'm on task, message me through the kiosk system. Anyone on board can be contacted via the kiosk, okay?"

Jill swallowed. "Okay."

"Am I overwhelming you?"

"No," she lied.

Erin laughed. "Would you like some time in your suite before dinner?"

"Yes, I need to change my clothes."

"We better leave now then. I'm sorry I didn't have time to give you a more thorough tour. I expected the helicopter to arrive a bit earlier than it did. Would you like me to walk you back to your suite?"

"I think I can find it. It's just down one flight and towards the back of the boat on the left, right?"

"It's in the port-aft section, yes, E517."

"When will I see you next?"

"Whenever you'd like to."

"I'm sure you have things to do, and babysitting me doesn't need to be one of them."

"Your scheduled obligations are on the kiosk, and I'm sure the printed version has been delivered to your suite already. I have to coordinate with the person overseeing the museum set up after dinner for an hour or so, and then I'm mostly free. If you need me, you can dial my room directly. I'm in S309." Erin found a post-it note and wrote it down for Jill. "Otherwise, why don't we meet for breakfast in the morning and go from there?"

"Great idea," Jill agreed.

"How about the casual buffet on deck seven, say eight a.m.?"

"Sure. Sounds good."

"Okay." Erin handed Jill a small folded paper. "This is the map of the ship. I put a star next to your room and one next to the office. That way, if you need help or feel a little directionally challenged, you can show someone and they can help you."

"Thanks Erin, you've been so helpful."

"I've only begun to help. There isn't much about this ship that I don't know, Jill. Please feel free to ask me anything. My role this week is to help you, so take advantage of that. I insist," she stressed.

Jill nodded, intending on utilizing the encyclopedic blonde.

"Oh, one more thing. See the light at the top of the door?"

"I see it."

"When it's green, no one is standing in front of the panel-so you can open it up. When it's red..."

"Don't open the door. Got it."

Erin closed the door behind them and pointed out the button system on the right side. There were five identical unmarked buttons. By pressing a two button combination, Jill could access the room whenever she wanted to. "Okay then," Erin said. "I'll see you tomorrow morning at the latest. Have fun exploring."

"I can't wait. Bye." Jill waved, watching Erin walk away from her. Taking a deep breath, Jill stood in place for a moment and simply looked around. The windows opposite her showed a large deck and Lake Michigan beyond it. She wanted to go outside and breathe for a few minutes, enjoy the scenery, and explore the cruise ship, but she had dinner plans. She looked down at her left hand, now absent the ring she wore the day before, and sighed. Quinn would love this, she mused. Map in hand, Jill headed back to her suite.

*   *   *

By morning, Jill felt much more confident in her surroundings. Her body had adjusted more to the motion, her calves tensing to compensate to keep her steady. She awakened before the sunrise and hit the upper level track for some exercise. She returned to her room to find Debi already gone, so she quickly showered and found a cup of coffee at a cafe on deck six. It was going to be a beautiful day.

She set her camera down on the lounge chair to enjoy a few minutes of peace before her day started. She knew that Debi wanted to introduce her to some of the other staffers, but beyond that she wasn't sure what all her day included. She had a good hour before she was scheduled to meet Erin for breakfast.

Jill curled her knees to her chest and rested her mug beside her. The ring was back on her finger, sparkling in the sunshine. She didn't want to think about anything from home today. This was a work trip, but it was also supposed to be a break. She couldn't help worrying about Uncle Dave, feeling guilty that she was here and not there. Quinn could handle it, she thought. After the last few years of knowing him, Jill knew he could handle anything.

Chapter 12

Saturday 4pm, departure day, Chicago, IL

"People watching" had always been one of Jill's favorite pastimes while growing up, but the ship's disembarkation was a whole new level of intrigue, she decided, leaning against the railing of her spot on deck six. Since Jill had arrived on the ship earlier, she was able to watch the prior week's guests disembark when it docked in Chicago. Small boats and water taxis treaded water in the distance, bearing signs with destination names like Navy Pier. Individuals in an array of souvenir clothing paraded slowly from the side of the boat underneath Jill.

The platform system extended like an arm floating on the water connecting to the dock. She had been standing against the rail for a half-hour, and she still couldn't wrap her mind around how the system worked. From her vantage point, she could see well beyond the departing guests but also onto the dock, where behind a partition, men with long mirrored poles checked underneath large silver containers. Others guided dogs around rows of luggage.

Down the railing, two other employees took their mid-afternoon break on the deck to watch the commotion. Jill couldn't help but listen to their conversation.

"What are the dogs looking for?"

"Aren't they searching for drugs?"

"I doubt it. The man who searched my room wasn't looking for drugs."

"I wasn't there when they searched mine."

The wind picked up and Jill lost the next comments, but heard enough to take mental notes. The confidence she had felt earlier today was beginning to shake. The security updates she'd noticed as she toured the *New America* as well as the boarding of the secondary protection team she watched now made her feel just a little uneasy. Her planned breakfast with Erin had turned into three minutes in the buffet line together before Erin was called away. Since then, she had spent the day meeting random people aboard the ship and trying to stay out of the way when groups were called for disembarkation.

Sucked in to the drama and tidbits of conversation that floated up over the deck, Jill pulled a lounge chair close to the edge and sat down. She curled her knees to her chest and perched her camera on them to re-see what was happening through her viewfinder.

"Well, fancy seeing you here!" Erin called out.

"Good afternoon," Jill welcomed. She moved her stuff off the lounge chair next to her and Erin sat down.

"I just thought I'd take a few moments of rest. I guess you had the same idea?"

"Exactly," Jill smiled. "I was feeling a little overwhelmed by it all."

"Saturdays are always the craziest. It'll get worse later on. Once per week, we're flooded with a group of individuals who are utterly disoriented. By the end of the trip, everything smoothes out."

"It really is a different dynamic," Jill agreed.

"Would you like to see more of the ship?"

"Sure," Jill said.

Erin gained her feet and led the way upstairs.

"How is the museum exhibit going?"

Erin groaned. "It's going to be perfect, I know it. It's just getting there that's the hard part. Have you taken any shots?"

"Well, normally I'd be going crazy with it, but Debi told me that I wouldn't be able to keep any of the film or memory cards."

"Oooh, right." Erin nodded, sipping her coffee. "I didn't even think of that. Hey, breakfast was so rushed that I forgot to ask you... how did you like dinner last night?"

"Oh, goodness. It was wonderful!" Jill smiled. "Quinn is amazing with food so I am decently spoiled, but what I had last night was unreal." Jill reached down into her camera bag and pulled out a long cream colored piece of paper. "I got this from the waiter. It's a copy of last night's menu. Did you know it was called Great Lakes night? Look at this menu, Erin!" Jill exclaimed.

Erin looked it over, enjoying Jill's excitement. She had seen it before, but played along. "Very nice, indeed. What did you have?"

"I had the morel mushroom ragout with wild leaks appetizer. I chose the Great Lakes fish chowder with saffron for my soup and grilled duck breast salad. For my entree, I had peppercorn seared venison tenderloin. It was accompanied by Native American fry bread. I topped it off with a wild blueberry frozen souffle."

Grinning Erin added, "I gained three pounds just hearing about it."

"Me too, but it was worth it."

"I loved it. The food here... my God! Even the coffee is wonderful." "Well, I'm glad you had a good time. The spinning didn't freak you out?"

The Lighthouse Room, Jill learned last night, was a completely round restaurant with walls of glass and large skylights located throughout it. In seventy-five minutes, the restaurant completed one 360 degree revolution, allowing its guests to enjoy the entire surrounding skyline during their meal. Having never been in a spinning restaurant before, Jill was nearly undone by the combination of waves constantly underfoot and a room designed to slowly spin. She didn't think she'd like it, but her body quickly adapted to the motion and she found herself enjoying the experience.

"No, not until after I got used to the movement. Chase would love the place... oh, sorry," Jill said, catching herself. "Chase is my boyfriend's younger brother. He's in culinary school."

"Don't you mean fiancé?" Erin asked, pointing to the ring.

"Oh... right. Yes, he is." Jill shook her head, still a little bewildered by everything. Erin looked expectant, and Jill realized she had spaced out again. "It is all so new. He asked me to marry him just before I left for this job, and to tell the truth, I feel a little off."

Erin laughed. "It's okay to be a bit wiped out. There is an adjustment period to being on a big boat, you know." Erin explained. "And to the crazy schedule. I have wanted to spend more time with you. Then this morning was so rushed..."

"Don't even think of apologizing about that. I am sure that I'll be rushed too, once I have my subjects to photograph."

"It all starts tonight," Erin said and began humming the theme song from Jaws.

"I bet I'll learn all kinds of things. Just watching this process is amazing."

Erin grinned. "Yeah, I agree. Are you interested in grabbing an early dinner? I know Debi needs you from six o'clock on, right?"

"That sounds like a plan... but I'm starting to get concerned that all I'll do this week is eat."

"We could grab something light. Do you want to try the food court?"

"Sure. And would you mind showing me the enrichment center?"

"Ooh la la, the spa, you say?"

"I overheard a couple talking about their favorite moments from the trip--and they both said they loved the spa the most."

Erin smiled widely, switching into her tour guide voice. "Well, follow me madam."

They didn't have to walk far before Erin began her textbook like explanation of Jill's point of interest. "On a ship where every inch of space counts, 48,000 square feet were devoted to the Enrichment Center, a space of celebration for the body and mind."

"You sound like a brochure," Jill teased.

"It's because I worked in advertising for a while," she confessed. "Seriously, though... this place is brilliant."

"The planetarium and IMAX are both inside, right? So, it's not like all that space is filled with people being massaged and pools and whatnot."

"That's right. The Center houses the convertible IMAX, the planetarium, the classrooms for the College at Sea program, the museum, an 8,000 volume library, and rentable offices. Also, don't forget about the pool," Erin said as they walked through the steel and glass doors. She didn't need to continue, because the pool was now visible and required no real introduction.

The pool seemed more like an indoor lake with a waterfall on one end that resembled something she'd seen at Taqhuamenon. The roof was translucent pale pink and, according to Erin, retractable, though it was currently closed. Surrounding the pool were a few actual living indoor trees and lush potted foliage. There were lounge chairs as well as hammocks in the crooks and bends of the room, allowing for privacy as well as gatherings.

"Wow," Jill whispered. She raised her camera to her eye, because she just couldn't help it, and took a few pictures. The atrium was vacant now since vacationers were busy leaving, but Jill imagined that it would be every bit as inviting when filled with guests.

"The water comes right from the lake. It is naturally purified and heated when needed," Erin explained. A phone rang at her waist, and she picked it up. "Debi, hi!" She paused, listening. "Yes, we're on our way." She exchanged a few other comments and clicked the phone off. "It's time to go to work."

Jill looked up and smiled. "Sounds good to me."

*   *   *

The arrival of Candidate Walker and his entourage was nothing less than comedically grand. Jill had been instructed to wear a suit and was thankful that she brought the only two she owned. Today's was an old charcoal grey number from her college days with a crisp white shirt underneath. Jill had pulled her hair into a loose knot and applied some make-up for the occasion when she witnessed Debi take thirty minutes to perfect her own. When Debi was finished preening, she looked glossy and beautiful in a sharp black pinstriped suit that probably cost her a fortune.

Standing on the arrival platform, camera in hand, Jill felt clueless about fashion. She felt even worse when Erin greeted her with a sympathetic smile after she glanced over Jill's clothes. The parade of black limousines was impressive, but the people who emerged from them looked like they should have been walking a red carpet. She was ready with her camera as Erin gave names to those she photographed. Most of the names didn't mean anything to her, but once in a while Erin would shock her with a family name that was a major household appliance or common product. Erin oohed and ahhed over the jewelry and dresses. "That must be Armani," she'd giggle as she pointed out individuals that Jill needed to photograph.

This was not intended to be a quick embarkation and disbursement, Jill realized, as servers circulated with trays of tidbits. People mingled and chatted while slowly making their way from the pier onto the floating arm and directly to the upper deck where the lounge chairs were absent and an orchestra played cocktail music. A buffet of more delicious looking items as well as two ice sculptures greeted the guests. Jill's mind was blown, not by the food or decor, which were both incredible, but by the way guests were checked in--there was no line for these people. Rather, cruise line staff members and security detail floated amongst the crowd, keeping meticulous count and track of individuals as they chatted with others. At random intervals, guests would be invited in small groups to join the festivities on board--the whole process was elegant.

Jill decided that she would have to ask Debi how exactly this was organized, but not at the moment. Debi was knee-deep in making impressions, extending comfort, and casually mentioning features of the ship for guests to enjoy. Jill took most of her direction from Debi between mingling and followed her intuition for the rest.

"Jill, take a break. Let's grab a snack," Erin suggested.

"Are you sure, Erin? I don't want to miss..."

"You've been photographing these people for well over an hour. Walker will still be another twenty minutes, I think. And I'm just dying to try the gazpacho."

Persuaded, Jill joined her new friend at the feast. She piled a small plate with salsa and tortilla chips. As she turned around, careful to protect her camera, a man bumped into her, causing the plate to tip and salsa to splatter against her white blouse. Erin gasped and the man fell over himself to help, which almost caused a larger disaster until Jill separated herself from him.

"Oh no, Jill."

"Yeah, this was my one white shirt. Maybe I can just button my jacket over the shirt for the time being."

Erin shook her head. "Don't let these people see you soiled, Jill. Give me the camera and go."

"But the arrival... and the speech."

"Go, now. The ship pulls anchor and actually starts sailing in nine minutes. Worse case, you've ran me through the basics, if you don't make it back. We can send your shirt to the ship's cleaning staff later."

"Okay." Flustered, Jill handed over the camera and walked briskly back to her room. Nine minutes to traverse half the ship's length and five stories, she thought, quickening her pace.

*　　*　　*

Thirteen minutes later, Jill jogged through the corridor on deck five, rounded a corner, and smacked hard into the black suited chest of a security agent.

"What the..."

"Sorry, Sir. I need to get through here."

"No, you don't," he corrected.

Shocked, Jill stepped back. "Excuse me?"

"Miss, this staircase is restricted during the speech. Only members of the staff and those with security clearance can be allowed to access this space right now."

Jill looked down at her chest, but realized her badge had come off when she changed shirts. "Dammit. Listen, I'm a photographer. My name is Jill Traynor and..."

"Nice try, but the photographers are all upstairs. I don't know if you're rebelling against your parents' idea of a vacation, or if..."

"My name is Jill Traynor. I accidentally spilled salsa on my shirt and ran down to change. My assistant, Erin Nettles is in my place right now. I share an Erie Suite with Debi White."

The agent raised an eyebrow. "I know Debi." He reached into his pocket and pulled out a palm pilot, apparently searching for verification.

"Of course you do. Everyone does. And this makes no sense. The ship is secure, isn't it?"

"This is the staircase that Candidate Walker is using tonight. And, you're clear. I apologize, Miss Traynor. Next time, please wear your badge."

"Thank you," Jill huffed, quickening her pace. She slid into the crowd, found Erin, and took over the camera.

Candidate Walker stood behind a podium in front of an American flag with the city skyline glowing as a backdrop as he finished his remarks. Jill didn't pay attention to the speech as she focused in on a few excellently framed shots. The party continued after the speech was finished, guests mingling with crystal glasses in hands. She wasn't sure if the skyline, now shrinking in the distance, or the jewels anchored in the hollows of ladies necks sparkled more.

Chapter 13

Gulf Shore General Hospital, Ft. Myers, Florida

Dr. Crawford was a petite woman of stature, with a sharp tilt to her head and a keen look of brilliance in her eyes. She addressed Dave sharply, but not unkindly, as she explained the importance of open communication. She wasn't thrilled with his vanishing act, but knew better than to lecture him on something that couldn't be helped at this point. Quinn leaned against the nondescript wall of the hospital room and listened to her explain what exactly she was going to do in the operating room, the risks and procedures in clear English.

The explanation scared the hell out of Quinn, but he was thankful that this woman was responsible for Dave's well-being, as much as any human could be. He made a conscious effort to remember details for Jill. She would demand to know everything and fatigue was fighting Quinn's ability to a good job with the telling.

It had been a long day. Last night, they arrived at Dave's home exhausted after living through the chaos of airplanes and airports. Quinn tried to call Jill, but didn't have any luck, so he left her a voicemail message. He opened the blinds a bit, realizing the sun had gone down already. Dr. Crawford finished answering Dave's questions and said good night. Surgery wouldn't take place until Monday morning. Dave needed to regain some strength.

"Man, you look beat." Dave chuckled, knowing he must have looked horrible himself. "Why don't you get out of here. Go out and have dinner, go home."

"I'm good."

"Yeah, but there's a CSI marathon on Spike, and the hospital gets that channel. I'm just going to hang out here and fall asleep in a little while. Go ahead. You've got my keys, right?"

Quinn pulled the ring out of his pocket, jingling them in his hand. "Yeah, but..."

"I insist. Come back in the morning, and you can talk my ear off about all your business plans."

"Okay," Quinn said on a laugh. He hugged Dave.

"You know, Quinn... whatever happens, tell Jill..."

"Hey! You're going to be fine. Tell Jill yourself."

Dave opened his mouth and then closed it. "Okay."

Chapter 14

Black gloved hands slipped the card key into the lock and paused, because there was always a moment-- one moment--when the lock clicked open that even the best laid plans could be ruined. The most skilled intruder would be stupid not to feel that heartbeat's worth of panic, the wildly thumping heart and rush of adrenaline that reminds the mind of life. Someone could be waiting on the other side of the door. He could be smarter, stronger, better. He could somehow know the plan; somehow see past the facade to the intruder's true identity, because nothing is perfect. Every plan has a ripple, a flaw, a tragic mistake, known or unknown, but regardless--exploitable.

A furtive glance confirmed that the hallway was still clear, and the intruder swung the door handle down and stepped through. The door shut quietly. Relief. The room was empty. The bathroom was just ahead. This was not a hunting mission or an excuse to toss this suite for contents, or to spend time looking for information. The plan was precise.

The toothpaste was on the counter near the sink. The black gloved hand dipped into the long trouser pocket and pulled out a syringe. In moments, the needle was inside the toothpaste, contents flowing nearly effortlessly into the tube. When finished, the cap was clicked closed and the perpetrator left the room. The black gloves were tossed into a trash can near the stairs leading up to the bars on deck six. The closest one was populated by individuals easily recognized. Jill Traynor smiled and waved. The hand formerly gloved shot up and gestured toward a group of other individuals, indicating someone else would be a moment or two longer. I'll see you later, Jill. Much later.

Chapter 15

"We're spending the whole day at lake?"

"At sea, Jill. Yes."

"This body of water is a lake, Erin," Jill argued, pointing vaguely toward the water from their window view. "I know. I live on Lake Huron. I wake up everyday and there it is, outside my house."

"Note to self," Erin said and laughed. "Letting Jill drink too much makes her sense of humor a little on the feisty side the following day."

Jill smiled back, not denying it. "I am only telling you what I know to be true."

"The cruise term is "at sea." I'll see what I can do about getting it changed for you."

"That's all I ask." Jill sipped from her coffee mug. In an hour, the *New America* would sail beneath the Mackinac Bridge. Jill was ready, with cameras and tripod nestled next to her in the booth. "And where are we going?"

"For the love of breakfast! Jill, are you serious? We're going to Apostle Island National Lakeshore and Bayfield, Wisconsin. Didn't Debi give you an itinerary?"

"I keep meaning to read it, but there's always something more interesting to do. If you weren't here, I definitely would have read it."

"That's comforting."

"Sarcasm really doesn't suit you, Erin." Jill teased, enjoying their banter.

She laughed. "Uh-huh. You still don't have a clue what you're doing today."

"I didn't really know what I was doing yesterday, but I didn't get to bed until four in the morning, so something must have been right."

"God Jill, that was only five hours ago. Are you still drunk?"

Jill shook her head. "No, of course not. I'm feeling a bit feisty is all. I really don't know what has come over me. I usually take my work very seriously."

"Ooh, look alive. It's the boss," Erin whispered.

"I thought I might find you two up here," Debi called.

"Good morning, Debi." Jill smiled. As late as she had gotten home, Debi had been even later.

"I stopped by the office and looked through your files, Jill. Very impressive work. I am pleased you decided to join us this week."

Jill's expression might have been shocked, but a strong wave of nausea rippled through her, overwhelming the conversation. She staggered a bit and Erin grabbed her arm to keep her steady.

"Are you okay?" Erin asked.

Debi smiled. "Poor dear. I had a little too much to drink last night as well."

Jill nodded. "I'm glad you like the work."

"There are two on-ship events, which, of course, you know about, but I want to draw your attention to a few individuals I want you to focus on." Debi handed a sheet with names to Erin. "Also, Gordon Lightfoot is flying on board this evening for a concert. We'll want to take pictures of the meet with Walker."

"Sounds good."

"And tomorrow is a really full day, but what can I say? That's the life." Debi eyed the equipment. "You're taking pictures of the bridge pass, hey?"

"I've never been under it before, so I thought it might be a cool idea."

"What would be even neater is if we could somehow get the ship in the picture too." Debi laughed at her suggestion. "Okay. I've got to go. I'll see you later. Say, noon in my office?"

They nodded and Debi left, pausing to chat with one of the guests.

Erin wrinkled up her face. "I wonder what this is about." She looked up to find Jill's face in a foggy daze. "Jill-what is up?"

"Erin, is the helicopter being used this morning?"

Erin shrugged her shoulders. "I have no idea, but I can find out. Why?"

"If you can get me permission, I could use the helicopter to get pictures of the ship going under the bridge."

Erin grinned. "I am liking this idea. Of course I would need to come along to hand you lenses and things."

Embellishing, Jill replied, "I simply couldn't do it without you."

Erin left for a few moments to make some phone calls and clear the way for the two of them to take a short ride. Fifteen minutes later, she returned, smiling. "All we need is a signed okay from security," she said.

Jill approached the first agent she could find, realizing too late that she knew him from last night's fiasco.

Instead of looking for another agent, Jill decided to plunge forward. "I know you and I have gotten off to a rocky start with the whole staircase bit last night," Jill began.

"Don't forget the moment when you decided to step on my foot," the agent grumbled.

"That was an accident."

"Or how about when you complained about me to my supervisor and couldn't remember my name?"

Jill had forgotten about that and now wished she could back down or hide in the corner. "As we've already established, I was more than a little drunk and I never knew your name, I didn't forget it," Jill muttered. "I apologize and hope you will forgive me for all of that."

The agent looked at the request slip Jill handed him. "You want to use the helicopter to take pictures of the *New America* going under the Mackinac Bridge?"

"Yes! And I need someone from security section to approve it."

The agent reached into his pocket and removed a pen. She watched as he scribbled a name across the page.

"I really am sorry about last night. Hopefully, I didn't cause any trouble."

"I've signed already. Please go before my other foot gets stepped on or worse."

"Thanks." Jill turned and started walking away.

"Jill?" The agent called out.

"Yeah?"

"My name is Rob."

Jill smiled over her shoulder. "Thanks, Rob." The communications unit at Rob's belt beeped and a voice spoke loudly into his ear.

She paused when she heard her name mentioned, but shook her head knowing that would be bizarre. She was about to resume her mission, when he called out.

"Ms. Traynor!"

"Rob, you're just..." Jill's voice trailed off as she caught the look in his eyes. "What's wrong?"

"My superior has asked for your help. We need you and a camera."

Jill didn't ask any more questions. She took her camera bag from Erin.

"What's going on?" Erin asked in a whisper.

Jill shook her head. "I don't know, but I'll find you later." She followed him without question, because she had seen that look before and knew exactly what it meant. Something was seriously wrong.

She followed Rob silently, knowing he either

didn't have answers or couldn't give them to her. They approached mid-ship, walked up to deck seven and then in a starboard direction. The area was cordoned off by velvet rope instead of yellow tape and guarded by similarly suited men. A few guests milled in the area, curious. She couldn't see anything from the rope line, so whatever happened, they'd given it a decent perimeter.

The Captain spoke with two agents in a low voice. When he spotted Jill, he stopped.

"Captain, this is Jill Traynor," the Secret Service man said. "She's a special photographer brought in by Debi White for the event--but she has background in crime photography. She'll be an asset."

Jill's eyes widened, wondering how or why the man knew that.

The Captain nodded, holding out his hand. "Good to meet you, Ms. Traynor."

"Likewise, Captain." Jill shook his hand firmly. "How can I help?"

"Do I need to tell you that this is a closed lid?"

"I have signed a number of confidentiality agreements. If there's a list of those I can and can't talk to on board, I'll need an appraisal."

The agent in charge crooked his head to the side. "Follow me."

Jill walked to another set of stairs. At the bottom of the platform, a dead man lay with his legs snapped back at contorted angles, his arms in odd directions. She swallowed audibly, looking over the scene with her eyes before she used her camera.

The Captain asked, "Do we know what happened?"

"The witness says that the man put his hands to his head and staggered into the flight of stairs."

"So, he wasn't on his way down them?"

"There's no way of knowing, but he seemed to have a headache."

Jill said nothing and performed a calm face, as a wave of nausea churned her stomach. She removed the lens cap from her camera and framed out several pictures of the body, the stairs, and the area surrounding the scene in all directions. When she was finished with the preliminary round, she stepped back and allowed them to move the body.

The late forties victim was identified as Brent Schultz, a campaign contributor and guest of the party. He traveled alone, according to the manifest, a fact that intuitively troubled Jill, but she couldn't put her finger on why.

"You don't suspect foul play, do you?" The Captain asked in a loud whisper, the mark of a man who is not used to being quiet.

"No, Sir. I believe it was an accident," The agent in charge responded. "Jill, if you could make two stacks of those photographs as well as a disc and bring them to my office, I'd appreciate it."

"Sure thing, Sir," Jill said soberly. "Is there anything else I can help with?"

"Don't discuss this with anyone but the individuals you see here." The agent's open arms included the Captain, himself, and Rob. "Understood?"

"And if someone asks where I have been? Or if I

know anything?"

"If an individual already knows about the death, you can confirm that you were present at the request of the Captain, but not any details."

Rob spoke up. "Sir, when I found Ms. Traynor she was accompanied by Erin Nettles... I requested that she bring a camera."

"It is currently a confidential matter, Agent. Ms. Traynor, you cannot discuss any details with anyone. Am I clear?"

"Yes."

"Good. Thanks."

Jill nodded and walked out past the rope line. Debi stood on the other side of it. Her mouth fell open when she spotted Jill.

"What are you doing here?"

"The Captain requested my presence." Jill repeated the phrase the Captain provided to her.

"What happened?"

"I can't discuss it, Debi. I'm sorry."

"Jill, when something happens on this ship, I need to know about it."

"You'll have to find out from someone in there."

"Are you trying to pull something?"

"Not at all, Debi. I was told not to speak about it."

Debi crossed her arms over her chest, visibly rattled. She nodded curtly and focused her attention on the agent at the line. Jill slipped past Debi and made her way through guests and servers down the hallway, then the stairs, until she found her office. She set her camera on the table carefully then loaded the card from her camera into the computer. She tasked the computer to print two sets then burned a disc.

A year must have passed in the time Jill waited for the pictures to print. She scowled at herself and her exhaustion and sank deeper into the chair with each print, knowing she wouldn't consider drinking as much again this week. She was not on vacation, she reminded herself silently. Thirty minutes passed before they were finished. She gathered them into an envelope, slid the disc into a sleeve and then added it to the pile, and set out for the security office. No one she knew was there, so she sealed the envelope, signed across the seal, and gave the file to an aide.

When finished with the task, and uncaring of the time, she found her way through the hallways and staircases back to her room. She found her bed quickly and fell asleep on her side, with her knees curled to her chest and her arms crossed over her head as if to block out the world.

Chapter 16

Bayfield, Wisconsin was a charming hillside
community with pots of brimming flowers, quaint
shops, and old charm. Regardless of how quaint the
area was, in Jill's mind all she could see was the dead
man's limbs snapped into strange angles from the fall.
She kept asking herself questions. Did he die before he
hit the ground? Did the fall actually kill him? She
hadn't been interested in anything like this for a long
time. But then, Drummond Island was a peaceful place.
There hadn't been anything to be interested in for a
long time. She shook her head and tried to focus on
Bayfield. She couldn't really experience the area if she
wasn't paying attention.

The area was home to the Apostle Islands, which
Jill learned were named by French missionaries who
thought there were twelve instead of twenty-two. It was
one of those rare places that people went to be alone in
a crowd of people. Jill took everything in with her
observant mind and began to seep into a slightly
different era for a moment. Although there were
different reasons involved, Bayfield was one of those
places that hit her like Drummond had--she would have
to come back.

The ferry boat ride from Madeline Island was
lovely, and Jill took advantage of being on the boat's
return trip with Candidate Walker, gathering several
candid shots after the meet and greet with the
Governor. Secretly, she envied those who spent the day

kayaking amongst Apostle Island National Lakeshore. She hadn't been kayaking in a while and longed for the freedom and solitude of the open water.

With seven lighthouses inside its borders, sea caves, beaches, sandstone cliffs, old fish camps and miles of hiking trails, Jill was tempted to ignore her duties and simply explore. She noticed a group of individuals with binoculars, books, and notepads leaning over the ferry's rail and pointing.

"Who are those people?" Jill asked a crew member.

"Bird watchers. There's a fancy name for them, but basically they come here to look for birds. Bayfield has over a hundred migratory species."

Jill grinned. "Okay, thanks."

"Last week, someone confused Bayfield for Madeline Island and went around looking for all the black bears."

Jill grinned. "Doesn't it have the largest black bear population per square mile in the U.S? I think I read that today."

"Yes, it does."

The ferry docked and Jill said goodbye to her new friend and walked off with the rest of the cruise ship tourists, jostling her bags in her arms, surprised to find Erin pacing anxiously.

"Jill!" She waved. "I thought you might have missed the ferry. There were so many warnings about making sure to get on the right ferry back to Madeline, otherwise..."

"You look stressed," Jill dead-panned.

"Well, I am... what kind of a nightmare would it be if you had missed the boat? Most of the tourists don't really understand the two boat system. I came back hours ago because I didn't want to risk not getting back on the ship. And you're laughing! I can't believe you're laughing at me," she exclaimed, but began laughing in spite of herself.

"Erin, I live on an island. I set my watch to a ferry system. I know when to get back on the boat. If there's anything I know, it's when to get on the boat." Jill beamed at Erin. "Guess what I got to do?"

"Meet the governor?"

Jill rolled her eyes. "Well, when you say it like that it takes all the fun out of it. And, I really didn't meet him. I just photographed him meeting Candidate Walker."

"Did it go okay? I've been worried ever since you talked me into taking the morning off."

"It went great." Jill waved off Erin's concerns. "But it looks like you bought some things," Jill pointed to the sack slung over the other woman's arm.

"Yes. I bought a nice jacket that says Apostle Islands and some great postcards. I also picked up a t-shirt for a friend back home. It's tie-dyed; she'll love it."

"Did you have fun?"

"I had a ball, thanks."

Jill smiled, walking with Erin toward the water shuttle dock. "You don't take days off, do you?"

"Not really, no."

"Tsk," Jill teased. "So... we leave soon, right?"

"In forty minutes all passengers have to be loaded back on board. Judging by the crowds, I don't think there are too many of us left. What did you buy?"

Jill smiled. "Two dress shirts and a skirt. I also picked up an apron. Whenever someone from work goes on a trip, we try to bring back something for the kitchen."

"For the barbecue business?" Erin asked.

Jill grinned. She hadn't given Erin a very detailed description of her company. "Yes," she agreed. It had tickled her to find Three Bobbers sauces in the same store where she bought the apron. Of course, it was becoming more common all the time, but still... something always made her strangely giddy when she saw them in new places.

"They wouldn't have left me, you know."

"Oh. Why is that?"

"I was on the same ferry with Walker. They wouldn't have left him."

*   *   *

When Jill reached her room, she was surprised to find Rob waiting for her. "Fancy seeing you here... Oh, wait! Is this my room?" Jill chuckled at herself, earning a smile from the tall agent.

"Ms. Traynor, your presence is requested."

"By whom?"

"FBI Special Agent Doug Riley."

"Really? The FBI?" Jill raised an eyebrow. "Is he the man investigating Mr. Schultz's death?"

Rob smiled. "Yes, indeed."

Jill opened her suite door. "Come on in, Rob. Let me set my stuff down."

Rob followed her into the room.

Jill set her stuff on the bed, but grabbed her purse. "Do you think I'll need my camera?"

"I have no idea. Would you like me to call?"

"No. I'll bring it. Let me just call Erin quickly and tell her I might be late. We're supposed to have dinner."

Rob waited for Jill to make alternate plans with Erin and then led her out the door. "Why don't you use your beeper?"

"Excuse me?"

"You were given a staff beeper, right?"

"Uhm, yeah. I have that thing that Debi can get a hold of me with when I need to be somewhere."

"Well, that's its first priority, sure. But Erin has one; you could beep Erin when you need her. Didn't anyone show you how they work? It's just like a standard beeper. You pick up a house phone and call the number then you can type in a message with alpha-numeric code."

"I can beep Erin?"

"Certainly, yes."

"I wonder why she didn't beep me when we were out..."

"Only works on board the ship. It's a different kind of technology."

"Ah... how does one ever keep up with the tech

stuff?" Jill asked no one in particular.

They reached their destination on deck seven where Rob escorted her to a conference room. Behind a long table/make-shift desk sat a suited man bent over some paperwork.

"Agent Riley?" Rob called.

The man smiled and stood up. Jill noted that he was at least ten years older than Rob and four or so inches shorter. He stepped forward, offering a weathered hand. He wore glasses low above a large nose and, to Jill, he looked more like a detective than an FBI agent, but she wasn't sure what made her think that. Perhaps the beige pants and button down print shirt. In the movies, FBI agents were young and wore black, but real life was different, Jill realized. The Secret Service on board the ship, on the other hand, really did wear black. Jill mentally pinched herself and refocused on the current scene.

She shook his hand and smiled. "I'm Jill Traynor."

"Good to meet you, Ms. Traynor. I am Special Agent Riley, please call me Doug. Thank you," he nodded a dismissal.

Rob left the room, closing the door behind him.

"Please, Ms. Traynor, have a seat."

Jill sat down in the chair Doug pointed to and waited. He grabbed a file folder from his side and joined her at hers. She tried to be quiet, but she couldn't. "It seems strange that the FBI was brought in on this," she said. "It seemed like the Captain was confident this was an accident." She watched his face, looking for a reaction. The truth of the matter was that

Jill simply did not believe in accidents.

Doug eyed her over the folder's edge. He set the photographs down on the desk and looked at her plainly. "My eye tells me you have some experience with this," he gestured to the photographs.

"Yes, Sir."

"What happened? Were you in a C.J. program?"

"Criminal justice? No, no. Crime is interesting, always has been. I'm just a photographer. I've taken a few classes in forensics, crime theory, other stuff, but everything I've learned has basically been through field photography work, sometimes for the police."

Doug nodded, seeming to be in some decision making process that Jill couldn't quite discern. "You want to ask me something, don't you?"

"The investigation must be connected to the candidate, right?" Jill hurried on. "I don't want to overstep my boundaries."

"Speak freely, Jill."

She could see the scene in her mind. The narrow stairs and dim yellow lighting; she brought the man into her mind and pictured the fall. As tragic as his death may have been, it shouldn't have sought federal attention. "Well, if a man gripped his head and groaned and then fell down a flight of stairs in a building somewhere, would it interest the FBI?"

"Probably not."

"Then you must think there's some kind of foul play. Otherwise, the circumstances and the eye witness account would have closed the case by now, right?"

Doug eyed her, wondering if she'd find the

answer. He gave her a moment.

"State lines," she grumbled.

Doug grinned, amused by the moment, regardless of the circumstances. "That's right. The only reason I am here, is because the death crossed state lines. If it isn't an accident and someone needs to investigate, it's the FBI's jurisdiction because the ship crossed over state boundaries."

Jill scowled at herself. "That was stupid of me, sorry."

"No, it's a good question. Frankly, it may have been the first one I asked as well, if I were in your shoes." He paused. "Jill, I would like you to take some pictures for me. I could do it. I have my own training in this sort of thing, but I'd like your eyes with me on this. These photographs are sharp, and you were there early; you heard the bits of conversation that I missed yesterday. Would you mind? You're under no obligation, of course."

"I don't mind. What am I shooting?"

"Brent Schultz's suite. I haven't seen it yet. To my knowledge, no one has been in there besides two security agents."

"Okay. Now?"

"If it's okay with you, yes."

Jill stood up, ready to help.

Doug consulted a file and grabbed the card key from it. "Deck four, H-441." He led the way down two flights of stairs to the correct side of the ship. He pushed his glasses higher on his nose. "Is this the room?"

"Is it odd that it's not marked in any way?" Jill questioned quietly.

"No. That was to keep guests calm."

"You know, I expected to hear more about it."

"Well, it's sad and unfortunate, but no one here really knew him. His family and friends back home will grieve, so why should the people here? I think that's how the guests are thinking about it," Doug offered. He opened the door. "Oh, hold on." He reached into a bag and pulled out gloves. He handed one pair to Jill and donned another pair.

Jill slung her camera strap over her shoulder, put on the gloves, and followed Doug through the door.

Huron Suites were the next step up in space and luxury from Jill's own accommodations. The sitting room was significantly larger than the Erie's and the decor was just a bit more luxurious. Neither individual wasted time concerning themselves with thread count, as they each looked at the way the room had been occupied. The space was neat, organized--the man was probably organized in life, and thus, the same on vacation, perhaps, she speculated. Jill stepped into the bathroom. She liked to look at it with her eyes before closing in with the viewfinder. A used towel was draped over the bar, dry now. The toiletries were neatly arranged on the counter and in the medicine cabinet. She took pictures of everything.

The bedroom closet was the same:organized in one neat row were pants, shirts, and jackets. She noticed Doug poking through the trash can's contents.

"Do you think he traveled for work?" Doug asked.

She smiled, almost having vocalized that same assessment. "Something like that, yes." At Doug's request, Jill took pictures of the trash contents, the bedroom, the way the chairs had been moved a bit for better television viewing.

A noise behind them had Jill swiveling on her heels to face a small framed housekeeper.

"Oh, excuse me, Senora."

Doug stood quickly. "No, wait. Come in. What is your name?"

"My name is Maria Sanchez."

"Is this one of your regular rooms?"

"Yes, Sir. I was told it was okay to clean. Sorry."

"Don't worry about that," Doug said calmly. "Did you meet the man who was staying here?"

"Yes, Sir. I introduce myself to everyone on the first day. Mr. Schultz."

"Did you notice anything strange about him?"

"Sir? No, Sir. I clean the room." She had a confused expression, and Jill couldn't tell if it was the language barrier or if she was simply unaccustomed to someone asking her these kinds of questions.

"How about the room?"

"Sir?"

"Did you notice anything unusual at all about the room?"

"Eh... no, Sir."

"Okay, thank you Ms. Sanchez."

"Is it okay to clean the room now, Sir?"

"No. Someone from security will tell you personally when it's okay. Otherwise, don't let anyone clean in here."

"Okay." The maid smiled and left.

"Just a precaution, Jill. Even us small city FBI agents can be thorough."

Jill held up her hand to stop his thought. "I'm not knocking small, Doug. I'm from a small town. I get it."

"You know, your name sounds familiar to me. Maybe I have seen some of your work? My wife hauls me to an exhibit or two every year."

"It's possible," Jill replied, not wanting to talk about herself or her work. She stood back and looked over the room. It seemed absolutely normal, save for the possibility that it was too organized. She thought about her own room and the necessity to keep it tidy because she had a roommate. Of course, if she were staying on her own, she'd bet that it would be just as clean and organized. Beyond that, she couldn't see anything... no remnants of a personality, no strange behavior revealed by shining a light on personal space. Doug opened the suitcase and found it empty. There was little to photograph.

"Is there anything else you'd like me to shoot?"

"No, I think we've got it, Jill. Where is your office?"

"Midship, deck six, behind the photography wall. I've got a ship beeper. It's my room number plus B."

"Okay. Will you make me a disc of those? You

can drop it by my office or let me know and I'll come to yours."

"I'll drop it off."

"Great. I'm going to make arrangements to fly out then."

"Is this confidential?"

"Who are you wanting to tell, Jill?"

"No one, really. I share a suite with Debi White, my supervisor. Erin, my colleague might ask questions."

"Do you know anything about the case that's new? Anything secret?"

Jill considered. "No, not really."

"Go ahead, then."

"Okay. Well, I'll see you later then." Jill smiled, turning to walk out.

"If I don't see you again, thanks."

"Take care, Doug."

Chapter 17

As small as Jill's office was, she appreciated the structure. She loved her office at home, but it didn't utilize vertical space quite as well as this one did. She had shelves and drawers, small cabinets and cubbies in every conceivable square inch. She sat down at her desk and called Erin's beeper, leaving a message that she would be an additional thirty minutes. She started the computer's process to transfer the data from the camera card to a disc and spent the wait-time looking at earlier photos. Debi's list included individuals she wanted pictured with Walker. Jill was using it as a checklist, but she still couldn't place all the names to faces, so she'd have to get Erin's help.

Something in the wall beeped, a warning to Jill that the wall was about to swing open. Debi smiled when she saw her and took the second chair, allowing the wall to close behind her.

"Hey, how was your day?"

"Good," Jill smiled. "I got lots of really good shots of Candidate Walker with the governor, and many other individuals."

"A nice assortment of places?"

"Lovely ones, yes. Let me show you the one I'm most proud of," Jill said, bringing a file from today's trip up. She scrolled quickly through those from the suite.

"What are those?" Debi asked.

"Agent Riley asked me to help him photograph a suite," Jill explained.

"Oh, wow... this whole thing with Mr. Schultz's death has been such a public relations nightmare," she confided. "I have been fielding questions all day, which should really be teaching me something. If you try to keep something quiet, everyone talks and talks about it. If you tell everyone, the story goes away and no one gives it another thought. We should have just announced what happened. I've had people who needed assurance that the food is safe to eat." She sighed. "Full disclosure. The man had a headache, he fell down a flight of stairs and died. It's tragic, but that's the way it goes sometimes."

Jill frowned, considering. "The problem with telling everyone is, well... what if we don't know all the facts. If we tell everyone a story that we believe is true, and then they found out it wasn't, it will be worse."

Debi's attention shifted to the screen when Jill pulled up the intended slide. "Oh, Jill, that's art."

The photograph was of Candidate Walker leaning down to listen to a small girl whisper in his ear. In the foreground, there were potted plants from one of the Bayfield streets. In the background, there was a pristine old town store front with an American flag waving above it. The crisp colors gave great contrast and framework with Walker as the clear focal point.

Jill smiled, pleased that Debi liked it. "Thank you."

"Excellent work."

"After dinner there's a cigar and brandy event.

It's not on my itinerary, but if you want me to attend, I'd be happy to," Jill offered.

"No, don't worry about that one. Let's give him some breathing time. Do you have dinner plans?"

"Yes. I'm meeting Erin as soon as I get this disc to Agent Riley."

"Okay." Debi smiled awkwardly. "You know, I'm going that way anyway. If you'd like, I can drop it off for you. Are you ready for the fireworks social?"

"Yes. It should be beautiful."

"The Walker team had to get special permission from the governor to shoot fireworks over Split Rock Lighthouse. I don't believe it has ever been done before," Debi commented.

"Erin and I will both be there. Is there anyone specific I should be aiming for?"

Debi considered that for a moment and then insisted on seeing everything that Jill had up to this point, which meant almost forty-five minutes of conversation and a new list of individuals for Jill to seek out. By the time Debi left, Erin had beeped Jill three times.

Jill finished the disc and dropped it into the same type of envelope as the last one. She sealed it, signed her name across the seal, and locked up her office. It didn't take long to close the distance between her space and Doug's conference room. He wasn't in, so she left the disc and paged Erin back.

*   *   *

After dinner, Erin and Jill walked back through the maize of staircases and hallways to Jill's suite. They had about one hour before they were expected to be on deck, and Jill couldn't quite shake a sense of unease. She had just begun explaining her feelings to Erin, when Erin cut in.

"Have you used the box?"

Jill looked at her dumbly.

Erin couldn't help but roll her eyes at the woman she would now call a friend. "Jill, I didn't explain the technology for the fun of it all. It actually has a purpose. Come here," she beckoned, leading Jill to the television console.

Erin used the touch screen to lead her through the menu options until she reached the clinic site.

"This connects me with on board doctors?" Jill asked.

"Not yet, but that's the idea. First, you explain your feelings."

"Do I type them or speak them?"

"Just talk, Jill. When you're ready, press the icon on the screen that says 'begin'."

Jill laughed at herself. She placed her hand above the button but waited. "But Erin, I don't think there's anything wrong with me. I think it's the case."

"The case? Since when did something become a case?"

"Brent Schultz," Jill explained. Erin had heard the man's name from Debi originally, but by now the story was public. "I haven't been involved in something like this in a long time."

"Well, I don't mean to be rude, but all you've

done is taken some pictures, right?"

Jill smiled. "Yes, that's true. It just feels like old times."

"When you used to take pictures for that police department you mentioned?"

"I've worked a little more closely on cases than that, but yes, that's the idea."

Erin shrugged. "Well, it can't hurt to put your finger against the wand and rest your head over there. These services are free to everyone at this time because it's in testing. Everyone who boards the ship is encouraged to use it and even those in great health usually learn something about themselves. Humor me."

Jill nodded and pressed the button. She explained her dizziness and other symptoms and then pressed the stop icon when she was finished. The computer guided her through a series of questions including the physical points of having her finger scanned and resting her head against the gizmo hidden by a small closet door. When finished, the screen said that her results would be sent through the ship's email program and if she needed a further consultation, she would be guided to a meeting through the television/computer system.

When finished, Jill had to admit that she was impressed. "How long do you think it will take?"

"By the time we get back from the shoot, we'll definitely have them."

"You're not kidding, are you?"

"No."

"Unreal." Jill sat down on the chair opposite

Erin, her mind spinning. "Excuse me for just a minute, Erin. I need to make a phone call."

"Would you like me to step out?"

"No need," Jill said, shaking her head. She dialed Doug's conference room and waited. The line was picked up immediately.

"May I help you?"

"This is Jill Traynor. I'm the photographer on board, and I'm looking for Agent Doug Riley. He was using the room. Is he still there?"

"I'm sorry, ma'am. Agent Riley is no longer on board the ship. I was instructed to clean the room."

"Thank you," Jill said and hung up the phone. Puzzled, she sat back for a moment. "My encyclopedic friend," she began.

"Uh oh."

"Is there any way to access if a guest has used the medi-system?"

"Those are confidential records, Jill. I can access my ship-mate's system, but only because she has never changed the standard pass code. I wouldn't know this room's pass codes or any other's."

"Well, sure you do. You just typed it in for me."

"Only because you told me what it was," Erin countered. "Why?"

"My mind is still wrapped up in this case. Don't worry about it, Erin. I'm sure it's nothing."

Erin stared at her for a few moments. "You think Mr. Schultz might have used the system?"

"Well, didn't you tell me that guests are informed about all the on board features?"

"In detail, yes."

"If you knew about the system and felt ill, why not use it?" Jill speculated.

"I don't know."

"You would use it," Jill insisted.

"You didn't think of using it," Erin said pointedly.

"Yes, but most people don't tune out technology quite the same way that I do. If he used it, there has to be a record of it."

"There's no way to figure that out, Jill."

"I wonder if Doug knew about the system."

"Hmmm." Erin made a show of looking over Debi's list of subjects to photograph, a clear indication that she couldn't discuss confidential information.

Jill didn't want to let the thread lie, but Erin wasn't going to be able to help her with this chore. She tucked the information away, just in case she had the opportunity to talk to Doug again. Jill grabbed them each a bottle of water from the refrigerator and sat down, ready to talk about work. A knock on her door was a pleasant interruption.

Jill stood and opened the door, surprised to find Rob standing outside in casual dress as opposed to the on duty wardrobe of a black suit and earpiece.

"Rob!" Jill smiled. "How can I help you?"

Erin waved from the couch.

Rob shrugged a bit, grinned when he saw Erin. "I was wondering if I could buy you ladies a drink."

"What a sweetheart, considering that there are open bars upstairs for the party," Jill teased.

"We had such a good time the other night, I thought we might want to do it again-and this time, I'm off duty so you know..."

Erin stood up and laughed at the man's comments. "Unfortunately, it is our turn to be on duty."

Jill nodded. "We're shooting the shindig."

"Got ya. Well, it can't last all night, can it? I'll be in one of the bars. When you're done working you should come find me."

"We will most likely do that." Erin intoned.

"Thank you for the invitation."

"Ladies," Rob gave a small bow and exited gracefully. Jill shut the door behind him and giggled.

"Someone likes you," Jill teased.

"Perhaps," Erin smiled. "You should call Quinn. We've got twenty minutes before we have to work."

Jill smiled, missing him. "Okay. I'll try again."

Chapter 18

The ICU waiting room seemed to be the exact same size and shape as every other hospital waiting room Quinn had visited. He wondered if there was a manual about how hospitals are supposed to look, and if designers tried to make them as impersonal as possible. Of course, Quinn had been fortunate to not have to be in too many waiting rooms in his life. He found that he really didn't have the patience for waiting on health status.

What was worse, in Quinn's mind, was the strict no tolerance policy on cell phones. All cell phones must be shut off. As a result, he had been out of touch from Three Bobbers, Chase, and Jill each and every hour he stayed by Uncle Dave's side. It wasn't a problem, especially since Chase was out of state, and Jill was damned near totally unavailable, but he liked to be in touch with the troops at home. DeeDee surely had it under control, but it was better to know than to wonder, to speculate that everything might not be operating smoothly.

Uncle Dave was in the operating room now. Dr. Crawford had finally cleared him for surgery after two delays. Needing to stretch during the second hour, Quinn let the waiting room attendant know that he was taking a walk. Once he cleared the cell phone barrier, he reached into his pocket and grabbed his cell. He listened to the charming noises bringing the small marvel to life. The screen read, "three missed calls." He called his voicemail.

"Brother, you should see the property out here. I was a little skeptical, but Brenda has shown me the possibilities. I'm taking lots of pictures. I can't wait to talk to you about it all. Hope Uncle Dave is doing well. And if you talk to Jill, tell her to keep me in mind out there. Some of those small towns have recipes that have been handed down for generations. Call me if you can."

Quinn smiled, deleted the message. He listened to two messages from Jill, scowling when he realized he had just missed her last call. Quinn clicked out of his voicemail. Knowing he wouldn't get through if he called her back, he turned off his phone again and headed toward the cafeteria. A large cup of coffee sounded like a plan.

By the time Quinn returned to the waiting room, cell phone off, the occupants had changed a bit. He quickly recognized a woman with auburn hair from Uncle Dave's pictures. He sat down next to her. "Karen?" Quinn asked.

"Yes. Are you Quinn?"

He nodded and held out his hand. "Nice to meet you."

For the first time, he noticed her tense neck and shoulders accentuated by a stern frown. "If that man wasn't already under the knife, I'd be putting him under one, myself. He didn't tell me he was in the hospital."

"You didn't know he was sick?"

"Oh, yes. Of course I knew that. I had planned a trip to Arizona to visit my sister-well, golly, almost a year ago now. I was going to cancel and that dratted man promised me that this was a fine time to go. I get home and sure enough, there's a message on my answering machine from Dave. That son of a..."

"Well, he probably just didn't want you to worry."

"Don't you take his side, young man. It is my right to worry. I've been a part of his life for four months now. I think I am entitled to worry. So where's your Jill? I would love to meet her."

"It's a bit of a long story. Can I get you a coffee?"

The switch in the woman's face was something short of a marvel. Karen softened, and nodded her head yes in reply.

Although Quinn didn't really want to tell her the story, he knew she would somehow have all the details before the second cup was empty.

Chapter 19

Considering the size and population of Drummond Island, the annual fireworks display is said to be nothing short of spectacular. As a result, Jill was expecting something smaller since the crowd was smaller, since the venue seemed smaller to her way of thinking. On the other hand, the individuals on board were money trees and couldn't possibly be impressed with anything short of a dazzling display of sky glitter.

Working the shots as Erin pointed out individuals from the list, Jill canvassed the event with the art of a dancer, taking the time to ooh and ah as the crowd did. This wasn't the Captain's ball or the grand gala, but the individuals aboard the deck were dressed to the nines. Jill felt her plain shirt and pant combo were clear identifiers that she was not one of the guests. Erin, on the other hand, had used the ten minutes of personal time to utterly remake herself. A matching set of pear shaped diamonds glittered from her ears and neck. The size and caliber were no match for the bling present, but she looked very nice, and Jill made a mental note to tell her so later.

Debi caught Jill's eye and smiled broadly. Jill captured her in a picture with those she chatted with, returning the smile. They kept going, gliding through the group smoothly for the better part of an hour even after the final fireworks had exploded.

Erin signaled a server, grabbing two flutes of champagne. She handed one to Jill.

"I take it this means we're done?" Jill asked, accepting the glass.

"I think we nailed it, but of course, you're the boss."

"Ha!" Jill guffawed before taking a sip. She wrinkled up her nose.

Erin laughed at Jill's face. "You're not much of a champagne drinker, are you?"

"I like Corona."

Erin smiled and finished her drink with one long swallow. She winked at her friend. "I'll have to remember that. Are we ready to meet Rob?"

Jill shook her head. "Not me. You go ahead though. I want to hear all about it in the morning."

"You're not serious? You have to come."

"No, I really don't. You two kids need some time together," Jill teased.

"What are you going to be doing?"

"I'm going back to the room. Perhaps the office for a while. I might check out what's playing at the IMAX tonight."

Erin nodded. "I'll meet you in the morning, then?"

"Isle Royale tomorrow, right?"

"Yes. It's beautiful, Jill. You'll love it."

"Okay. Don't get too trashed. Have fun."

Erin tried to keep her excitement at bay, but giggled nervously when Jill shot her a knowing look. "Okay, so I like the guy."

"I know. Give me that list and the notebook. I'll drop off everything at the office. You just have a good time," Jill insisted.

"Thanks."

Jill shuffled the items from her hands into her camera bag and simply carried the rest. She was happy to finally understand the ship well enough to not need the map, and she walked without incident to her office. At the party, she had entertained the idea of getting an hour or so of work in before she retired for the evening, but now she thought better of it. She could work in the morning before the first shoot.

One thing she could appreciate about this group of individuals:they all socialized quite late, which meant the floor surrounding her room was very peaceful, and the festivities in the morning wouldn't begin at an unreasonable hour. A destination fund raiser, as Erin explained, favored flowing alcohol and merriment followed by rest. The objective was to keep the guests happy.

Jill clicked the lock in the door. Hanging from a cabinet door handle was an opaque white plastic bag from the laundry. Even though she had purchased a couple of new shirts on land, it was nice to have her favorite shirt back. She tore open the bag, perplexed to find not one but three shirts plus a skirt and nightgown. It took her less than a minute to realize she had mistakenly opened a bag of Debi's linens. Jill hung the pressed items in the closet and folded the nightgown. She opened Debi's top drawer. On the left were various pajama items and on the right, socks. She tucked the gown into the drawer and attempted to close the drawer but it stuck. She reached her hands in and yelped as if bitten when the drawer vibrated unexpectedly. She opened the drawer fully. Something inside a sock vibrated again, and before she thought about her actions, she had unfolded the socks and flipped open the cell phone nestled inside.

The screen showed a text message in clear black font: Fingerprints Matched. Operation Go.

"What the hell is this?" Jill whispered to herself. She closed the phone, slipped it back inside the sock and to the back of the drawer. Fingerprints? She thought. What the hell is Debi doing with fingerprints? And why was the phone hidden away? Jill had watched Debi use no less than three communication devices so far this week and never once this cell phone.

Of course, there could be a dozen easy explanations. The message didn't mean anything specific. It could be some part of Debi's job that Jill simply wasn't familiar with. It could be personal, but Jill didn't know how something personal would relate to fingerprints or an operation.

"Why did I even look?" Jill questioned herself in a fierce whisper. And honestly, she thought to herself, there was very little she could do. If she confronted Debi, she might wreck her chances of finishing out the week. Debi might think she was snooping inside her drawer. If she went to someone other than Debi--and the next question might be who--she'd probably be laughed at. It was most likely nothing.

Jill allowed herself to relax more fully. She was jumping to conclusions, guessing at answers without knowing the proper questions. Two points circled through her head that she couldn't explain away: How many people deal with fingerprints? And what operation was Debi told to go forward with? Running through her experiences with her roommate thus far, she had no reason to suspect any strangeness. Jill shrugged off the information, rolled her eyes at her own paranoia, and wondered if this was a long term side effect from her assault.

In the back of her mind, where Jill filed away pieces of information, this one rested on top of the stack. Wanting to numb her mind to thoughts, Jill turned on the television console. The menu screen showed that she had mail.

She followed the instructions, opening a message from the on board clinic. She read the message aloud. "Dear Ms. Traynor, thank you for using... blah, blah, blah..." She whispered, skipping ahead to the important details. "...request a consultation with a doctor to determine details about apparent pregnancy." Jill stopped cold, her eyes and mouth opened wide, her heart hammering against the walls of her chest. "Oh my God."

She stood up and paced the room slowly, returning to the screen again and again. Eventually, she hit the print button and read the information on paper. A baby. Quinn's baby. "Our baby," she whispered quietly, looking down at her still flat stomach. She patted her tummy gently, surprised by the well of tears in her eyes. She went back to the keyboard station and sent a message to the doctor with her availability, requesting an appointment. She changed into her pajamas in a fog of images, totally overwhelmed by the surprise.

She crawled into bed, but could not sleep. Quinn would be floored. She indulged herself with images of them taking boat trips and traveling, and the pictures she could take. Her home came into her mind and she considered the rooms, wondering what changes could be made now before the construction began. She considered names--perhaps Cliff if it was a boy, maybe Lily if it was a girl. Of course, she couldn't name a baby without even asking Quinn. Jill stared at the diamond ring, wishing she could tell him right now, share her excitement with him, and see his face.

Chapter 20

"Turn it off," Quinn whined, swatting blindly. "Please turn it off."

"What?"

"What does he want us to turn off?" An older woman's voice crooned.

"The light," he mumbled, irritated. "Chase, leave me alone."

"Someone's chasing you?"

"Is he dreaming?"

Quinn managed to open an eyelid but slammed it shut. He turned his head and risked an eyeful. "What the hell is that?"

"It's called a sun," the woman dead-panned. "It's mighty hard to turn off."

Quinn gathered his bearings. "Florida," he breathed.

"That's right. You fell asleep in the chair."

"Where's Uncle Dave?"

"Is he on this floor, dear?" The older woman leaned in close to Quinn, patting his shoulder.

Quinn shook his head to clear it. It all came back

to him now. Late last night, Dr. Crawford had told them the news. Uncle Dave had made it through surgery, but had a difficult time coming out of the anesthesia. He had to remain on the ventilator. Quinn looked at the individuals surrounding him, the motley crew of loved ones staying late or coming in early to visit their own. "How long have I been asleep?"

The waiting room volunteer smiled. "I reckon all night, sir. You were sleeping soundly when I came in this morning. Betty told me you'd been there since the wee hours."

"Where's Karen?"

"Who's that?" A teenage girl snapped gum loudly.

"Never mind," Quinn shook his head, still quite disoriented.

He wandered out of the room and found a restroom to splash water against his face. The hospital bathroom reminded him of those at War Memorial Hospital in the Soo. Then, it had been Jill in the hospital bed, and he'd rarely been alone. Pete and Kate Dombrowski, Chase, the Eby's next door, Mrs. Barber, and others took turns sitting with Jill. They had been there for him and taken shifts of looking after him and his business. Now, he was taking one long shift for Jill. Of course, he respected and admired Uncle Dave. The man was as good as family and would be once Jill became his wife--but this was about her. Flying to Florida and leaving his business interests behind for a few days was about her.

He dried his face with paper towel and exited the bathroom, working his way down to the ICU corridor to Uncle Dave's room. He leaned against the doorjamb, hands idly in pockets, wondering how long he'd be here. The nurse was inside with him now, running some kind of test or whatnot. She smiled when she noticed him.

"Hey, there."

"Has Dr. Crawford been in?"

"No, she's not in yet. Dr. Morse has looked in on your uncle through the night. It might be a good time for you to go home, get a shower, sleep in a good bed."

Quinn raised an eyebrow.

"You slept in the waiting room."

"How do you have time to keep track of family like that?" Quinn asked, surprised. He'd watched the long, hard hours that nurses put in. He had always been impressed.

"Just the cute ones, sugar." She laughed when he blushed and moved past him. "You get on out of here for a while. Get some fresh air, a good meal. He'll still be here when you're rested."

Quinn grinned, accepting the suggestion as a good one. "Okay, then. I'll be back in a few hours. You've got my cell number."

"Sure do."

"Thanks."

Chapter 21

Isle Royale was isolated in the chilly waters of Lake Superior, a considerable distance from land, Jill realized, looking over the information Debi provided. One of the staff members held a microphone on stage and talked about their destination.

"...It's richly forested surface, remote location, and the fact that it is teaming with wildlife make Isle Royale National Park a paradise for those that truly want to envision what our fore fathers looked upon so many years ago." Loon song sounded from the PA system, and the guide chuckled merrily. "Northern lights dance across the sky at night. The call of loons, just like that one, beckons. You may see an eagle or osprey gliding through the wind. This, ladies and gentlemen, is the jewel of *New America*'s destinations this week. While the National Park system has an average visit time of four hours per guest, a typical stay at Isle Royale is three and a half days. Isle Royale is forty-five miles long. You will be landing at the Northeast end, near the Rock Harbor Visitor's Center. A Park Ranger will greet you and..." The man paused, as the PA system rang with chimes. "All passengers holding a B ticket: please approach the gate." A flurry of individuals rose and moved toward the exits. Jill glanced at her ticket even though she knew it had a "D" on it. Her turn would be soon and she needed to get below deck.

For reasons unknown to Jill, the breakfast photo

shoot had been the most efficiently timed event yet. Debi let them leave barely forty-five minutes after they began, an unprecedented occurrence. Now, Jill was busy trying to talk Erin into hiking with her.

"Do you see these thighs, Jill?"

Not knowing how to answer that, Jill simply waited.

"These are not the thighs of a hiker."

Jill laughed merrily, unable to shake the good mood she woke up with. "We'll go on an easy hike. You'll love it."

"Jill, I'm going to be visiting this island every week for the rest of the season. I'll have ample opportunity to take in a hiking adventure, just not today," Erin argued.

"If you hadn't consumed so much alcohol last night, you wouldn't be feeling hung over," Jill teased.

"Thanks, Mom. I really appreciate that sound bit of wisdom. You go. Have fun, take lots of pictures. I am going back to bed for a couple hours while I have the chance."

"Okay. I'll see you later then." Jill left Erin in her office and made her way back to her room. Having never visited Isle Royale before, she couldn't have been more elated. She filled a knapsack with binoculars, her camera, two large water bottles, a sandwich she snagged from the kitchen, and a variety of energy bars. She also brought the National Park trail map she grabbed from the visitor's center with the intention of walking Stoll Trail. She couldn't be more excited when she finally boarded the ferry and journeyed the short ride to the island. She hitched the strap of her bag over her head and inhaled the clean Isle Royale air. The spruce, fir and pine trees welcomed her yet made her feel a bit homesick.

She longed to bring Quinn here. This island was every bit the beauty that Drummond was, but with more flowers and less people. The water was somehow even clearer. There were no roads to mar the beauty of this place. She made a mental note to watch the time and set the alarm function on her watch to stop her from losing track. Jill couldn't help but fetch her camera before she'd walked even a quarter mile. She found cala lilies, fireweed, and blue flag flowers, which were beautiful violet colored starbursts of petals with hints of yellow. She took pictures of dozens of them, so caught in the beauty of the land that she almost missed seeing a cow moose and calf, near small trees, close to the water's edge.

She first hiked to Lookout Louise, then doubled back and took a trail that led her to the north side of Isle Royale over looking a bay and small tent camping area. She moved on to Rock Harbor. Realizing she had made great time, she checked the distance and hiked Stoll Trail North to its end. Jill wasn't sure if it was Isle Royale or the news she had received that made her light on her feet, but she didn't think it mattered. She was giddy with happiness, thrilled that she could spend the first full day of knowing about the baby growing inside her surrounded by nature.

Someday, the three of them would come here, she thought, smiling. She hadn't told a soul yet. She knew it was right to tell Quinn first, but she needed to talk with someone. Jill felt like she was going to burst. She focused on the footpath ahead of her. The trail was rough, winding close to the water at several points along the journey. Hearing loon song, she paused by the water and found the binoculars. It didn't take her long to spot the black and white birds floating peacefully in the water.

She took pictures, including a few excellent shots of a small fishing boat anchored off Raspberry Island. At Five Finger Bay, she recognized a number of individuals from the ship already in rented kayaks. Inspired, she paid the fee and nestled herself into a rented kayak. She placed her bag safely between her legs and paddled calmly out into the bay, stunned at the placidity of the water. She allowed herself to float for a while and took time to eat her sandwich and drink from one of the water bottles. She paddled around slowly, allowed herself a moment to dream.

Wasn't it a gift that Quinn had already asked her to marry him? If he hadn't, would she be worried now? She didn't think she would. Knowing Quinn loved her was one thing, but having a family was another. They weren't ready in the way that a couple makes plans and sets aside money ahead of time. She laughed at herself, knowing money wouldn't be an issue. The business was on a phenomenal course and there wasn't anything to be worried about in that respect. Quinn would see that the new construction was finished well before the baby's arrival, plus or minus a few changes. And they would be great parents--with Uncle Chase a beloved part of the baby's life. She had never thought of herself in a maternal way before, secretly marveling at how women back home were able to work hard and raise children well. She wasn't scared.

Perhaps the fear would come later, she mused, but it was nice not to be afraid for the moment. Fear had been the rule rather than the exception for the last two years, and she felt free now. Responsible, she amended mentally, but free to live a good life with a man who loved her. Looking outside the small kayak, she was stunned at the clarity of the blue water. She could see all the way to the bottom. At first she wasn't sure how far that was, but after a time she guessed the small stones resting on the bottom were over thirty feet down. She paddled for a while longer before she returned her kayak, and made her way back to Rock Harbor.

She found a park employee selling tickets for a tour aboard the MV Sandy. By traveling with the boat, she could see the Harbor Lighthouse, Edison Fishery, and the inner passage. She checked her watch and purchased a ticket. The boat wasn't leaving for another thirty minutes. She took the time to visit the gift shop, where she found a book on the early days of Isle Royale before it was a National Park. Afterwards, she tried her luck with the payphone, shocked when Quinn answered.

"Hello?"

"Quinn, is it really you?"

He laughed, delighted to hear her voice. "Hey, Babe."

"How are you? How's Uncle Dave?"

"He made it through the surgery. The doctor thinks he's going to be fine. They went through a rough patch when bringing him out of anesthesia though. He's still intubated. The ventilator is breathing for him."

"Oh no," she breathed raggedly. "Quinn, is he going to..."

"One of the nurses told me she really believes he'll be fine. Sometimes it takes a while to unthaw. I fell asleep in the waiting room last night. We have to shut our phones off when we're in the hospital, which is why I keep missing your calls."

"Of course. That makes sense. I wondered if you just had bad signal or something."

"How is the cruise?"

"It's good. The work is strange--I've never done anything quite like this before. The occasional wedding and whatnot for friends, but nothing quite like this. I mean I'm really not a portrait photographer. I guess I got the job because they want candid shots." Without saying it, Jill realized with a start that her qualifications were not suited for this work. She was known in some circles for her scenic photography, but portraiture was something other photographers worked toward exclusively. Why was she brought onto the ship? Who requested her? Jill realized she'd have to question Debi, and she let it go for now.

"It's strange to think of you being on a ship. I know cruises are common, but you seem so far away."

"Isle Royale is quite a hike from Drummond, Babe."

"I know, but I keep thinking that you're in the Caribbean or somewhere exotic."

Jill smiled. "Yes, I know what you mean." She turned back looking towards the interior of Isle Royale and mumbled, "I am."

"What did you say?" Quinn replied, not sure he heard her correctly.

"Isle Royale is exotic," she clarified.

"Is it gorgeous?"

"I am bringing you back here as soon as we have

a chance."

"That's great. What about the dead guy?"

Leave it to Quinn to drop the polite language, she mused, smiling. Her body ached with missing him. "Nothing new. Something strange last night though." She quickly filled him in on the text message, something she herself had stopped thinking about once she learned she was pregnant.

Quinn listened to the whole of it, wishing he could be there with her. "It could be anything, hon. I hardly think it's something to be worried about."

"How many people have anything to do with fingerprints?"

"More and more people all the time. Hell, I cashed a check down here and had to stamp my fingerprint right on the check. Weird as hell."

"I guess I'm a bit spoiled on Drummond, hey?"

"Maybe so. Debi's hidden phone is weird, but not bizarre. I think it would be better for everyone involved if you said nothing at this phase. The people who are on this cruise sound pretty connected. If this goes well for you, it could mean more jobs. Don't burn bridges here, Jill."

Jobs, she thought, glancing down at her tummy. How would he feel about his pregnant bride traipsing around on jobs? Of course, he didn't know yet, and she wasn't going to tell him over the phone. She desperately wanted to see his face. "Have you heard from Chase?"

She changed the subject abruptly. "Yeah. I guess he agrees with Brenda's assessment. It's the perfect property."

"It's in Oregon, right?"

"Yep. It's not too far from Portland, if I remember correctly. I've never been out there. It might be a nice excuse for a trip."

Jill grinned. "Next time I go on a trip, you're coming with me."

"Same here, Babe. Traveling is just not the same without you."

Watching from the payphones, Jill noticed the crowd beginning to assemble on the dock, ready to board the MV Sandy. "I am about to go on a boat tour, Babe. I've got to get going."

"Go ahead."

Chapter 22

Agent Doug Riley's office, located in Milwaukee, Wisconsin, was an absolute reflection of the man. It was small, but fortunate enough to have a window with a view. The walls were barren of commendations or awards and degrees--which wasn't to say that the man hadn't earned them, just that he had never quite found the time to hang them. He flipped on the light switch and tossed the Schultz case file onto his already cluttered desk. The light on the brown phone blinked, indicating a message, but he ignored it for now. He shrugged out of his sport coat and picked up his phone and pressed down the memory key for his boss's secretary.

Doug spoke before Martha could deliver her greeting. "Martha, it's Doug. Can I get fifteen minutes with Devonshire?"

"Sure thing, Doug. He's open now if that works for you."

"On my way." Doug set the phone down, grabbed the report he typed from home, and made his way to the office of Special Agent in Charge Charles Devonshire. He was seated across from Devonshire's desk in under five. He gave his oral report in no nonsense terms, taking the other man through the chain of events exactly as they appeared to have happened. When the initial telling was over, Devonshire looked through Doug's notes.

"The body is in autopsy?" Devonshire asked.

"Yes, as we speak. So far, I've seen nothing to suspect foul play. Granted, it's a bit strange for a man of apparent health to trip down a set of stairs and die... but it does happen."

"What about the family? Anything suspicious? I don't see any notes in your report."

"Burrows did the initial interviews. He's next on my list of people to talk to." Agent Burrows was a temporary partner replacement for Doug, whose last partner had been promoted and moved to the Chicago office. So far, it hadn't been a good fit. The temp partner was a minute short on communication and an hour short on diligence. Doug didn't complain.

"Doug, Burrows isn't here. He was called to assist on a case in Minneapolis."

It was of no use to ask Devonshire if Burrows completed them before he left; he obviously didn't know. Doug puckered his lips together grimly. Talking to the family was the worst part of it. "Well then, I'll have that information for you shortly."

Devonshire nodded. "Keep me updated. There's bound to be some political pressure if this turns out to be anything more than a natural death."

Doug nodded, recognizing his cue to leave. If Burrows hadn't done the interviews, it was possible that no one had contacted the family at all. He sat back down in his office chair, flipping through pages until he found the contact information that Debi had provided him.

He took a breath and dialed the number.

An upper-middle aged woman, judging by the

voice, answered on the third ring. "Hello?"

"May I speak with Mrs. Schultz, please?"

His question was met by a soft chuckle. "Well, my name hasn't been that for a few years. It's Mrs. McConnelly now."

Doug shook his head. "I'm sorry, ma'am. Perhaps I have the wrong home. I'm looking for the wife of Brent Schultz."

"My name is Carolyn, and that's me."

"Ma'am, my name is Doug Riley. I am an agent employed by the Federal Bureau of Investigation, and I am afraid I have some bad news."

"About Brent?"

"Yes, ma'am. He passed away this..."

"Four years ago, this September. How could you possibly have bad news?"

"Ma'am, I don't understand. You're telling me that your husband passed away years ago?"

"Why are you calling me? You don't know that he's dead?" He sensed irritation and confusion across the phone line.

"Well, the man I'm calling you about passed away a few days ago. He was on a cruise boat in the Great Lakes. The name on his driver's license is Brent Schultz, and his contact information led me to this address, and to you."

"I'll be damned," she whispered. She was silent for a moment. "I don't know what's going on over there, but my Brent died from cancer. Damned cigarettes. Do you smoke?"

"No ma'am," the agent replied.

"I held his hand in mine when he took his last breath and I was there when they put his casket in the ground. I don't know what the man was playing at but that ain't my husband. I have a new husband now, a good man. He doesn't smoke, never has." Her voice broke on a sob. "And I don't really want to talk about my Brent today. Sun's too high in the sky for that."

"I'm sorry to disturb you, Mrs. McConnelly."

"What was your name again?"

"Doug Riley. I'm at the Milwaukee office."

"Find out who this man is, Mr. Riley. I don't know why someone would want to take on Brent's name, but it can't be good."

Doug listened to the phone line go silent and then beep in his ear. He set the phone down with a dull thud. "No, it can't be good," he whispered. He dialed Devonshire's secretary. "Martha, I need a few more minutes with him."

*   *   *

Special Agent in Charge Devonshire's earlier calm was a bit ruffled. His jacket had been thrown off, tie loosened, and sleeves rolled to his elbows. "This better be good, Riley. I've just been ordered to send Clint and Lacey to Minneapolis. I am now utterly shorthanded, and I need you to join Russell on..."

"I'm afraid I'm not going to be able to do that," Riley interrupted.

"And why not? Did you talk to the family?"

"Yes. Brent Schultz is dead."

"Well, no shit, Riley. Didn't you bring the body back with you?"

"No, Sir. I mean he's been dead for years. I spoke with his wife, now remarried. The contact information led me straight to her."

"Stolen identity?"

"Perhaps. I just sent the fingerprints to the lab. I would like to change his death from natural to suspicious. And I'd like to go back to the ship. If someone killed him, the answer is on board."

"You'll need to contact the Secret Service, tell them what you've discovered and that you're coming back."

"I'd rather not give them specifics. It might hamper the investigation."

"Doug, the man on that ship could be our next president. If something is hinky, the service team needs to know about it. We're not taking any chances here."

Doug nodded. "Very well."

"You'll need to take someone with you."

"Who? Burrows is gone. Clint and Lacey just left, right?"

The other man nodded.

"I have been utilizing someone on board."

"Secret Service?"

"No, Sir. A civilian. Her name is Jill Traynor."

"Traynor? Why does that ring a bell?"

"I've been asking myself that same question, I just haven't had time to research it. She just seems too interested. I don't know whether I should be impressed or concerned."

"You think she could be connected to the Schultz case?"

"No," Doug said quickly.

"Martha!"

The secretary popped her head into the office.

"Have you heard of Jill Traynor?"

Martha considered it for a moment and slowly nodded her head. "Yes, Sir. She's a photographer."

"I wouldn't know..."

"You know her from the Canadian diamond case a couple of years ago. She tracked down Lieutenant Colonel Ortiz. Remember the billions of dollars that were donated to the government? Traynor is responsible for figuring that out. She was beaten to death, nearly didn't make it. The newsletter did a large story on her. I think there's more, but I don't remember the rest of it."

"That's Jill?! I knew I recognized her name from somewhere. Can you get me more information, Martha?" Riley asked.

"Sure. Give me some time and I'll send it over to you."

"If this checks out, get her to sign a non-disclosure, consultant status. We'll pay her the civilian rate, make it official. This is only until I can send someone out to help you. Understood?"

"Yes."

"And keep in touch. I want regular updates on your progress."

"Yes, Sir." Doug turned. "One more thing... can you weigh in with the coroner? We'll get faster results if your name is attached to this."

"Sure thing."

Chapter 23

This evening's event, unlike many of the others, was indoors in a plush decorated room over-looking the waterfalls of the enrichment center. The tables were set up to face a stage and podium area, but the design of the room was specific to allow people to mingle and not become caught up in bottlenecks. The room had a feeling of spaciousness, even with the large crowd. Wearing her pantsuit, Jill circled through the guests, taking pictures. Her mind wandered a bit as candid shots became more difficult when the candidate spoke from the podium.

Behind her, two guests spoke in whispers.

"You know he won't be talking about this on CNN," the man whispered to his companion.

"No kidding. I haven't heard any of this and I've been a supporter right from the start."

Puzzled at the intrigue in their voices, Jill refocused her attention back to the candidate. Mid-sentence, she paid attention. "...policy has not served America's best interests for far too long. We will no longer be a member of the United Nations or NATO. We will no longer place more importance on the concerns of other nation's than on our own well being. I will reinvest the billions of dollars spent in foreign aid on the citizens of our own nation, and we will rebuild and take back this land for our own!" The group broke into applause.

"In our hearts and minds, we have the will to be a great nation but the yoke of burden has weighed heavy on us all until our backs are bent from the strain. I will remove that yoke allowing each of us to stand tall and allowing our hearts and minds to soar!"

At that the group erupted into applause, and the candidate paused for a moment. Jill bit her lip in disbelief. What? She thought, paying closer attention to the men behind her.

"He is actually going to deport aliens?"

"Even those holding green cards," the man replied.

"That's just talk, Ben. What he wants to do can't be done. Congress will never allow it."

"Don't be so sure. According to his plan, we will have a much smaller military. In fact, there is talk that the Army would be done away with in favor of the Marines. Our Navy, Coast Guard, and National Guard would expand. The monies saved on foreign aid and a smaller standing Army would go to things like new schools and free tuition to community colleges. He wants to rebuild our inner cities and create a government sponsored medical program." Grinning, the man added, "And, of course, futuristic weapons to keep us all safe."

"Bill, he's going to change the world. He wants to pull troops out of the Middle East, Germany, and South Korea. He's going to build a wall on the Mexican border. It will happen. Down deep, the American people want it. They're tired of seeing their children die for ungrateful bastards like the French. We bailed them out in two wars and they hate us. We send money by the truckload overseas to foreign governments so they can buy weapons to shoot at our sons."

Bill nodded his head in agreement, and the two men clinked glasses. "If he wins the oval office, he'll fix this country. Or die trying."

"Well, he's got my vote and my money. But I'm concerned about your last comment... he might die trying."

"I am worried about the death threats also. There have been a lot of them, but it's not the nuts I'm worried about. It's foreign governments. I'm concerned about old allies like South Korea or Israel. That's why he has the Secret Service detail already. Normally, there isn't a need for protection like this."

"I heard about a few of them," the man commented. "They won't get him. Walker is smart and well protected."

"For the country's sake, I hope you're right. I fear that this is just the beginning."

Jill raised an eyebrow, intrigued. She couldn't help eavesdropping. It was simply part of her nature. She moved away from the men, found Walker in the viewfinder, and captured a picture.

She paused behind a small table of women who were also talking. "Well ladies, I spoke with Diana this morning, and I can tell you that she's concerned about that man who died."

"Is she trying to get Walker to back out of the race?"

"No, nothing like that. She believes in him, supports his decision--but she's worried. She doesn't like the Secret Service detail, either. I told her it was only going to get worse and that she could come take refuge at the ranch anytime she needed to get away."

"Oh heavens, Clare. Let me know if she comes, we'll make a week of it. It must be fabulous to own a spa."

"Hell, who are you kidding? You practically live in one with all those trips to the Golden Door."

No longer interested, Jill moved on, taking more pictures as the speech ended. Erin tapped her on the shoulder a bit later. "Debi says we can be done for the night."

"Really?" Jill asked, hopeful.

Erin grinned. "You should see your face. Now I wish I hadn't exaggerated. We actually have two more pictures to take. In a few minutes, they're having some sort of cheese dedication and then..."

"I'm sorry. You didn't say cheese, did you?"

"Yes. There's a major contributor from Wisconsin who is giving a speech. And then... You know, Jill, why don't you let me finish this up? You look tired."

"Don't be silly, Erin. I will finish."

"Are you sure? I really don't mind staying a while. Some of these people have been drinking all day and the conversation is getting interesting," Erin confessed.

Jill smiled. "I was thinking the same thing."

"There are quite a few people talking about your dead guy."

"Oh?"

"Yeah. Some of the staff, and the guests for that

matter, think that something's up. Oh, there's the cheese. Look, Jill."

Jill looked in the direction Erin pointed. Two staff members rolled a cart with one large wheel of cheese, as promised, onto the stage area. Jill found a position and clicked off a few pictures, while a contributor made a toast and the cheese was sliced and served for the guests to try. After they had finished making the rounds, Jill whispered, "I have now seen it all."

"Me too! Do you want to go over to the lounge later? They're playing charades."

"No, I don't think so. I'm going to take the equipment back to the office and maybe get some reading done," Jill lied. She actually had to make her doctor's appointment, but she didn't want to field Erin's questions.

"You're lying, but you're a sweetheart. If you actually had told me you were going to work, I would feel guilty and need to tagalong. This way, I have plausible deniability."

Jill winked. "That, my friend, was the idea."

Chapter 24

Less than two hours later Jill found herself back in the office after she finished the doctor's appointment. She looked down at her belly every few minutes. Occasionally, she even succumbed to touching it or saying hello to the cells that would become a living, breathing entity. She couldn't stop beaming. The on board doctor confirmed what Jill had learned in an email. She was absolutely pregnant, and according to the doctor, approximately five weeks along.

The door to Jill's office opened with a mechanized whir. Erin slid through it and hit the button for it to close behind her. She looked... flushed, Jill decided.

"My goodness, what a night!" Erin declared.

"I am not sure I have seen you quite this peppy yet. And I definitely didn't expect to see you here tonight. It must be the luxurious morning snooze you took while I was out there seeing the world and whatnot."

Erin shrugged noncommittally. "Rob got called in, so I thought I'd come say hello."

"How did you know I'd be here?"

"Because you're always in here if you're not on a shoot." Erin said and on impulse spun around quickly on the office chair. Both of the women laughed. "I feel like a kid!"

"A little return to childhood is a good thing now and again," Jill said. "Or perhaps it is romance I see glittering in your eyes. You're gone for him, aren't you?"

"Who?" Erin asked maintaining a serious expression for just a moment before she grinned wildly. "Okay, so I might have a crush on our favorite agent."

Jill smiled up at her. "Love is a beautiful thing."

"Love is a bit too strong of a word for this experience, but yes, I generally agree. Except when it only lasts one week, and then it's pitiful. I'll spend all next week pining, I'm sure of it."

"Will Rob be with the campaign until the end?"

"I think so. I haven't wanted to ask, but I got that impression. Lots of traveling. It must be hard after a while. At least with the ship there's something of a home base."

Jill considered that for a moment, wondering if she could handle the lifestyle. She didn't think so. And of course, with a business, an engagement--there was simply no way she could handle it. And a baby, she thought gently. She smiled to herself, bit down on a giggle and looked back at the computer screen.

Erin sat down at the adjoining desk. She flipped through the pictures Jill had printed. "Okay, next week I don't care what has to be done. I am going hiking. These are amazing, Jill." She paused, chewed her lip on an idea for a moment. "You were hired by the ship, right? A special assignment, no doubt--but Debi hired you, not the campaign?"

"Yes, that's correct."

"That means that Magellan has ownership of

these photos, not the Walker campaign, right?"

Jill shrugged. "Debi made me sign dozens of pages, and I have no idea what it all meant because there was no time to read it. All I know is that I can't take any of it with me unless I get permission. Why?"

"I'm seeing a product line for the shops on board in my head. A calendar, a coffee table book perhaps. If I can work it out, are you interested?"

"Well, I don't think I would have any part of it," Jill admitted. "The product doesn't belong to me."

"Oh, hell. I can probably get you a standard financial package. I know the right people to talk to. I have to get through Debi first, though. Hmmm. Something to think about. Make sure you leave me your agent's contact information."

Jill scribbled Dean's name, phone number, and email address onto a post-it note and handed it over.

Erin filed it away in her binder. She spent the next several minutes tidying the office. Jill worked on cropping a picture, humming to herself while she worked. She used the publishing program to play with the floral scene, manipulating colors simply for the enjoyment of it.

"Ah, Jill..."

Jill picked her head up from her task. "Yes?"

"Don't we have four memory cards?"

"Yes, four."

"There are only three here. I wouldn't even question it, but you pulled the one from the camera after the shoot, right?"

"That's right." Jill frowned, rising to see for herself. She looked around the office. She checked her camera. "I don't see it."

"Well, it's not like we're missing pictures. I know you download them everyday."

"Don't worry, Erin. We'll find it."

"On a completely off topic, I figured out why everyone is talking about Schultz again," Erin said.

Jill spun her desk chair around to face her friend.

"Agent Riley is returning to the ship."

Jill's eyes widened. "Are you sure?"

"I don't know how the word spread so fast, but Rob told me himself. He had to cut short our after-dinner drink to attend a meeting. Apparently, their shifting something about the security detail. He couldn't tell me anything more than that."

"Do you know when he'll be here?" Jill asked.

"No clue."

If Doug was returning to the ship, something must have been off with the investigation--which supported Jill's suspicions. Jill closed out of her file, and leaned back in her chair, drumming her fingers against the desk.

Erin glanced at her. "You look bored."

"Restless," Jill corrected. The truth was that her palms simply itched to be doing something productive. She had organized and reorganized the pictures, charged her batteries, taken every conceivable extra shot she could work in. She could take part in the ship's

New America

entertainment, but she had done some of that the night before. And this morning, she'd spent the whole day having fun. If Riley was returning to the ship, he must have a reason. She'd bet anything that he uncovered doubt concerning the natural death. He was returning to investigate, which meant maybe she could help him. But how?

"I think I'm going to peek in on the museum exhibit," Erin announced. "I'd like to see how everything is going. Would you like to come?"

"Yes, I'd love to." Perhaps, it was just the thing she needed to clear her mind. "The museum is generally your baby, right?"

Erin smiled, leading the way out of the office and adopting her 'tour guide' voice that she so loved. "Yes and no. Currently, we have a professor visiting from the Chicago Institute of Arts. He is acting as our curator for the summer and handling the two major exhibits. He's also teaching some of the classes available on board.

"There is talk as to what will happen with the museum next. One of the higher ups in Magellan wants to partner with a university and either offer fellowships for individuals wanting to live on board and teach a class in the college, or simply hire a curator. I have been working closely with the current museum director, because it's something I care about, and I am also in charge of the mini-exhibits that are specific to the group on board. They require less square feet and less materials, but almost as much preparation. I think it helps the museum to have one of the business agents, like myself, directly involved. As one of my college professors once told me, business people think differently than artists--for the most part, that is."

"What is the current exhibit?" Jill asked.

"It's a collection of political artifacts on loan from the Smithsonian accompanied by a dynamic display from Candidate Walker's life. It's relatively small on the scheme of things, but I think it has turned out nicely."

When they finally reached the large opaque glass doors, Erin beamed at Jill. "I can't wait to see what you think." She allowed Jill to enter first, watching her face for a reaction.

Much like the spa, the room was taller than she expected. Large red, white, and blue banners rippled down from the ceiling in swoops, giving the room texture and ambience. Red, white, and blue balloons were caught by nets in the corners at interesting intervals. The floor of each display case was covered with political confetti and rained down from the ceilings of various national conventions. The walls were alive with dynamic displays of other era clothing, photographs of political leaders, and pins from campaigns. Although Jill had never considered herself to be overly political, she could certainly appreciate an artistically created exhibit. "Erin, this is beautiful."

She could see that Jill meant it and smiled. "Thank you."

"I thought you said this was small."

"Oh, it is. After this week, the museum will be closed for one week to bring on a paleontological exhibit from the Royal Tyrell Museum. I won't have much involvement with that one."

"You're bringing dinosaur bones on board?"

Erin's face was positively giddy. "Yep. I can't wait. I've always been a bit of a geek. And I love that our home base is Chicago. I go to the museum there and visit Sue every chance I get."

"Sue? Jill asked.

"You're not a dinosaur fan, I take it?" At Jill's blank face, Erin laughed. "Sue is the world's largest T-rex skull. The Field Museum of Natural History bought it some years back for two million. My parents and I were there when they put her on display for the first time." Erin rambled on, but Jill had stopped listening.

Something clicked in her mind. The fourth memory card was in her shirt pocket. She placed it there so she wouldn't confuse it with the others and simply forgot about it. She still had the pictures from Brent Schultz's suite. One of the crew members called Erin over, so Jill was saved from embarrassing herself. She took the opportunity to view the giant-sized scrapbook that generously held a broad collection of articles and clippings from Walker's life.

Erin returned to her side. "It turns out there's a bit of a problem with one of the computer's here, so I'm going to help out for a while, okay?"

"Sure. No problem. Thanks for bringing me here, Erin. I love it."

"Call me if you need me."

"Thanks." Jill took a few more minutes to look around before she made her exit. She kept her pace controlled and even, barely containing her excitement to do something productive. When she got back to her suite, it didn't take her very long to find the card tucked away in her blouse. Thankfully, she hadn't sent it out to the cleaners.

Before returning to her workspace, she stopped and purchased a bag of gourmet chocolates for Quinn from the store, and then on impulse bought a second one to nibble on for herself. She settled into her office with her treats and loaded the card into the drive.

The first file she opened was of the crime scene itself. She looked at the staircase, the body, the angle of the limbs with a critical eye. She didn't know quite enough about forensic science to determine anything concrete from the photos. She set those aside for the moment and opened the file from Brent's suite.

The pictures of the bedroom, the dining area, and bathroom were all so very typical. There was nothing in the pictures that she hadn't mentally filed away, nothing that shocked her now that appeared ordinary then. She wasn't sure what she expected, but it wasn't the same nondescript findings she had come upon earlier. She zoomed in on areas that included the trash can, the crumpled paper on the desk, but found nothing. In the bathroom shots, she studied the toilet, looking for any kind of sign that the man might have been sick. She looked at the floor, zooming in and out.

On the countertop were simple things, a toothbrush, toothpaste, glass, one used washcloth, one wrapped bar of soap, one opened. She moved to the next picture: the medicine cabinet this time. Inside there was shaving cream and a razor, a travel pack of q-tips, hair product, a prescription bottle, and a bottle of aspirins. The prescription bottle interested her. What kind of pills was he taking? Could they support his natural death? She tried to zoom in, but the label was tilted, and the bottle was twisted just enough to make the drug name indecipherable.

"Damn," she whispered. She looked through the rest of the pictures, trying to interpret something from the opened closet doors. Nothing. She found nothing to indicate suspicion or foul play. It was simply an ordinary display of a rather organized man's room. She looked through the pictures one more time before giving up. At the end of her search, she moved the files into a locked folder on the desktop and replaced the memory card.

She would find something, she knew it. Tomorrow, she would have to look harder.

Chapter 25

Wednesday Morning

She dreamed of pill bottles, babies and butterflies, but she didn't have a coherent thought about any of them. Of course, the pill bottle was from Brent Schultz's medicine cabinet. The baby was hers, and the butterflies sounded like a good idea for a nursery theme if the little one ended up being a girl. She took her time getting dressed, wary of the business slacks and blouses she wore for the job. One of the things she enjoyed about being a photographer was that she rarely needed to dress a certain way. Any job that allowed her to wear jeans and her trademark t-shirts was a winner.

Jill tip-toed out of the bedroom, careful not to wake Debi, and relaxed when she closed the bedroom door behind her. It was the first morning that Debi hadn't beaten her out of bed. Jill smiled at the small pile of new things on the coffee table. Debi might have stayed out most of the night, but at some point she splurged on new open-toed red heels. Jill admired them for a moment then shook her head. She had never been a big fan of dressing up.

Jill gathered her hair at the back of her neck and secured it with a clip while she glanced out the window. From her view, Jill could see the colorful cliffs and town of Pictured Rock National Lake Shore. She checked the clock. Her first shoot today was on land

and didn't take place for a few hours. Jill slipped her card key into her pocket and wandered. Her thoughts kept returning to the pill bottle in Schultz's suite. Somewhat mindlessly, she made the trek from her room to Schultz's.

"Your partner is not with you today? Do you need to go back into the room?"

Jill turned when she realized someone was talking to her, recognized the housekeeper from Schultz's room. "Excuse me, what did you say?"

"You need to go back in, yes?"

On impulse, Jill nodded her head. "Yes, thank you."

The petite, dark-haired woman unlocked the door. "You know, I remembered something."

Just then a guest interrupted their conversation, requesting more towels from the housekeeper. Jill spotted plastic gloves on the small cart and pocketed one, while never taking her eyes off the door. When the housekeeper returned, Jill listened.

"The day that man died, I saw a woman enter this room. She had blond hair, about your height. She wore a nametag."

"She worked on the ship?" Jill asked, sharply.

"Yes, miss. I don't know who she is. I didn't see her closely."

"Okay, thank you. You can leave me in here, if you like. I know you have much work to do."

The woman smiled kindly. "Thank you." She turned and closed the door, leaving Jill unsupervised in the dead man's suite.

Jill pulled the glove from her pocket and slipped her hand inside while she walked to the bathroom. She flipped on the light switch and opened the medicine cabinet. Nothing. The prescription bottle was gone. Could Doug have taken it? She didn't think so. Stepping back carefully, she looked over the scene, comparing it with the pictures still clear in her memory. The vanity was different and missing something.

Thirty seconds passed before Jill realized that the toothbrush and toothpaste were absent from the countertop. Why would anyone steal the toothpaste and brush? They wouldn't, unless they were somehow incriminating. Items that she hadn't paid attention to now jumped out at her. She noticed a white cream smudge on the mirror, residue inside a glass. Did Brent brush his teeth and rinse with water in the glass? Did he mash his pills and mix them with water before he took them? Jill chuckled harshly at herself, but didn't want to risk anything else being stolen.

She moved to the bedroom closet and removed the laundry bag from the shelf. She carefully placed the cup inside the laundry bag and sealed it, feeling a touch ridiculous. What would happen if she was caught in here, she wondered. Would anyone believe that she was trying to help? Probably not.

Jill looked long at the rooms, checked pockets of pants and shirts, hoping for some small definitive detail to point her in another direction. She looked closely, carefully... and found nothing.

Chapter 26

"Doug, it's Martha. I've got the information you wanted."

Riley held his hand over his other ear, trying to block out the noise. He was about to board a helicopter that would taxi him out to the ship. He had flown from Milwaukee to Houghton. Since the ship was anchored at Pictured Rocks, it was the most convenient way he could get out there. Arranging the flight, however, had been long and complicated. Milwaukee wasn't a bursting metropolitan, but it was certainly a great deal easier to book a chopper there. Doug walked further away from the noise and stepped into the nearby building. "Go ahead."

"She's an orphan, Doug. Her parents were targeted and killed in a plane crash along with over one hundred others. She was the only survivor, raised by her grandparents. She got involved with our work by learning how to use a camera as a child. She has worked with a number of different police officers, mostly in a photographer's capacity. She's attended a few forensic workshops and taken a few classes in criminal justice. She came onto our radar when she solved a murder and counterfeit case on Drummond Island in 2003.

"She also determined who robbed two banks in northern Michigan and solved several murders associated with the case, one of which was a member of

John Dilinger's gang."

"The gangster?"

"Yes. And most recently, she tracked down the rightful owner of a diamond mine's profits. The Michigan FBI team has a deep stack on Traynor. I talked with an agent there who has worked with Jill personally. Apparently, they consider her an asset. She digs into things that shouldn't concern her, but she always solves the puzzle she starts. She's a natural. Devonshire confirmed again that you can bring her in on this."

"Maybe she'd like a real job," Riley joked.

"I doubt it. She owns a seven figure culinary business."

"Jill does?" He tried to put this information in perspective with the woman he met on the ship. She didn't seem rich, he thought.

"Yes. She's a third-share partner with her live-in boyfriend, Quinn McCord, and his brother."

Riley shook his head. Perhaps he was the only idiot still working for the government, he thought. "Okay. Thanks, Martha. Tell Devonshire that I'm about to board the chopper. I'll call him in a few hours with an update."

"Do you want me to send this to your PDA?"

"No. I don't think I have signal here. Leave it on my desk, will you? I'll look over it when I get back home."

"Sure thing. Bye Doug."

Riley clicked off the phone then turned it back on. He still had some time before they would be ready to take off. He dialed the Medical Examiner's office directly, but reached a recording. He left a message and hung up, pleased when the pilot signaled him that they were ready to go.

*   *   *

As focused as he was, Agent Riley couldn't help but appreciate the beauty of his surroundings. He had visited the Upper Peninsula before, but seeing Pictured Rocks from the air was a surreal experience. Even viewing the cruise boat once again from the sky was a bit of a sight. The water was dotted with small boats and ferries running tourists back and forth from Munising. He looked to the north at the vast open water of Lake Superior, noticing an ore carrier on the horizon. Before the day was over, the ship would be at the Sault Locks, then the St. Mary's River, and on to Lake Huron. For a moment, he wished he could be on that ship with a lawn chair and a good book instead of on the *New America*. If something went wrong with the investigation, his career might never recover.

When the copter landed, Riley hit the deck and retrieved his luggage. He had a singular mission in mind. He needed to find Jill Traynor. He didn't even know why it was important to him, save for a nagging feeling of intuition that the woman could help. Beyond that, he would start back at the beginning with the crime scene, re-interview the witnesses, and count on the agents assigned to Brent Schultz's identity to provide him with the missing information. Schultz wasn't killed at random. Someone on board knew him and it was up to Doug to find him.

The Captain's aide greeted him and ushered him into the pilot house. "The Captain wants to be apprised of the situation at all times, Agent. As you did before, you'll have full cooperation with the ship's security. If you need help connecting to Secret Service..." He stopped when Riley shook his head. "Very well. We've cleared the conference room for you, so you can set up in there. Here's your pass card and codes, my number, contacts, so forth. Can I do anything for you at this time?"

"How do I contact Jill Traynor?"

The Captain's aid looked puzzled. Agent Riley watched as the man's eyes shifted and tried to place the name. Finally, he asked, "The photographer?"

"Yes."

"Debi White is her direct superior. Her information is on the sheet I just gave you. That would probably be the easiest way to reach her."

"I am going to be utilizing her as a personal assistant. Can you help me clear that through Debi White?"

"Yes, of course. I'll ask the Captain to contact Ms. White and free up as much of Ms. Traynor's time as possible."

"Good. Thanks." Doug moved forward, intending to begin right away. He didn't want to waste time with formalities and small talk. He didn't want to have to talk Jill into helping him. He hoped his instinct was right about her. This was an intricate, complicated case. She needed to be every bit as good as his gut told him she was.

Chapter 27

Although she had been near him at several intervals over the last few days, Jill had not had the opportunity nor the inclination to speak with Candidate Walker at all, unlike everyone else on the ship--guests and staff alike--who firmly believed this man would be the next president. Today, her reticence was going to make the day awkward, she realized, when the shallow draft boat she was escorted into was only large enough for about twenty individuals. Jill was given one of the prized seats, while Erin stayed behind to tend to other tasks. The candidate wanted to view the beauty of Pictured Rock up close, in a less "public" setting. The individuals on board were friends and aides rather than contributors, which seemed to be a delight to everyone, including Jill. This event didn't have the fake glossy sheen of being staged.

As the boat pulled away from the ship, the pilot introduced himself. Jill leaned back and enjoyed the ride. She took a few candid pictures of individuals on board, but didn't feel right about the timing, so she put her camera away for a while. The boat slowed for long looks at Indian Drum, Rainbow Cave, Flower Vase, and Lovers Leap. The pilot, or narrator, as Jill thought of him, told stories from his own life and local legend about the cliffs. She listened for a few moments.

"Picture Rock National Lake Shore was founded in 1966, as our country's first National Lake Shore. It covers 71,400 acres and is made up of sandstone cliffs, sculptured by nature over thousands of years. The Lake Shore also has extensive sand dunes, sandy beaches, forest, inland lakes, streams, and waterfalls. Many of our visitors like to hike, camp, fish, swim or just picnic. There are several lighthouses here. To our left," he added, which made the group look in the direction he suggested, "is Grand Island National Recreation Area. Of course, what people really come here for is the natural sculptured cliffs that rise out of Lake Superior and are at times a rainbow of colors."

The cliffs at Bridalveil Falls towered high into the sky and allowed soft white water to flow over the juts and crevices. Jill couldn't resist photographing each place, then capturing images of the candidate gazing up at the cliffs, or a romantic shot of the couple together. The boat slowed near the beach. A young woman approached Jill. "Miss Traynor, thank you for taking minimal pictures today. We all feel you've been doing an excellent job from some of the proofs we've seen."

Jill smiled, pleased. "Thank you. I didn't know anyone from your group had seen my pictures yet."

"Ms. White brought a small sample of the work over. You've fulfilled your duties here today, but you are more than welcome to stay and have lunch with us if you'd like."

"I appreciate the offer, but I brought my own lunch. I didn't know when we'd get back to the ship. Thanks anyway." Jill glanced beyond the woman, startled to see Walker staring intently at her. A shiver coursed through her spine and she looked away quickly, suddenly uncomfortable.

The woman glanced off to the shore, spotting a park ranger near the team from the ship that was busily setting up a picnic. "I wonder if the ranger wants a photo with Candidate Walker," she mumbled.

"I'd be happy to take one if that's the case," Jill responded.

The group disembarked the boat slowly. Jill heard the aide ask Walker if he wouldn't mind a picture with the ranger. The man in question came closer to the boat.

When Walker left the boat, he was surprised when the ranger walked right past him.

Jill turned around to dig her camera back out of her bag when she heard someone call her name.

"Jill? Is that you?"

She snapped her head around, recognizing the voice and grinned broadly. She had met the ranger a few years ago while photographing Pictured Rocks in the autumn. "Hey! How are you?" She called back.

She snapped her bag closed and shook the man's hand.

He lowered his voice, guiding her away from the group. "I came over to make sure no one is lighting a fire today. We're on high alert for fire danger, and when I glanced down I thought I saw you."

"How have you been?"

"Just fine. I can only stay a minute. I ordered a sub from town."

"Ooh, can I get a ride?" Jill asked.

"Sure thing."

"Are you coming back this way though?"

"Wouldn't be trouble to bring you back."

"Sounds good," Jill said. She followed him into the truck and when she spotted a payphone, she asked him to drop her off. "Just pick me up right here, okay?"

The ranger nodded and she hopped out.

She tossed a few quarters into the machine and called Quinn, whose phone went directly to voicemail. Prepared this time, she tried the hospital's phone number and asked for Dave Kinney's room.

"Hello?"

"Ohmygod. Uncle Dave?"

"That's right, darlin." His voice was thready, but he had obviously come through the anesthesia problems.

"How are you?"

"Feel like someone opened up my chest and stole a piece of my heart," he whispered.

Jill laughed, her eyes tearing a bit. "I am so glad you're okay."

"Thanks."

There was a shuffling noise and a woman came onto the phone. "Jill? This is Karen."

"How is he doing, Karen?"

"He's doing so much better. Dr. Crawford says she thinks he's going to be fine. Of course, then she told him about the diet she wants him to be on. He's not quite well enough to grumble, but I can feel it coming."

Jill smiled. "I'm so glad you're there."

"You just missed Quinn. Dave is trying to shoo him back to Michigan, but he's sticking for the time being. He's such a good man, Jill. He's been a big help."

"I'm sorry I can't be there."

"Nonsense. We're getting along just fine."

"That's good. If there is anything I can do..."

"You're doing it. Quinn told me all about your exciting opportunity. Are you meeting famous people?"

Jill smiled. "A few." She continued the pleasant small talk until she spotted the National Park truck approaching.

"I've got to go Karen. Hug Quinn and Uncle Dave for me." She waited until she heard Karen say goodbye, then hung up the phone. Instead of being returned to the beach, she asked to be dropped off at the top of a cliff she was shown last time she visited. They chatted for a few more minutes before Jill thanked him and started the walk down the hill. The switchback trail weaved back and forth around large pine trees. The trail was marked well and the footpath was nicely cared for, closely guided by a split rail fence. Plateaus, used for lookout points, provided handy areas for Jill to pause and take pictures from. In one spot, she could see a woman resting on a plateau further down and also the candidate and entourage on the beach below. Jill kept going and stopped when she reached the woman, surprised to recognize the housekeeper from the ship. She was bent over an open backpack when Jill approached.

"Hello!" Jill called.

The woman turned, startled. She smiled when she saw Jill. "Lovely day, si?"

"It's beautiful." Jill glanced up, appreciated the flawless blue sky and warm yellow cast of the sun. "Do you have the morning off?"

"A few hours, si. You too?"

"I just finished. See you later," Jill called, knowing the woman would probably prefer some peace.

Even though she wasn't asked to, Jill couldn't pass up the photo opportunity when she saw it. The candidate and his wife, along with many members of the group played a rousing round of beach volleyball. She watched Walker for a moment. She didn't agree with some of his messages, but was okay with that. His intent stare earlier still had her feeling mildly uncomfortable.

She took a few more shots, careful to frame the whole scene. The net was actually anchored in a shallow portion of the water, which meant everyone was in casual clothing or swimsuits. Jill paused on the hill before she rejoined the group and zoomed in and out for a variety of pictures. When finished, she looked back up hoping to wave to the housekeeper, but the plateau spot was empty. Jill shrugged it off and continued toward the beach, noticing for the first time that it was mysteriously absent of any Secret Service agents.

Chapter 28

Although Jill was required to work many hours, she also found time to enjoy herself. Today, for example, she attended the boat tour, but she couldn't imagine many better work opportunities. When she returned to the ship a bit ahead of her party, she was surprised to find Debi waiting for her in their suite.

"Hi, Debi!" Jill exclaimed. "I rarely see you unless it's at an event. How is your week going?" Jill set her equipment down on the coffee table and relaxed for a moment on the couch.

"Well," the blonde sighed. It was the first time Jill had ever seen her roommate and boss ruffled. "I..."

"Is something wrong?"

"Agent Riley has returned to the ship, and the Captain has instructed me to let you work with him."

"Doug's back?"

"Yes."

"He wants me to work with him?"

"Apparently so, yes."

"Only between shoots, right?"

Debi shrugged. "The Captain told me to accommodate him in any way I can, so it might be up to him... which is going to simply ruin the entire portfolio. Erin might be learning, but she's not you. Why do you think he needs your help? What is going on?" She asked.

Jill's heart went out to the woman. She knew Debi worked around the clock to make sure all went smoothly. "Debi, I'll talk to Doug. I don't know why he needs my help, but I am not going to abandon my obligations. The entire reason why I am here this week is to take pictures of this event."

Something flickered in Debi's face, but it was gone before Jill could identify it. "You must think I am being petty. If the agent needs your help then, of course, he should have it. You have already taken an excellent collection of photographs."

"Thank you."

The phone's melodious ring interrupted what Jill was going to say next. She picked up the phone from the end table. "Hello?"

"Jill Traynor, please."

"This is Jill."

"Good. It's Doug Riley. Have you spoken with Debi White?"

"I am speaking with her now."

"Excellent. When you're done there, why don't you come up to the conference room. I am sure you have questions, and she can't answer them. Okay? Can you be here in an hour?"

"I can be there in thirty minutes."

"Even better. Thanks." The phone clicked off and Jill replaced the handset. She smiled at Debi as she moved into the bedroom and fetched some clothing from her closet. "Duty calls," she explained. "I'm going to freshen up and then meet Doug. Can I do anything to help, Debi?"

Debi shook her head. "No. Go on ahead. You're free for the night, so hopefully you can finish helping the agent and be back in play for tomorrow. Mackinaw is going to be a big day, Jill. Will you be ready?"

"I'll be ready, Debi. My first commitment is to you and the contract I signed with this ship. With that said, I do not know what Agent Riley wants of me or what power he has to pull strings."

Debi understood. "Keep me posted if you can't do tomorrow's shoot."

Jill agreed and retreated into the bathroom to get ready for her meeting with Agent Riley. She turned the shower's hot water on, slipped out of her clothes, and stood under the warm stream for a minute, slowly working the knots from her muscles. When finished, she didn't bother with make-up, but dressed casually in jeans and a t-shirt. If the agent needed her help, he wasn't going to be concerned with her clothes, she decided. She fetched the glass that she had bagged from Schultz's room and placed it in her camera bag. She brushed her hair back into a ponytail, tossed on her sandals, and made her way out of the suite and through the ship to Doug's conference room.

She knocked before entering and was greeted by Doug's voice calling her to "come in."

"Ah, Jill, thanks for coming. Have a seat."

Jill sat down in a chair two down from him and placed her bag near her feet. "Debi said you need my help."

"If you're willing, I do. Are you willing?"

"Sure. What do you need me to photograph?" Jill asked.

"Nothing." Riley leaned back in his chair and studied her face. He watched confusion pass through her eyes before speaking. "Jill, I haven't read your file personally, but I hear it's the size of a book. And let's say I've heard the cliff notes version of it. The diamonds in Canada, the billions of dollars you tracked down for the government, the pennies--all of it. I have been authorized by my supervisor to bring you into the FBI in a temporary, consulting status."

Jill swallowed air, taken aback. "Consulting on what, Sir?"

"It's Doug, Jill. And the answer is this case."

"Didn't you believe it was a natural death?"

"We can talk about that after you sign the paperwork. I need help, and at the moment we're short on agents." He paused. "If it makes a difference, it is a paid position. Will you help me?"

"I've never done this before, but I'd be happy to help."

He shook his head, surprised at her humility. "Jill, you've solved more cases than some professionals." He slid a file folder across the expanse of table between them. "Sign the highlighted parts and we can begin."

She picked up her pen, hesitating. "I still need to finish the photography. I'll help you during every moment of in between time if you need me to, but I have to take the pictures."

With no choice, Doug conceded the point. "Very well."

Jill signed each indicated line and handed him back the folder. "What can I do?"

"Let me bring you up to speed with what I know so far. The man who died..."

"Brent Schultz," Jill supplied.

"Yes, but that wasn't his real name. It turns out that the man on board was using the documentation of a man who actually passed away a few years ago."

"So, who was he?"

"We have agents working on that question right now, but the truth is simply that I don't know. For some reason, a man took on another person's identity and boarded this ship. Let's not forget that he had to contribute a sizable chunk of money to even be a part of this fund raiser event."

"If he was murdered, there must be someone on board who knows who he really is."

"That's right," Doug agreed.

Jill considered it for a moment. "I have something that might help." She reached into her bag and grabbed the plastic covered glass. She handed it to him.

"What is this?"

"After you left, I realized that I had not destroyed the pictures like I was supposed to. When I ran across them, I looked at them once more and noticed a prescription bottle in the photograph. I was curious about what the pills were and if they could be related to the man's death. The housekeeper let me into his suite."

"You re-entered the suite?"

"Yes," Jill admitted without making excuses. "The pill bottle was missing."

Doug had noticed the same thing during his visit today, but couldn't help being surprised. "I saw that."

"The toothbrush and toothpaste were also missing," Jill continued, "which means, at least to me, that his death was no accident. Someone removed those items from the room after we had been there. There must be a reason."

Doug shook his head in disbelief. He hadn't noticed the other missing items. He leaned forward, thinking about everything she had told him. He crooked his head to the side and looked at her. "Was the name on the pill bottle Brent Schultz?"

Jill frowned. "I looked closely at the drug's name. To be honest I didn't look at the patient's name at all."

Doug opened another folder and pulled out the pictures she had made him. He flipped through the stack until he found the medicine cabinet. He squinted at the copy and moved aside so she could look at it.

"We can go back to my office and enlarge the image."

Doug stood. "Let's do it."

*   *   *

An hour later, Doug was on the phone with his superior, Special Agent Devonshire. "I have a possible name on the victim. Scott Grafton. Run it through the system and see if anything pops up, okay?"

As many times as she had looked at that picture, she had never thought to question the name, assuming it was the doctor's. Doug didn't even have to see it before realizing the potential clue. She listened to his side of the conversation with interest.

"Do we know for sure he was poisoned?" Doug asked.

Poison, Jill mulled as she considered the missing toothbrush and paste. How possible would it be to insert poison into a tube of toothpaste? It would be easy with the right tools, she figured. Plus, if the poison had any kind of an odor, the minty scent of the paste would probably mask it. What about the pills? Could someone have substituted different pills in the bottle or tampered with them in some way? Regardless, it was now a certainty that the man had been murdered. But why? She wondered. Who knew of his real identity?

Doug spoke for a few minutes, letting his boss know about the other missing items before he hung up the phone. "Well, it's official. We are investigating an open murder case."

Jill nodded. "What do we do next?"

"Devonshire is going to reach out with the name, see if he can figure out who this guy was."

They sat in silence for a few minutes, each lost in their own thoughts before Jill spoke. "The housekeeper mentioned that she saw a crew member enter the victim's room."

"When?"

"I'm not sure, but she said the woman had short blond hair, average build. She didn't know who the woman was."

"Well, we'll just show her."

"Like a line-up?"

"The ship has photographs of everyone on board. We'll have the housekeeper look through it."

"I didn't know that."

"Sure you did," Doug said. He pointed to her ID badge with her photograph emblazoned on the front.

Jill grinned. "Never mind then. I guess on some level I must have known that."

"Okay. Let's go back to the conference room. When we get there, I want you to contact the Captain's aide and ask him for the phone records for the victim's room."

Jill locked up her office while Doug gave her directions. "Doug, do you know about the kiosk system?"

"What are you talking about?"

She quickly explained the possible communication methods, medical system, and internet connections. She finished by saying, "I think it would be worthwhile to access those records too."

Doug nodded. "Good idea. Make the calls. I'm going to spend some more time in the victim's suite. When you get somewhere, come find me. I'll go get pictures of the crew and talk to the housekeeper. Let's try to make some progress. "

Chapter 29

If anyone had asked, Jill would have confirmed that Thursday morning arrived too early--much too early, since Agent Riley had kept her glued to a desk until the wee hours of the morning. After tracking down the information she needed, she stayed with it, checking and cross referencing all outgoing numbers. She attempted to connect those numbers back to the guests on board with very little success.

Unfortunately, incoming calls were more plentiful and not tracked by the ship's computer system. Jill didn't even want to breathe the thought that entered her mind sometime between three and four in the morning. If she looked at the entire ship's call log, it might be possible to search for someone who dialed the victim. It would be a needle in a haystack and probably not worth it--so she hadn't mentioned the idea yet.

This morning, Jill disembarked the ship with a pleasant face but a rather cranky disposition. Mackinac Island's itinerary was jammed with photo opportunities. She moved to the side of the plank and observed the crowd for a few minutes while she waited for Erin. Unlike other destinations, crowds poured off ferry boats with nearly the same speed that people departed the ship--and quite possibly, faster. She expected the cruise guests to get lost in the shuffle of her vision, but she could easily pick them out. They were not dressed in tourist t-shirts that seemed to clothe the throng of others. The cruise ship guests wore fine linens and looked like they were about to attend a tea party. Jill found that she preferred the t-shirts, even though she was dressed in a button down shirt and slacks.

Mackinac Island was a pristine, well-maintained, thriving summer community. Living only one hour away, Jill had visited the island a few times, but always in the spring and fall rather than summer. She took a moment to let her eyes sweep the buildings visible from her vantage point. From her peripheral, she noticed men from the kitchen transporting the special containers of ice. She lost interest when Erin called her name.

"Jill!" Erin rushed over, balancing a satchel, bag, and briefcase. "Good morning," she smiled. "I think I've got everything we need for the day. Have you sun blocked?"

Jill laughed merrily.

"I have to take care of our star photographer, don't I?"

They both laughed. "Where are we going first?"

"Well... we have about forty minutes before Walker arrives." Erin walked next to Jill. "Look at the flowers. They're beautiful, aren't they?"

"They're everywhere," Jill commented. She pulled the lens cap from her camera. "This place really is a postcard."

"Did you know that nine presidents have stayed here?"

"Not surprised," Jill murmured as she looked through her viewfinder. "Let's get some pictures of the boardwalk. Maybe we'll see some of our group."

Erin grinned and followed along, smiling at the passerby horses. "The no cars thing always rattles me a little."

Jill nodded. "I know what you mean."

"Is Drummond like this?" Erin asked.

"Lord, no."

Erin waited a moment and then rolled her eyes at Jill. "Okay, you are awfully distracted. What's going on?"

"I'm sorry. Doug kept me working until four in the morning."

"Doug? Agent Riley, you mean?"

"Yes."

"Doing what?"

"Sorry Erin, I can't tell you. I signed a non-disclosure form."

"This week has been lousy with those, hasn't it?" Erin murmured, more rhetorically than anything. "Is there anything you can tell me?"

"I've become a civilian consultant. It's very strange."

"What do you mean?"

"Well, I get myself into these situations sometimes... but it's usually for a reason."

"I don't understand," Erin admitted.

Jill paused, thinking about it for a minute. "When my friend Joe was murdered, I tried to help the local police because I needed to find some resolution. And now, I am being asked to help. It occurred to me, sometime in the midst of last night, that some of the things we learn in school are totally wrong." Jill side-stepped a horse drawn carriage and continued walking. "For example, we're usually taught to mind our own business. There comes a point, however, when that is simply the wrong advice. How would crimes be solved if everyone was willing to mind their own business? Sometimes, butting in is a good thing."

"You're rambling a bit, Jill."

Jill grinned. "I am tired. Stand over there, in front of the water. I'm going to take your picture."

Erin giggled, but she did as she was told, setting the bags at her feet. "Why on earth..."

"If I get to keep some of these, I am going to show your picture around and hook you up on a blind date every time you pass through the area... which means one blind date each week until the end of the season."

"Uhm, Jill. What about Rob?"

"He'll be traveling. You've got time to explore Upper Peninsula options."

"You really are in a mood, Jill." Erin smiled.

"What's that face?"

"The fudge. Can you smell it? Mmm-mmm," Erin said making a lip smacking sound.

"I can almost taste it." Jill took one more picture. "Let's get a snack. I need some sugar or caffeine or something to wake me up."

"Sounds like a plan," Erin couldn't keep the excitement from her voice. "I want peanut butter fudge in the most desperate way. I had a sample a few weeks ago from one of my co-workers in the museum. I haven't had a chance to make it on land since."

Jill held the door open for Erin, surprised to see Debi hovering over the sample table.

"Make it a pound of the chocolate chip too," she said. "Jill, Erin, hi! Can I buy you some fudge?"

Jill inhaled the sweet scent deeply. "I am going to buy my own, but thanks."

Erin moved right up to the counter and placed her order. She stood much like a deer caught in headlights and watched the workers make fudge.

"I just love this rocky road flavor," Debi admitted.

"Ma'am, your order is ready."

"My God, how much fudge are you buying, Debi?"

"These are gifts for some of the guests. I'm making baskets for twenty key contributors. A little something from each place we visited. After seeing the quality of your work, I'm including framed photographs too," Debi explained. She glanced at her watch. "You're not going to miss Walker's carriage ride are you?"

"No, we've got fifteen minutes still."

"Tell me you're not operating off the old itinerary, Erin."

Erin flipped open her satchel and retrieved the

leather folder housing the itinerary. The women compared notes while Jill made her own selection of fudge, thinking of the team at Three Bobbers.

*　　*　　*

"I feel so glamorous riding in a carriage," Erin admitted, leaning back against the plush seat.

"The pictures of Walker and his wife in their carriage are some of the best yet. Walker setting the canon off was a good one, too."

"Do they really have a canon blast everyday?"

"That's what the tour guide said. I don't think he would lie about it," Jill teased.

"And now we're on our way to the Grand Hotel."

"Not on our way, Erin. Almost there." Jill pointed forward.

The tall pillared building looked almost majestic against the clear blue sky. American flags waved proudly, greeting the entourage of carriages. Everything about the building and grounds was aesthetically balanced, regal, and pristine. No longer remotely tired, Jill stood in the carriage and then climbed on top of the seat.

"Ah, Jill..." Erin cautioned.

"Shhh," Jill whispered as she braced her arms together, holding the camera steady. In her frame, she caught the Walkers' carriage in the foreground and the Grand Hotel behind them. As if Jill had willed him to turn with her mind, Walker looked over his shoulder and smiled. Jill took the picture and sat back down, beaming. "That one belongs on a cover," she boasted.

"Time? Newsweek?"

"Oh, I'm not picky." At that, they both laughed and were still having fun when the carriage rolled to a stop. Jill took time to pet the horse and moved on, ready for the tour and social event ahead. "As soon as we are done here, you and I are going for lunch. I am starving."

"What do you mean? We've got fudge."

"We need a meal, Erin."

"I could have had the kitchens pack something for us."

"Oh, isn't it time for something local?"

"I keep hearing people talk about the Pink Pony. Have you been there?" Erin asked.

"No, but it sounds fun."

Jill and Erin fell into step with the private tour group. Erin did the talking when it was time for a group photo, and Jill stood back, ready with the camera. Walker's aide let them know that they could break for a while. Apparently, there was a meeting they wouldn't be needed at and were given a time to return by.

"Debi's itinerary said she was going to be arranging the event tonight. Do you want to go see if she needs help?"

"Of course," Jill replied, repacking her camera into her bag.

It took some time to locate their fearless leader, but when they did, Jill stopped Erin from blithely rushing ahead. Debi was cornered by a man gesturing wildly. Jill walked that way slowly, surprised now that she hadn't recognized the ice carver sooner.

"What kind of imbeciles are working for you?

Can they not count? Five cases! Five! They bring me six! Do you know what you've done?" His volume increased as Jill approached.

She couldn't hear Debi's response, but noted the way she placed her hand on his arm, tilting her head a bit to the side to appear less threatening.

"You have jeopardized the sculpture for the final gala! My ice has to be kept in constant temperature! I have worked for..." His voice became inaudible, but his stance appeared threatening.

"Debi, can I be of some assistance?" Jill offered.

The ice carver spun on his heels. "How is she going to help take pictures of a ruined sculpture?" He yelled. "Do you know why a Volkov sculpture is great? Because excuses are not tolerated! I'll never be able to show my face again if the ice is ruined!"

"Mr. Volkov, the crew is on their way over to take care of the ice. It will be taken care of, I assure you. Furthermore, if the final sculpture is compromised it will not be considered your fault at all. I take full responsibility for this incident, and I will communicate the error to the Walkers."

The tall Nordic man seemed to calm. "Fine," he nodded abruptly and moved away.

Debi took a breath.

"Are you okay?" Jill asked.

"He is just such a tall man," Debi said, trying to inject humor into the situation.

"What happened?"

"A mix-up is all."

"Can Erin and I do anything to help?"

"No, Jill. Thanks, though. I appreciate the offer. I'll see you later."

"Food?" Erin asked.

"Yes. Good idea."

Chapter 30

After their luncheon, Erin ducked away to canvass the shops for gifts while Jill returned to the Grand Hotel to take exterior pictures of the grounds. According to the plan, there was going to be a formal processional of carriages this afternoon which they would need to photograph. This event, not limited to just the cruise guests, was drawing in financial backers and supportive politicians from across the country. Bizarrely enough, Jill was not required to photograph the island dinner and dancing extravaganza. There were separate photographers contracted by those throwing the event, and Debi hadn't wanted to start a turf war. There was, of course, an after hours event on board the ship accompanied by a midnight buffet. Jill planned to take the minimum amount of pictures possible and get to sleep as soon as she could.

When finished with the exterior shots, she found a rocker on the porch to sit down in. She had Erin's cell phone with her and used the opportunity to call Quinn. He didn't answer, so she dialed the office number. Deedee picked up the phone. "Three Bobbers Over Land Culinary Creations, this is Deedee."

"DeeDee, it's Jill."

"Are you on the ship? Is it luxurious?"

Jill smiled. "I am actually on Mackinac Island, believe it or not. How is life there?"

"Good. The business is operating pretty smoothly, but it's strange not to have the guys here. Chase flies into Kincheloe tonight. Noel is going to pick him up."

"I haven't heard much about his trip. Did it go well?"

"From everything he's said, I think so. I talked to Quinn about an hour ago. Have you talked to him?"

"No. I just tried but he didn't pick up."

"He told me that your uncle is doing really well."

"That is good news. Did he say when he's coming home?" Jill asked.

"He said he didn't know, but he didn't think he'd be too much longer. The doctors are going to send your uncle home in a few days, I guess."

Jill beamed into the phone, relieved. "That is so good. I can let you go; I know you must be busy."

"Billy has been complaining that I never leave the factory. I just want to make sure everything goes smoothly. If Quinn knows I can handle it, he might feel good to take a vacation or get away for a while. And Lord knows Quinn and Chase need a break, you know?"

"I'm glad you work for us, Deedee. Who knows what we would have done this week without you." Jill smiled and said her goodbyes. She waited out the hour before the processional by walking through the building and grounds. When the carriages began arriving, she photographed the event and returned to the ship.

*   *   *

Jill hadn't even made it back to her suite before she found a phone to call Doug. He picked up quickly.

"Riley," he barked.

"I'm back on board..."

"Meet me at the buffet for dinner. Thirty minutes."

"Okay." He clicked the phone off in her ear, which left her with dead air before she replaced her handset as well.

She made the zig-zag trip through the nearly empty ship in record time and found Doug filling a tray with food, exactly where he said he'd be. She gathered a tray and a plate and began selecting foods from the exquisite display. He nodded toward her but didn't waste time talking at this point.

They sat at a table near a window over-looking the island. Jill wasn't overly hungry, but smiled at the large volume of food she gathered for herself. Since Doug had even larger portions, she chose not to feel badly.

"What have you learned?" Jill asked before swallowing a bite of pasta.

"A few things," Doug began, appreciating Jill's style. He would have suffered through small talk, but wanted to get right to work. "We have discovered that Scott Grafton, our victim, was actually former CIA."

"What?" Jill was in threat of choking with her surprise, coughed and took a sip of water.

"There is more. This is where it gets interesting," Doug went on.

"Before the CIA, he was a Major in the Army stationed in Germany working with NATO. His father was also Army stationed in Germany in the fifties post

World War Two. His mother is a German. His father died when he was nine in a training accident. His mother did not remarry and raised the boy alone. Reading between the lines," Doug spoke very quietly now, "I believe he was working for NATO or Germany." At this he shrugged his shoulders turning his palms up in question. "Maybe the CIA. They're saying he went off grid. He requested a leave of absence earlier this year, and they haven't heard from him. It sounds fishy to me. The CIA doesn't simply let go of its operatives that way."

Jill looked into Doug's eyes. "I don't understand. I thought the Germans didn't like us. I would think they would want Walker in the Presidency."

"I'm sure the general population of Germany would be glad to see us go, but the government would not. They have done very well with the U.S. supplying their defense since World War Two. Like Japan, they have prospered. We pump millions into their economy in payrolls and foreign aid. For the same reason, all of Europe or NATO members would think the same way. They hate us and love us. Hell, almost every country in Europe has a national medical program because we supply the major part of their defense."

"So, if we leave NATO and the UN, Europe will have a lot of problems?"

Doug nodded. "Yes, exactly."

Jill looked down at her plate of food, giving the situation some thought. "Since Russia's decline, NATO is less important."

Doug sat back and said nothing, listening for the gears to change in her mind.

"What I don't understand is the CIA. Shouldn't it

get smaller if Walker becomes president? Walker's plan would generate less worldwide problems. That would be better for them." Doug was about to speak when Jill went on. "Of course, the CIA might want him in the White House. If we aren't physically in as many countries, we'll need a larger network of intelligence. Our enemies won't go away just because we're leaving their land."

Jill looked up, thrown off guard to see Doug smiling at her.

"You can't have it both ways, Jill."

Jill grinned. "I say Grafton was here to help. I think the CIA sent him."

"And why is that?" Doug asked.

"Because he is dead. Someone on board came to kill Walker and Schultz or Grafton, whoever the hell he is, he came to stop him."

"Wow," Doug replied, astonished by her thought pattern. "If all you say is true, and you can prove it, then you've got it, Watson."

Jill blushed. "Of course, I am probably wrong. But it helps me to try and understand the why aspect."

"I wasn't making fun of you. Hell, I'm impressed. Even if the theory is wrong, there is sound logic behind it."

Jill took another sip of water. "What else?"

"That's really all we know on that front so far, but I talked to the Medical Examiner. Grafton was definitely poisoned by something close to tricloroethane. It's not a true tricloroethane, because the real thing has a level five toxicity, and it smells like chloroform. The drug used on our victim was a hybrid. The lab tech said it probably had a modest odor that could be pretty easily masked."

"Like in toothpaste?" Jill asked.

Doug nodded. "They wouldn't have found it if they hadn't been looking for poison specifically. The autopsy revealed small hemorrhages in the lungs and brain. I think this drug was used so he would live for a time after ingesting the poison. The killer would want to separate the victim from the toothpaste, make it look like an accident. Trichloroethane is a heavy duty degreaser for machines and engines. It is a colorless liquid."

"Do you think someone got the liquid on board the ship?"

"No, simply because it's not the same chemical. I'm not sure how many lab techs would have figured that out. Other detectives might be thrown off, might believe he ingested the poison by accident. Anyway, the doctor said yes, toothpaste was definitely possible."

"Okay, then we are still looking for links between the victim and others on board, right?"

"That's right."

"And motive. I think he was killed trying to stop someone from killing Walker, or someone killed him because he came here to kill Walker."

"The CIA has an interest in someone on board, possibly Walker," Doug offered. "And there is a third possibility."

"What's that?"

"Maybe it has nothing to do with Walker. With

this group, it could be anybody. Do you know how many millionaires and billionaires are on this ship this week? There are business tycoons, current and future political giants. The truth is that we don't know nearly enough at this point. My boss is thinking along the same lines we are. He is extremely short handed, and yet he is sending us some help."

"How do we learn more?" Jill asked.

"Some of it we just need to wait for. There are agents now assigned to this back at the office. They'll be tracking down all the information they can find on Brent or uhm, Scott Grafton, rather." Doug paused and sampled some of the different items on his plate.

"I sort of have an idea."

"Go ahead."

"I wonder if we could access the entire ship's communication logs and look for individuals who called the victim's room."

"I didn't ask you to have them run a search on that last night?"

"No. I was under the impression from the tech guy that he couldn't."

"Well, he won't be able to tell you... actually, I have no idea. He should be able to tell you most of the victim's incoming calls. Did you get anything more off the kiosk after I left you last night?"

"No. He ordered room service once. He made reservations in the lighthouse room the first night on board."

"With someone?"

"It was a table for two, but there wasn't a second

name. He typed in guest under that spot."

"That's something we can track down. That's good work, Jill. What else? Where did he call?"

She shook her head, taking a moment to think. "He only made three calls from his room. One was off-ship. One was to the events' desk, and the third was to the Enrichment Center."

"Really?"

"When I talked to the receptionist there, he had an appointment for an aromatherapy massage."

Doug's fork paused before it reached his mouth. "You're kidding me?"

Jill shook her head. "No, I'm not. I thought it was strange too."

"It doesn't make sense. Let's visit the Enrichment Center a little later, see who else had appointments during that timeframe."

"Okay." Jill tasted an herb potato and sighed. "This food is amazing. I need Chase to come with me sometime."

"Chase McCord?"

"Yeah. I have mentioned him, haven't I? He's my fiancé's younger brother. He lives with us, owns the business with us."

Doug observed her for a moment. "You know, everything they said about you is true."

"Oh? What's that?"

"You have the intuition for this kind of work, the spark so to speak."

"Thanks. I'm not sure it's true, but if it is, I guess I come by it honestly enough."

"What do you mean?"

"Right before the cruise, my uncle told me about my mother. They think she was murdered because she was going to testify against a shipping company."

Doug had heard a brief synopsis of this, but played along. "Your mother was murdered?"

"I've only known about it since last week. It's not confirmed, but my uncle told me that the family always believed she was killed."

"Tell me what happened."

Jill filled him in on the few details she had learned and about the story of the plane crash she survived. It was good to talk about it. She didn't have a chance to talk with Quinn much since she learned the truth, and she sorely missed her therapist.

Doug finished his dessert and stared out at the island thoughtfully. "When this is over, Jill... I'll help you. I'll use every contact I have. I'll reach out to whoever has the answers and we will find out exactly what your mother knew, what happened."

Jill met his eyes over the table and felt tears spill onto her cheeks. She never took the time to sit with it, hadn't had the time, she reflected. She learned her parents had been murdered within a week of discovering there was a new life growing within her. In the meantime, she had sailed around the Great Lakes, taken a thousand pictures, and became a civilian consultant of the FBI. "I'm going to take a few minutes, if that's okay. Can I meet you back in the conference room in say... twenty minutes?"

"Take thirty, Jill."

"Okay. Thanks."

Jill excused herself, but she didn't walk back to her suite. Instead, she moved upwards, finding the highest deck on the ship. She stood at the railing and faced St. Ignace, the bridge, the water beyond it. The view was breathtaking, but she missed the rocks by the beach at home, the long endless blue.

She was so close to Drummond and her own private haven on the south shore that she felt its absence bodily. She would give anything for thirty minutes there with Quinn. She wanted to tell him about the baby. Of course, even if she had a way off the ship-- Quinn wasn't there. He was still in Florida.

The sun began its slip toward the horizon, still a distance off, but falling. Red and orange light spilled out across the clouds reflecting off the water. Jill stayed on the deck for only a few minutes longer. She looked one last time, longingly, toward Drummond, before returning to the conference room.

Chapter 31

The midnight buffet might have gone on un-photographed if Erin wasn't skilled in tracking Jill down. And since Doug was gracious enough to let Jill retire for the evening rather than return to work a few more hours, she managed to re-enter her suite a little after one in the morning. Bizarrely, she was wired instead of exhausted, but she didn't want to risk a return to the conference room. She simply couldn't handle another all-nighter.

Jill showered and dressed in pajamas, hoping the steamy water would help her relax. She paced around the room, feeling a bit physically restless and mentally drained. Taking refuge in the refrigerator, she found a few cans of pop and a half-eaten brick of fudge labeled Debi, as well as Jill's package, which Debi must have marked Jill. It was a little too sugary for this late at night, so Jill closed the door. Sugar.

Jill spun around on her heels and re-opened the fridge. The fudge wasn't sugar free--Jill remembered seeing a distinctly different label for such treats. This was full sugar fudge, the same kind Debi had sampled at the store earlier that day. Jill took a step back and sat on the corner of Debi's bed. She remembered back to the first day she met Debi, when the security agents checked through her bags. One included insulin and syringes to treat diabetes. There were plenty of diabetics who didn't follow the best health rules, but Debi didn't strike her as the kind of person that would ignore such guidelines. She was a by-the-book sort of person. As Jill sat there her mind jumped to the poison that had killed the guest that had fallen down the stairs. She couldn't remember the name but did remember Doug saying it was clear and had an odor. Clear, Jill thought a liquid that could pass in a sealed bottle for Insulin. She had hid the murder weapon in plain sight and no one was the wiser.

Jill stood and started pacing the floor. Her thoughts went back to the murder victim's room using her minds eye to look at every thing again. She had paced back and forth several time when nothing new came she reviewed all she new about the case and stopped when she came to the description the maid had given of the *New America* employee that had entered the room. Female, Caucasian right height and hair color, Jill shook her head to no one but herself upset that she had not come to this conclusion sooner, especially when she factored in the hidden cell phone and the strange message on it. Jill picked up the phone and dialed the number to the conference room. Doug didn't pick up. She dialed his suite number next, but hit the voice mail recording.

"Doug, it's Jill. I need to talk to you about Debi White. She is involved in our case. It's too hard to explain over the phone, but when I tell you the details I'm sure you will agree. She's not in the suite right now, but she may come back any minute. Call me and I'll meet you."

Jill ended the call and continued pacing the room. As she replayed events from the week, the conversation with the housekeeper stuck out in her mind. She wasn't with Doug when he questioned the woman, but she'd bet anything that he used the photos of those employees with crew status, something that

Debi wasn't.

Jill made notes for herself, feeling the exhaustion creep back over her. She hid the tablet of paper in her desk under a few magazines and crawled into bed. There wasn't much she could do without talking to Doug first, and besides, it was the middle of the night. She was still upset with herself that she had overlooked so many clues especially the hidden cell phone. Why she chose not to tell Doug about it was beyond her. Maybe it was the ship and everyone being so helpful and friendly or maybe it was because she liked Debi and in doing so didn't want to see the truth. As her eyes fluttered seconds before sleep her mind shifted to Uncle Dave also lying in a bed and then to Quinn and her unborn child.

Jill had lots to think about but it would all have to wait, in seconds she was fast asleep.

Chapter 32

Friday Morning

Jill grabbed the phone clumsily, waken from a dead sleep. "Uhm... hello?"

"Good morning. Is it Jill or Debi?"

"Erin?"

"Ah, Jill. I see you chose this morning to sleep in. Damn. I didn't mean to bother you. I'm outside your door. Can you let me in or should I come back?"

"You're where? Why can't you knock?"

"Jill, we can talk about it or you can just kindly let me in. Do you want me to come back?" Erin's voice trailed off as the door clicked open in front of her.

She held a tray of coffee cups. "Hi."

Jill plucked one from the tray. "Is this one mine?"

Erin nodded. "Yep, it's black. The latte is for Debi. Is she here?"

"She didn't come back to the room last night."

Erin wiggled her fingers. "She didn't come home at all? Maybe she got lucky! Good for her!"

Jill sipped her coffee, but smiled.

"Maybe I'll stop by her office then."

Jill sat down Indian style on the couch, holding her coffee cup with both hands. "What time is it?"

"A little after seven."

"Did I know you were coming this morning?"

"Well, no. I was trying to catch Debi. Apparently, there was some schedule shifting with Walker today, and I wanted to see if our itinerary changed," Erin said.

"As far as I know, we don't have to be anywhere until tonight's banquet at the Grand Palace. I intend on looking the room over this morning while they are setting up. Debi has reminded me of this event's importance everyday all week, practically."

"Do you need my help for that?"

"No, not at all. I'll probably spend most of the day with Doug. Where will you be?"

"I am going to make some calls for the curator, but beyond that I'll probably do some work in the office. I'll have my pager if you need to contact me." Erin consciously tried to lean back and control her smile to a normal proportion.

Jill squinted at her. "Okay. What's up?"

"Nothing." Erin glanced up at Jill's face and sighed. "Madeline at the Enrichment Center told me she would give me a huge discount if I wanted a mud bath and massage today. I've been trying to wheedle a good price from her for three weeks. Last night, when I got back to my room, I had an email from her."

Jill grinned. "Go on, then. I'll page you if I need you."

"Great." Erin stood up in a rush. "I'm off then."

Jill waited until Erin had left before she checked her phone and kiosk for messages. Nothing.

*   *   *

Jill showered and dressed in record time, knowing she needed to find Doug. On impulse, she grabbed her camera bag and tucked her pass card in her jeans pocket before she headed out. The conference room was vacant. She visited Debi's office next, but it was also empty. She sent Debi a message via the paging system, but knew the effort was useless with Doug. She left notes in both locations before she headed to the Grand Palace.

As expected, crew members were already busy at work, transforming the ship's finest dining facility into a forum for the week's keynote address and festivities. The ice sculpture, when finished, would be a six feet likeness of an elephant. She couldn't wait to see it. She surveyed the room looking for the best positions to take pictures from. Jill wandered into the main kitchen and then a smaller room, surprised to see the area transformed from pristine organization to utter chaos.

Jill stopped one of the wait staff. "What's going on?"

"One of Chef Guillermo's knives are missing."

She raised an eyebrow. "Just one?"

"The knives are hand crafted, one-of-a-kind works of art made by an artist who died last fall. They are Chef Guillermo's prized possession."

Jill was about to say that she understood, when her voice was drowned out by a woman's scream. Dressed in a cook's white garb, the woman's color nearly matched her smock. She stood in the walk-in freezer's doorway, her eyes tearing but locked in a stare with something inside the room.

The pale woman's right hand clenched the handle, her left hand shaking and pointing as her scream mutated into a wail. No one moved forward to comfort her, Jill realized, and sought to do so herself. She reached out to the crying woman but stopped when she fully realized what she was looking at. Inside the freezer, the ground was a blotchy mess of red and steel.

Blood, frozen in a pool and splattered across the floor, led back to a pair of red open toed heels that Jill recognized immediately. She felt bile rush into her throat as she couldn't stop herself from looking at the victim's face. Jill's legs wobbled beneath her, her breathing reduced to sharp gasps.

"Oh God, Debi!" Jill gasped.

Debi White's blouse was soaked red, her chest stabbed open and wounds frozen in blood. Her face was splattered, eyes wide open and terrified. Jill's eyes filled with her own tears as she tried to control the impulse to wretch, tried to force herself not to think, not to let this crime into her soul. She knew this woman for only a few days, but she respected her and liked her. She hadn't wanted to suspect her of anything, fighting to explain away the incriminating signs. If she had moved faster, searched the ship herself, Jill might have been able to save her life. Jill recoiled violently as stress tremors rippled through her body, one after another.

One of the cooks attempted to move past her, but she stopped him. She grabbed his shirt into her fist and focused each bit of composure she had on telling him what to do. "Call the Captain. Tell him what happened and that we need Agent Riley here now!"

The wailing woman had calmed some, now watching Jill. Turning, Jill realized that they all stared at her, all unsure of what to do, all startled by her reaction. Jill let the man go and watched him scurry out of the room to find a phone.

"I need everyone..." her voice cracked, and she took a moment to breathe. She had a difficult time forming words, crafting her sentence. Her therapist had warned her this might happen. Victims of violence never quite handle violence the same way again, Dr. Letters had warned. Jill sank to her knees, no longer able to stand. "I need everyone to carefully walk out of this room into the hallway. Do not touch anything."

She swallowed hard, motioning with her hands for people to do as she requested. She asked the man who made the phone call to stand at the other entrance and stop people from entering the room. She remained there, in a useless heap, staring at Debi's slain body- wounded as if the hands that once hit her again and again had returned. Jill pressed her chin against her chest and felt sobs echo from her body against the kitchen's walls.

There was no need to find Debi now, to confront her about Jill's suspicions. She was dead, murdered, Jill corrected.

She's dead. Jill looked into the freezer and recognized her roommate, but she saw her mother's body in flames, her roommate's body in ice. "Mom!" Jill whispered into her arms as her cries overcame her. She cried hard, unaware of when the kitchen's swinging door opened, and Doug rushed in ahead of the agents. They stopped abruptly, and Doug motioned for them to step back.

"Jill?" He kept his voice low, undone by her

distress. He looked into the freezer and sighed, returning his attention to Jill.

"Jill Traynor," he used her full name deliberately.

She raised her eyes to his. "She's dead, Doug."

"I know. I need you to come with me. You need some air."

Jill shuddered as if waking slowly from a dream. She couldn't take it in, couldn't wrap her mind around it. She took several long, focused breaths and attempted to calm herself. Doug waved the Captain and Service agents back in. He helped Jill gain her feet, but held onto her until he knew she was steady.

"Doug... it's Debi. Someone stabbed her. She's dead, Doug. I could have stopped this. I could have helped..."

Doug squeezed her arms, forcing her to look at him. "You couldn't have stopped this. Don't even spend a minute thinking that. I need you to breathe, Jill. You're in shock. I want you to sit in the hallway and just rest for a few moments."

"Is Jill okay?"

Jill recognized Rob's voice, and her eyes brightened a bit.

Doug seized the opportunity. "Will you sit with Jill in the hall for a few minutes? She's in shock. She needs to calm down."

"Sure."

"I need to go over the scene, Jill. I'll be right here if you need me."

Rob led her into the hallway and opened his arms to her. She hugged him tightly, crying against his chest for minutes, abandoning all thought until her ribs ached. Her heart ached, but she slowly rose from the emotional stupor. Rob instructed her to take deep calming breaths until she had completely relaxed. He let her sit in silence for several minutes. Finally, she picked up her head.

"Are you feeling better?" He asked.

She nodded. "Debi's dead," she whispered.

"I know."

"I'm sorry for crying all over you," she mumbled.

Rob looked into her eyes, relieved to see life returning to them slowly. "You can return the favor someday."

She smiled in spite of herself. "They need me in there."

Rob shook his head. "I don't think that's a good idea."

"No. It's okay, Rob. I can handle this."

He arched an eyebrow. Judging by the past fifteen minutes, he seriously doubted that. "Take some more time. Wait for Doug to come out. I'm sure he can take the pictures. You don't need to see her like that."

Jill wiped her eyes with her shirt sleeves and took one more raggedy, calming breath. "I didn't know her that well, but I liked her."

"I liked her, too."

"I was beaten to death nearly, a few years ago. I thought I had gotten over it--but sometimes..."

"You don't have to explain yourself to me."

"I know." She stood up, her knees still a bit shaky, but holding. "Thank you, Rob. I'll be okay."

"Are you sure?"

"Yes." One more deep breath exhaled slowly, and she looked at him fully. Her color had returned a bit, her eyes seemed to sharpen and refocus.

"Okay."

Jill walked back in through the swinging door. Doug caught her eye, looked worried for a moment, but relaxed again. The Captain looked at her a bit longer, and Jill presumed, less confident in her ability by the moment.

"Can you tell me what happened, Jill?" Doug asked gently.

"The crew was searching for a missing knife. I came in looking for you or Debi. One of the kitchen staff told me the chef's knife was missing. I was about to join in the search when the woman who is still crying in the hallway opened the door to the freezer. I didn't know what she was looking at. I reached out to comfort her when I saw Debi. I asked people to step into the hall and not to touch anything. Then I collapsed. Sorry about that."

"Jill, you don't have to be in here for this."

She shook her head and took one more deep breath. "I'll be okay."

Everyone wore gloves, and after requesting a pair, one of the service agents provided them. Jill removed the camera from her bag.

The Captain clenched his hands tightly.

"Dammit," he whispered. "What the hell is going on here?" The question seemed rhetorical, so no one answered.

Doug squatted next to the body, scrutinizing everything. He didn't touch her yet; he merely looked at the knife still protruding from her chest and a cleaver discarded near her on the floor. There were multiple wounds surrounding the fatal one. The body was leaned against a cart where one of the ice chests sat. The case was open, revealing a cube with a hole chopped into the top of it.

"Jill, do you see this?" Doug asked, referencing the ice block.

She nodded, fighting through the fog of her mind. She brought her camera up to focus and snapped several pictures. The Captain spoke to the security team in low tones before leaving the scene. He told Doug he'd be back shortly.

"Where's he going?"

"To talk to Magellan, probably. He'll need to contact Walker."

"Will he cancel the rest of the cruise?" Jill asked.

Doug shook his head. "I don't know, but I doubt it. He'll have to at least give the guests the option of leaving. There will be political pressure to finish. Walker isn't going to want his kick-off headline to be about murder."

"Dammit, Doug! There's a killer on this ship... we have to do something..." Jill stammered.

"Easy, Jill." He moved his eyes toward their small audience. He obviously didn't want to discuss it here. Doug added in a low voice only Jill could hear,

"We knew there was a murderer on board before Debi was killed. The only difference now is that this is open, obvious. There's no attempt at a cover-up or an accident. And the victim is someone we know."

Jill exhaled slowly, feeling anxiety threaten to rise again. She forced herself to calm, allowing her professionalism to take over. Jill looked through the entire freezer slowly, taking pictures from every angle. She tried to avert her eyes from Debi for the first few minutes, but then had to look at her, believing it was disrespectful to not really see.

Doug looked back at the men. "Would you mind giving us the room?"

Without argument, the rest of the group retreated from the room. After the door was closed, Doug spoke more freely. "I got your message about twenty minutes before I came here. The truth is, Jill, I was coming to the same questions you were."

Jill turned, surprised. "You were starting to suspect Debi's involvement?"

"Of something, yes. I saw surveillance footage from the Lighthouse Room during the night the first victim made the reservation. Debi was his guest."

"Debi had dinner with Grafton?" Jill asked, stunned.

"That's right."

"That doesn't mean that she..."

"That she was guilty? No, it doesn't. What if they were working on something? Or knew something?"

"I doubt this is a case of coincidence. Wrong place, wrong time?" Jill speculated.

"Jill from your phone message, I take it you have other reasons to believe Debi was involved with Grafton's murder?"

Jill nodded her head and told Doug all she knew or surmised, when finished Doug said nothing about her comments and asked no questions. He just nodded his head.

After a few seconds of silence Doug added, "I was in a meeting with one of Walker's aides when we got the message about Debi. I was trying to pin down some of her campaign connections, how exactly the system worked since she is a ship employee and not a campaign worker."

"She's new to this cruise though."

"Yes, and the owners of Magellan are contributors. You didn't think the name of the ship and the campaign both being *New America* is a coincidence, do you?"

Jill knew that, so she said nothing. "Doug, what is that?" On the wheel of the cart holding the case of ice was a brown smudge.

Doug peered closer. "One sec. Let me get a kit from security."

Jill didn't wait for him. On a hunch, she lowered her nose to the wheel and inhaled. She reeled back, coughing. "It's horse shit."

"What?"

"Dammit, Doug! This cart was on Mackinac Island."

He shook his head in confusion. "I'm not following."

"When I was on the island, I overheard Debi and the ice carver arguing about an extra case. He requested five cases from the ship and they brought him six. Someone switched it out."

"So what? This is a custom made container crafted in Norway. No one would be able to just switch it out. And why would anyone? What is so damned special about destroying a block of ice?"

Jill peered at the block of ice, the hole carved into the top of it. She turned her head, the idea solidly drawn in her mind. The light bulb flickered on in Doug's eyes as well. "You think the killer smuggled something on board the boat?"

"Or Debi did, and someone caught her," Jill corrected. "But yes, someone got something on the boat. I'm sure of it."

"Debi would have had other means, other chances."

"They checked her bag just as closely as they looked at mine, Doug. And I think we are jumping to conclusions. I need to find the manifest and prove this. We need to question the carver."

"What the hell did they bring on board?" He muttered.

"We better talk to Secret Service and Walker."

"You're right, but let's get the manifest first. I want to go in there strong. After you finish the pictures, you can go. Take this passkey; it will get you into almost any room on board. It should work on Debi's office. I have to make some calls to get her body moved off the ship. I want a crime scene unit to fly out first thing."

Jill accepted the key, realizing for the first time that the ship was moving, which meant it was already after ten in the morning. Mackinaw was an overnight destination, allowing people to fully experience the island and surrounding areas. "Doug, we need to make them cancel tonight's event. We need to get the people off the boat."

He pondered that for a moment. "It's not my call, Jill. The Captain can make it. Walker can choose to cancel, but I can't force everyone off the ship without serious cause and approval from someone way up the chain from me. We need to solve this and fast. I'm not sure how we'd do that without being able to question the people."

"We would use the evidence. There must be fingerprints or something..."

"Tell me. Did you find some in the first victim's room? Do you think we'll find some here?"

"Doug, this was obviously not a premeditated crime. Someone caught Debi in here, or Debi caught someone and she was killed for it."

He shook his head, but smiled. "Jill, three dozen different things could have happened. She could have planned a covert meeting here and something went wrong. Maybe the killer needed time to elapse before her discovery. We have no idea why Debi was killed or by whom, and the critical mistake would be to make assumptions."

Jill nodded slowly, feeling stupid. She had been so excited, so emotionally scattered, that she didn't pause to think before she blurted out that last bit. Doug was right--it could be anything. She finished the pictures quietly, seeing now that Doug was taking the scene into his mind. When she finished, she returned the camera to the bag. "I'm on my way to Debi's office."

"Okay. Come find me when you have the manifest." He paused and looked into her eyes. This woman wasn't a cop. He needed to ease up, demand less, but her eyes were crisp now--the emotion that had taken her down just a little while ago was mostly tucked away from view.

"Of course," she said.

"And Jill!" He called just before she reached the door. "Photograph the room first. Wear gloves. Let's see what you find."

Jill found new gloves on one of the kitchen shelves and kept moving. Her stomach rolled a bit and Jill paused, bracing her legs against the ship's movement. She closed her eyes and inhaled slowly, now looking at images of Debi's body in her mind. She leaned against the wall and practiced a breathing routine she learned from her therapist. She focused on Debi, fearing that if she did not, she would be thrown into reliving all similar experiences. The truth, Jill considered, was that she didn't really know the woman she shared a room with. She seemed friendly and efficient, but Jill couldn't say much more. She allowed herself to see the scene from the freezer and not dwell there. When she finished her breathing routine, she felt more focused.

Chapter 33

Dave adjusted his hospital bed so he was in more of a sitting position. He tossed his cards down onto the table between them, exaggerating his frustration. "I fold. Karen, why don't you call and get this kid on an airplane?"

Quinn chuckled. "Nice try, Dave. You're not getting rid of me that easily."

"You're going to have all my money soon. It's complete bullshit that you've never played before. Or maybe beginners luck?" The older man rolled his eyes. "I keep getting killed on the flop."

"I used to have a regular game of five card stud, but I haven't played Texas Hold 'Em. I've watched it on TV a bit."

Dave groaned. "You've done your duty. I am going to be fine. I'll be home soon and there is just no point for you to be here anymore. Fly to Chicago. Meet Jill. Spend a few days with her before you go home. It's a great idea."

"She docks tomorrow, Dave. There's no way..."

"Karen, take my credit card. Get him a plane ticket."

Karen grinned. "I've already got your card in my pocket, Hon."

"That's scary," he winced and they all laughed.

Quinn scooped up his winnings and put the cards away. "Karen, you're a jewel. You are going to come to the wedding with Dave, aren't you?"

"Of course I am. I have to meet Jill, don't I?"

"She'll love you."

"I'll double your gift if you get the hell out of here," Dave offered. "Jill must be stressed. She was supposed to have a nice, peaceful week of working. Even if this guy who you told me about fell down the stairs, it probably made her think of all sorts of things. She never catches a break."

"Yes, she has," Karen countered, smiling at Quinn.

"Thanks, Karen." Quinn looked Dave over. "You're sure you feel good?"

"As good as a man can in my place, absolutely. With Karen here, I am fine for you to go home."

"I am going to talk to the nurse about that, but if she agrees with you, then yes. I'll go." Dave slapped the call button for assistance.

"I am perfectly capable of walking to the nurse's station," he muttered.

A few minutes passed before the nurse stepped in and confirmed what Dave insisted. With some protest first, Quinn finally agreed to leave. He booked a flight for tomorrow morning, nonstop to Chicago.

Chapter 34

For an office on a ship where space was limited, Debi's was rather large. She had a nice dark wood desk that faced the outer door with chairs sat across from it. Behind her desk and along the adjacent walls, bookshelves reached from floor to ceiling. They held binders with small white labels, books about each possible destination in the Great Lakes, and a variety of other texts that held little to no interest for Jill. There was a second workstation at a perpendicular angle to the main desk. It held a computer, printer and fax machine. Already in gloves, Jill approached the scene as if a crime had taken place there. She took pictures from every angle, focused on the trash can, the desk, the shelves.

She started on the left side of the desk, carefully opening one drawer after another. She found the usual office collection and stopped searching when she found the manifest. Flipping through it, she confirmed her theory about the ice chests. She left Debi's office, locking the door behind her, and returned to the galley.

The door was now covered with crime tape. Rob was positioned outside of it, guarding the scene.

"Hey, Jill." His tone was somber, his face drawn tightly.

"Hi. Is Doug in there?"

"No. He went back to the conference room."

"Okay."

"This sucks, doesn't it?" He spoke quietly. "Did you get to know her very well?"

"No," Jill admitted. "I shared a room with her, but our conversations were limited to work mostly. I have spent most of the week just with Erin."

A small smile nicked the corner of his mouth, but he said nothing. Jill waved goodbye and turned, walking away, back to the conference room.

Doug had just replaced the handset when she arrived. "What did you find?"

"Six cases of ice out, five empty cases and one filled with ice back in," Jill reported.

"So someone definitely could have smuggled something on board, past security. They would have no reason to check it again. They didn't have the X-ray machine at this remote location. No one would suspect a weapon frozen in a large block of ice in a custom made chest that just left the ship hours before."

"We should verify that six left and one came back full. We need to be certain that they only used five at the Grand Hotel," Jill suggested. She wasn't going to make the mistake of assuming something again.

"Good idea." Doug picked up the phone and dialed the connection to the ship's security office. He explained what he needed while Jill sat in a chair, listening. When he finished the conversation, he shot her a thumbs up signal. "Just as you thought, Jill. They didn't check the cases."

"So..." Her face paled. She stood up, pacing the room. "Doug, we're talking about a conspiracy. We're talking about serious players, aren't we?"

"Talk it out."

"Okay. The ice carver only requested five cases, but got six. For him to get six someone on the ship must have changed that request--meaning someone was in on it. Someone on the ground must have been in on it, too."

"Your theory is that they removed the block in the case and replaced it with another block, right?"

"That's right. One with something hidden in it. But what? A weapon?"

"Don't lose your focus. Keep going."

"Okay. So, at minimum someone in the kitchen, someone on the ground. Then there is the person who needed to receive it."

"Couldn't that be the person in the kitchen?"

"I guess they could, yes."

Jill's face wrinkled then she flopped back down in her chair. "That's all I've got."

"Did Debi have access to the ice?"

"Sure," Jill answered.

"It's possible that she could have switched the order."

"I'm not sure she could move the ice without being noticed. Everyone knows Debi. If it was her..."

"If it wasn't Debi who switched the ice order, what was she doing in the galley? And Jill, there's no way she wasn't involved."

"The insulin, the pager. I know. She had a role, but to do what? Are we convinced that it's connected to

Walker?"

"To be cautious, we have to assume that it is. The smuggled item almost has to be a weapon of some kind, a gun most likely. One other point needs to be raised. There is a chance the ice chest was not refilled, but replaced. This would make it a lot harder to pull off, actually."

"If that is true, there are some powerful people in this," Jill said.

Doug agreed. "Those cases would not be easy to replicate." He glanced at his watch. "I have to call my boss then meet with the Captain."

"What do I do now?"

"Go back to your suite. Look through Debi's things. Wear gloves and photograph everything. If you find anything, call me. Also get me Debi's cell phone." Jill nodded as she walked away.

Chapter 35

The Captain pointed to a seat across from his desk. The lead agent of the Secret Service team, Agent Potts, sat adjacent to Doug. A man from Walker's campaign sat in another chair off to the side. "Tell me what you know, Agent Riley."

"At this time, Sir, it isn't much. Someone has smuggled something on board through an ice chest." Doug took a few moments to explain exactly how that happened, and what they had learned about Debi White and Scott Grafton, the first victim. When he finished explaining the facts, he sat quietly for a moment.

The Captain glanced out his office window and scowled. "I am responsible for their deaths."

"Sir, I believe they were both involved. I just haven't figured out how or to what end," Doug stated. "You couldn't have done anything to stop it."

"It happened on my ship, Riley. It's my responsibility."

Potts cleared his throat. "We have tightened security already. The candidate barely blinks without one of us knowing about it, but I am worried about the gala tonight. It's a wide open space. Everyone who will be there looks like they belong there. We can have guests walk through a security station to get in. We'll move the metal detector upstairs. The truth is that we're already on our way back to Chicago."

"We should cancel the gala," Doug voiced.

Until this point, the campaign man had been silent. "Captain, can I have a few minutes in private?"

"Yes. Excuse us, gentleman."

Agent Riley and Agent Potts stepped into the hallway. "What was that about?" Doug asked.

"The campaign man is explaining reality to the Captain. They are not going to deport these passengers. There would be an ocean of political fall out and bad press. And they won't cancel the gala." Potts spoke in a harsh whisper.

Doug said nothing, but waited.

When they were brought back into the office, Potts' fears were confirmed. "The ship will sail to Chicago. Doing anything but finishing the cruise would be a disaster."

Doug didn't wait for him to go on, "Well then, let's lock Mr. Walker down in his suite. No one in or out and cancel the gala."

"We can lock Mr. Walker down for the time being, as you requested. We can increase security around him, but the gala has to go on. The whole cruise is based around this final event."

Doug remained silent, knowing the decision was not in his hands.

The Captain stood up. "Thanks for coming in. Keep me up to date on what you discover, Agent Riley. The decision to cancel the gala isn't mine. I suggest you take your concerns to the candidate."

"I will, Sir."

Chapter 36

Jill sat on the edge of her bed, overwhelmed by Debi's death. She knew she needed to finish searching through her roommate's things, but it was too real now. She had been able to calm and separate herself from what had happened earlier, but looking through her clothing and personal items brought on a wave of sickness and memories that Jill hadn't wanted to face. The phone rang, disrupting her thoughts for the moment.

"Hello?"

"Jill, it's Doug. I just got out of the meeting with Walker." He filled her in on the decisions made.

When finished, Jill was incensed. "Why didn't they listen to you?"

"I'm a mid-level agent out of Milwaukee. I told them everything we've learned, but they don't think it's enough to warrant canceling their plans. They made some security adjustments on their own before the meeting and they think that's enough, but that's it."

"Shit," she muttered.

"Have you found anything in the room?"

"No not yet. I'm not done searching, but I can't even find the hidden cell phone."

"That's odd."

"I thought so."

"Okay. Two agents are going to arrive any moment. They'll step in and take over some of this. I need to contact my boss and let him know what is going on. I need to brief the incoming agents and bring them up to speed. I'll call you when I'm done, okay? There's a good chance they'll want to talk to you also."

"Okay. I'll talk to you later, then." Jill waited for his goodbye and hung up the phone. She hadn't lifted her hand when it rang again. Shaking her head, she picked it back up. "Hello?"

"Jill Traynor?"

"Yes."

"This is Wayne Walker's personal secretary. Please hold for Mr. Walker."

Why was Walker calling her, Jill wondered. She took a breath and waited for the secretary to connect them.

"Ms. Traynor?"

"Hello, Mr. Walker."

"Could you spare a few minutes to come talk with me?"

"In person?" She asked then felt like an idiot.

"Yes, in my suite. Do you know where?"

"Yes, I do. Now?"

"If it's not too much trouble."

"I can be there in fifteen minutes, Sir."

"Thank you."

The call ended with a click. Jill set the phone down, reeling. Mechanically, she moved across the suite, ran a brush through her hair and switched out of her comfortable clothes into the button down blouse and slacks she was saving for later. The most likely next president of the United States had just requested a personal meeting with Jill Traynor, Drummond Island photographer. She didn't understand why, but her body carried her through the motions to Walker's suite of rooms.

Jill waited in the foyer near the secretary's desk, taking in the opulence. This, Jill knew, was merely one of the eight superior suites on board. The Walker entourage held all of them. Jill had been impressed with her own room, but the level of luxury within this one was stunning. Her survey of the room was stopped short when the secretary led her in. The next room was incredible, positioned in the aft of the ship with a tinted glass wall, allowing a full unobstructed view of the water. One of the wall sections was actually a door leading to a large L shaped deck outside.

In the living room, there were two sixty inch Sony HDTV's. Jill could see into a room with open French doors, noticing a billiard table and bar. In the middle of the living room floor was a modern art, free standing waterfall. Jill had no more than taken it all in when Walker joined her. He was accompanied by security guards who remained inside the room, but positioned on different walls.

Walker stepped forward and reached his hand out to shake hers. "It's a pleasure to meet you, Ms. Traynor."

"It's Jill, Sir. Thank you. It's nice to meet you, too."

Walker turned to his secretary. "I'm not to be interrupted, okay?"

"Of course, Sir. Your next appointment is via telephone with the RNC chairman," the woman reminded him before leaving the room. At Walker's gesture, the agents moved to guard the living room from positions outside of it.

"Please, Jill, have a seat. Can I get you a drink?"

Jill sat down, but hesitated about the beverage.

"I am going to have a scotch and soda. I would like it if you joined me. We have a full bar. I can make you a mixed drink, wine, beer."

"Do you have Corona?"

He smiled. "Yes, I do, actually. One moment. I'll be right back."

Jill watched him step into the adjacent room, allowing herself to revel in the surrealness of the experience. She watched him candidly as a human, rather than the subject for her camera this time. He moved with a sense of ease that most people didn't share, and she found herself admiring that. He handed Jill her drink and sat down on the chair across from her. "You and I have a lot in common."

Her eyes widened as she sipped her beer. She paused, surprised that she hadn't considered her pregnancy for the moment. She set the drink down. "I don't mean our political views. Hell, for all I know you might even be a Democrat. We don't come from the same part of the country either. I'm a Texan and you're a Michigander, but we do have a lot in common."

"Like what, Sir?"

"We were both raised by our grandparents, and later, grandmothers."

Jill was a bit bewildered that he knew all this, but she said nothing. Truthfully, she admitted to herself, she didn't know what to say.

"Did anyone tell you that you were requested by name?"

"As a second choice, yes. I wasn't told who requested me, or why."

"The who is easy: I did."

Jill blanched. She couldn't quite wrap her mind around that before he continued.

"And I asked you to come talk with me to tell you why. Do you know a Paula Kinney?"

"I had a great aunt by that name, yes." Jill replied.

Wayne nodded his head. "Your grandfather's sister."

"She died when I was a child."

"I know. The first time you and I met was at her funeral. I believe you were ten or so at the time."

"You were at her funeral?" She repeated, dumbly. "How did you know her?"

Candidate Wayne Walker took a long swallow that finished his beverage. He set the glass on the table next to his chair and leaned back, ready to tell Jill a story.

"It was 1949. My parents decided to go on a Great Lakes Cruise," Walker waved his hand in the air encompassing his surroundings. "It was much like this one, really. Your Aunt Paula was also on that same ship. It was called the Noronic, the Queen of the Inland Seas." He paused, but saw no recognition in her eyes, so he continued.

"The Noronic was an older ship, but one with a perfect record. She was still considered the grandest ship on the lakes. We sailed from Detroit and landed in Cleveland, taking on more passengers. From there we went to Toronto. We landed at the Canadian steamship lines birth at Pier 9. My parents and I toured the city by day and then returned to the ship. We had dinner and then they went out to a night club." Walker shrugged his shoulders. "They tipped one of the stewards to look in on me." He smiled at Jill, "I can't imagine someone doing that today, but back then it was fairly common."

Jill watched him, trying to second guess the reason he was telling her this story. Her face was patient and encouraging, but she couldn't help but wonder what this was about. She had studied the photographs, knew the lines and creases of his face well--but he never looked authentically human to her before. He looked like someone she would watch on television or someone in a textbook, but not a flesh and bone man sitting before her, obviously unsettled by something.

"In no time, the ship was all but abandoned. Most of the crew was on land having a good time. There were several of us kids left on board to have fun ourselves. We never paid attention to the time. Hours slipped by. When I became tired, I decided to call it a night." He paused and sat in silence for more than a few seconds. Finally, he smiled at Jill and went on. "It was around 2:30 am. I was just heading toward our state rooms when a steward came running around the corner and knocked me down.

"He was highly agitated. He told me..." The candidate paused, collected himself. "He told me that the ship was on fire. He told me to head toward the pier, and I did. I didn't second-guess him. He was always nice to me. This was the man my parents trusted--so I went. I made my way to the open deck, but I was cut off from the pier side and the gangplank. The deck was chaos.

He took a breath, continued. "People ran in every direction, yelling and screaming out names of loved ones. I could hear fire truck sirens whirring around me. The world had gone mad. It was utter pandemonium. I was just over ten years old, and I had no idea what to do. The mob on deck was moving toward the bow, and I was swept along with them. Some people tried to climb down the ropes that tied the ship to the pier. Others jumped onto fire trucks' ladders. Some screamed as they jumped overboard."

Jill could see it as he retold it. The varnished wood everywhere, the faint scent of lemon oil in the air, the late forties clothing styles wrapped around the bodies of people vacationing across the Great Lakes. She could feel her heart racing as if she were ten years old, as if her parents were partying ashore, and all she had to do was find them to save her life.

"I was terrified. I sat down right there where I stood near the side of the ship and cried. A man in uniform knelt down by me. He asked me if I could swim." Walker paused. "I don't remember saying anything, but the next thing I knew I was flying."

She could feel it, the energy of being thrown through the air into the unknown, nothing but blue-black water filled with screaming humans beneath her.

Jill shuddered.

"The man picked me up and tossed me over the side. He told me to take a deep breath, to plug my nose and kick for the surface. Swim away from the ship, he said. I sank into the water, down and down. I thought it was over. I knew I was going to die." He met Jill's eyes and held them.

She knew what it was like to die. To be beaten by some kind of force, to have everything loved lost in one moment. Jill squeezed her arms tightly over her abdomen and watched the man's face carefully. Somehow, this man survived. She felt the water, thick and airless, surrounding her as if she had been there-- and waited for the moment when he would reach safety.

"Someone pulled me to the surface. I remember strong arms surrounding me, holding me tightly. This beautiful woman saved me and many others that night. She and another man in a small boat pulled people from the cold water and rowed to the pier, unloaded, and went back. I watched from the pier for several hours. There was so much confusion no one paid me much mind. She wore a white dress. I know it sounds silly, but she looked like an angel."

Angels. Was her mother an angel? Jill went back in her mind and imagined the truth of her parents' death rather than what her mind had created as a memory. She felt the warm, strong arms of a body, a life given to save her own. And she knew what this man had felt, because she herself had been saved. More than not, she wondered why.

"The woman who saved me was Paula Kinney, Jill. Your aunt."

Jill swallowed air in ravished gulps, stories her uncle told her floating to the surface of her mind. Her mother's arms still wrapped around her, her aunt's arms wrapped around him. She didn't know what to say. There was nothing appropriate, nothing worthy.

Jill stood up and faced the window. She remembered Aunt Paula's audacious sense of humor and courage. From all the stories Uncle Dave had told her, why hadn't he shared Aunt Paula's tale? Maybe he didn't know, Jill realized.

The phone next to Walker beeped. He pressed a button and told his secretary to hold the call. Jill covered her mouth with her hand, but turned to face him. She was shocked to feel tears drip down her cheeks and onto her arms. "I'm sorry. I am just surprised. I have never heard that story."

"Both of my parents were killed in the fire, Walker shook his head slowly, they had returned while I was playing, I didn't know, he added in a low voice almost inaudible."

"Both of my parents were killed in a fire, too," she whispered. But she didn't remember, couldn't know. She looked into Walker's eyes and knew that he had stood on that pier and watched the ship be engulfed in flames, smelled the air filled with dying souls and wood varnish choking the sky.

She remembered documentaries of burn victims watched over the years. She felt the scar on her arm more keenly than she ever had before. Her parents had been burned alive. His too. For the second time that day, Jill felt her legs give out on her, and she sat hard onto the couch and buried her head in her hands. Walker reached out and touched her face gently. He moved next to her on the couch and offered her a shoulder to lean on. "I am sorry. I am so, so sorry," she said. She looked down at the uneven scar on her arm. He slid his sleeve up toward his elbow and showed her scars on his arm.

He didn't say anything for a moment, but when he did, he spoke quietly. "My aunt picked me up and took me home to my grandparents in Texas. My mom was from Michigan. I was born in Detroit and lived there until my parents were killed. In Texas, there is a saying that you are not a true Texan unless you have made and lost a fortune several times." He smiled softly at this. "You see my great, great grandfather started in cattle and then oil and from there he moved to land speculation. Today his legacy has been diverted into technology. The problem with this saying is that my family never lost it."

She wondered about the connection, where he was going with all of this. "Well, that's fortunate." She wiped the tears from her eyes and tried to calm her beating heart.

"I am running for the presidency of the United States, Jill."

"I know."

"I want to give this country back to its citizens. I want to make it safe to walk our streets. To give it back to English speaking people and for the rest of the world not to fear us." He realized he was making a speech and stopped. "You see, I believe I was saved for a reason. I believe in things working together for the greater good. I was saved so I could help this world, our country, Jill."

She said nothing, overwhelmed by the emotional tide within her.

"I know stories of your heritage, Jill."

"The Kinney women?"

"And earlier, yes."

"Paula Kinney saved my life for a reason, Jill. And from all that I have read, I believe your mother died to save yours."

She could no longer control the tears as they poured unchecked from her eyes. This was too much. All of it was simply too much. She wanted to leave this room, curl up under the covers at home, and wait until it passed. She didn't have the strength. Instead, she asked, "Sir, why are you telling me this?"

He paused, considering his words. "I have enemies. There are many here and around the world who do not want a man of my vision to set foot in the oval office. I know about Debi White and Scott Grafton, who have both died this week. I know that you are working with the FBI agent on board."

"Okay," she said, still hearing no answers.

He took a breath, and for the first time she saw the stress visible in the lines around his eyes. He is nervous, she thought.

"I feel at ease knowing that you are on board."

Jill's mouth fell open and she shook her head. This time she found strength to warn him. If she had been quicker, she might have saved Debi, but she hadn't. The truth was that Jill was cursed, she knew. It was wrong to let him believe she was somehow a good luck charm. She said, "Sir, we have discovered that something has been smuggled onto the ship. We don't know what it is. You could be in danger."

"My life was saved by your aunt, your heritage, Jill. I believe I was saved for a reason, and that you were also saved for a reason."

"I am just a photographer. I can't save you," Jill stammered a bit.

He was about to speak, but she cut him off. "No, you must listen to me. People die around me. All the time. Most of my life has been spent between funerals. I am not keeping you alive. In fact, I am the worse kind of energy you can have on board with you. Please..." her voice broke into a sob, and Jill felt her heart twisted and wrenched from her body for this man--scared to death of losing his own life, already having survived too much.

"I didn't mean it that way, but don't worry. I am going to be the next president, Jill. I don't believe you are cursed. I asked you here because I want you to come to work for me."

Her mind went still. She closed her eyes slowly and reopened them. Did he not hear anything that she had said? She needed to leave, not continue working for him on the ship. "What?"

"I know you have photography work, and that you own a business--but I want you to consider coming to work for me."

"In Washington?"

"Yes."

"Why?"

He hesitated. "When I saw the opportunity to bring you on board, I took it, because I believe in fate. You are an extraordinary woman, Jill. I don't know why things have worked out the way they have, but I want you to consider my offer. Will you give it some thought?"

At this, the phone beeped from the coffee table. Walker glanced at his wristwatch. He had been keeping the Chairman of the Republican National party waiting for nearly twenty minutes. "I have to take this call, Jill. I'm sorry that we've run out of time. Give it some thought. I'll be in touch. Probably not for a few weeks."

Floored, Jill stood up slowly.

"No matter what happens, I want you to know that I think about your Aunt Paula everyday. I am thankful for her everyday."

"Thank you, Mr. Walker." Jill shook his hand. "I'll show myself out."

"Very well." He picked up the phone.

Jill left the room, damned near speechless, legs shaking.

Chapter 37

Slowly, Jill walked back toward mid-ship. She returned to her room first, running the conversation back through her mind. She hadn't even thought to ask what kind of a job Walker wanted her to do. Did people ever say no to a president? She pushed those thoughts aside and absently dragged her suitcase out from the closet. Sometimes a mindless task was a good ingredient to sort out her thoughts. Jill turned the music system on low and folded clothing she knew she wouldn't be needing before tomorrow. She wondered if she would be able to go home or fly to Florida when the ship landed. Would Doug ask her to stay? If she thought about that now, she realized, she might just panic so she pushed that aside as well. It was important to start over, to replay steps.

Jill was convinced that Debi's insulin and needles package could have provided the poison and the tool to kill Scott Grafton, whether or not she merely carried the items on board for someone else, or injected the poison into the toothpaste herself was another matter. She was without doubt involved, which brought Jill back to the first victim. If the man was on board to harm someone, and Debi discovered it, why didn't she just report him to authorities? Bringing the poison on board in the first place was premeditated. She must have known the first victim. At this point, there was no way to know why Grafton was on board at all. Whatever his reason, Debi must have objected to it.

Jill finished cleaning out most of the items in one drawer, so she moved to the next. She grabbed the two pairs of extra socks from the drawer, setting one out for the next day. Jill shook her head, muttering. This morning, she had specifically recalled seeing her lucky clover socks in the drawer. Jill crouched down, examining the drawer. When unsatisfied, she pulled the drawer off of of its track and set it on the bed. There was a gap between the wall and where the drawer system stopped. Pulling out the bottom drawer, she found two pairs of socks at the bottom. One was her lucky pair, while the second must have been Debi's. She pulled them both out, muttering a thank you toward the ceiling when she found the cell phone.

Jill flipped it open, scrolling through text messages. They were largely not understandable, one or two words that didn't relate to anything that Jill recognized. She noted the message about the fingerprints that she discovered earlier in the week. The next one she could read said: Check fax 2200. Shred.

Debi received a fax.

Jill abandoned her packing project and headed upstairs. She approached the woman behind the desk with a cautious smile.

"May I help you?"

"My name is Jill Traynor. I am the photographer for this week's events and am also aiding Agent Doug Riley with the on board investigation."

"Yes, Miss. How can I help you?"

"Can you tell me where fax machine 2-2-0-0 is located?"

The woman looked strangely at Jill through her

glasses. "Our fax machines are not numbered. They do have a serial system but it is much longer than four numbers."

"Oh." Jill's face fell. "I received a message to check fax machine 2200, and I just assumed..."

The woman smiled. "2200 is military time for 10 pm. You must have had a fax come in last night. I can check and see if it's here for you."

Jill inclined her head. "Please," she replied, knowing it wasn't there.

When the woman returned and apologized for not having it, Jill returned to Debi's office feeling a bit stupid. She used the passkey Doug gave her to get in. She checked the tray and Debi's shredder to see if there was anything waiting to be destroyed. Of course, there wasn't. The remnants had even been emptied. Jill sat down in the office chair, considering her fax machine at home--the reel of carbon paper inside it that held duplicates of each page transmitted.

Jill unplugged the machine from the wall and opened it up. She found the reel, slowly unraveled the pages. The first several were directly related to political events and the week's agenda. When she saw her name on one, she stopped. The pages following included a brief bio and a memorandum that cleared Jill of suspicion.

"Suspicion?!" Jill said out loud, shocked. She continued reading, unrolling the film to the next page, which was again about the ship. She cruised through several more before being startled by the logo on the top of the page. This one was clearly marked from the FBI, addressed to Agent White. It included details about the first victim, his CIA and NATO affiliation, and how Debi could find him. She was directed to incapacitate him, to have him removed from the ship without arousing questions. Triggered by something Jill had seen in the cell phone, she flipped it open, comparing the page for keywords.

One of the text messages said: sol n fatl. err.

Sol... solvent, solution? Fatl... for fatal? The text message was dated the same day, but after the victim had been discovered. Was it possible that Debi had been instructed to simply get him off the ship? Could his death have been an accident? Jill didn't know what happened, but she knew the FBI wasn't in the practice of taking people out. It was against the law, so unless Debi was... something else, she hadn't been told to kill the man.

Jill kept going through the film reel and found a biographical sheet on Scott Grafton. The picture was nearly impossible to decipher, but the page's intention seemed to be to help Debi locate the man. He was regarded as a critical threat.

Finally, the time stamp in the upper right corner matched the text message's referral. The page was a dossier on a secondary threat to the candidate. The assassin was female, early thirties. The picture included was taken ten years earlier, and because Jill looked at the carbon, totally unclear. Believed to be on the ship in a contributor capacity, believed to have South Korean ties, Jill read.

She sat back and took a breath. The page clearly identified this woman as an assassin, which confirmed that Walker was still in grave danger. Standing on shaky knees, Jill rolled the carbon paper back up, tucked it into a bag, and locked the door behind her. She hurried to the conference room to find Doug.

A man in a black suit jacket sat at the conference table met Jill's eyes when she walked in without knocking.

"Oh, I..."

"Yes?"

"Is Doug here?"

"Agent Riley is in a meeting. Can I help you?"

"I am Jill Traynor. I need to speak with him."

"He is currently with Secret Service, among others. Can I help you?" The agent repeated his question.

"No, thanks," Jill left the conference room. She didn't want to bring this to anyone but Doug; didn't feel right about explaining her discoveries to another agent. Instead, Jill approached the agent guarding the door of the Secret Service's makeshift office.

"I need to speak with Agent Riley immediately," Jill told him.

"I'm sorry, Miss. He isn't available."

"Please, try. I need to talk to him. I discovered something that he needs to see."

The agent frowned but spoke into his microphone. "The photographer is here to talk to... Okay. I'll let her know." He turned to Jill. "No interruptions. You'll have to wait."

"Dammit, listen to me. I know about a threat to the candidate. I have evidence. I am a civilian consultant to the FBI, and I need to speak with Doug. This isn't a question about how many pictures to take or what to do next. It's important. Are you listening to me?" Jill's voice rose with each word.

The door popped open and Doug peeked his head out. He took one look at Jill's face and stepped out. "What's wrong?"

Jill explained her findings to him in clear, quick terms.

Doug invited her into the office, asking her to explain it again with the secret service present. When they were finished, they contacted the candidate's secretary and requested a meeting. Since Walker was inside his suite showering and preparing for the gala, he could not be disturbed at the moment. As soon as he was finished, she promised to get them in.

Chapter 38

One hour later, Doug and Jill stared at each other. Jill was dumbfounded. The candidate refused to cancel the gala. Even after everything they had found, he absolutely would not change his plans. They increased security measures and began the search for the second assassin as well as her means to kill Walker. Each member of the security force was nervous about the night ahead.

Back in the conference room, Doug didn't have answers any more fulfilling than those Jill had already speculated. He let her leave, needing time to confer with the agents and call his home office. If Debi was truly working for the FBI, he should have been made aware--and now they had to flush that out.

Jill wandered back to the suite, surprised to find Erin sitting in the hallway, her legs drawn up to her chest and her face red from crying.

"Oh, Erin..." In the chaos since discovering Debi's body, Jill hadn't given a thought to her assistant.

"It's true? She's dead?"

Jill kneeled beside her friend and hugged her. "I am so sorry."

After a moment, Erin pulled back, making an effort to control her tears. "I have been in mud and massage all day in the Enrichment Center. My masseuse didn't know. When I came out, someone had just come in talking about a murder in the kitchen. Then minutes later I ran into a co-worker in the hall and found out it was Debi. God, Jill. You have to tell me what happened."

"Why don't we go in the room? I'll tell you everything I can."

Erin sniffled. "Okay."

Jill pulled her along into the room behind her. She grabbed a few bottles from the mini bar and made Erin a drink. She sat beside the teary eyed woman and explained some of the details to Erin, eliminating specifics. As Jill considered it, there wasn't much she could tell her besides the fact that Debi had been murdered, and that Jill believed it was connected to the first victim's death.

"I don't get it. Why Debi?"

Jill didn't know what to say to that, so she smiled gently. "I don't know." Jill glanced at the clock. "Listen, if you don't want to work with me tonight, I totally understand."

"Work?"

"At the gala. I have to photograph the gala." And try to spot an assassin, she thought, but didn't say. "Maybe it would be better if you just tried to relax. I know you liked Debi."

"They're still having the gala?" Erin looked incredulous. "Why aren't they cancelling the event? It doesn't make any sense."

"This is Walker's big official speech. He's not going to cancel."

"Well that's just... ergh!" Erin exclaimed. "How

can he expect us all to carry on as usual? She was a friend and coworker."

"I don't know too much about politics," Jill offered. "But I'm totally willing to work the night by myself. I have to work. It's in my contract."

Erin was silent for a moment. "I'll help. It's my job, too."

"Are you sure?"

"Yes, it's better than thinking about it. We need to get started, don't we?"

Jill smiled sadly. "I want to freshen up a little then go down. Typically, we'd be there already but under the circumstances..."

"Meet in thirty?"

"Sounds good."

Chapter 39

If tension could be physically manifested into an object, Jill thought it might just be personified by the ice carved elephant. By now, the whole ship was aware that Debi White had been murdered and that it had something to do with ice. Guests actually sneered at the giant elephant in passing. The elephant stood six foot tall with its right front foot on a map of the United States. The map itself was over a foot thick. Around the edge, carved into the ice, were the words *New America*. Under other circumstances, Jill knew she would have found a few hundred people mocking an impressive ice sculpture amusing. Today, she couldn't generate any extra emotion.

Jill tried to focus on photography, but she found herself scrutinizing the guests' faces, looking for small characteristics that matched up with the fax. She had spent hours staring at their faces, cropping and enlarging photographs, framing these people in her viewfinder... and she didn't recognize the woman. Someone from the FBI had used a program to recreate the picture. It still wasn't photograph quality but it was definitely good enough to draw a match from, and still nothing.

For all the tension around him, Candidate Walker approached the podium with confidence and ease. He didn't seem nervous at all--and ten minutes into his speech, Jill realized that as a result, the people relaxed.

"Isn't this the damnedest thing?" Erin whispered.

"What?"

"Everyone has calmed down. Five minutes ago, a waiter dropped a plate and that woman in the purple jumped literally out of her chair. Now, look at her."

Jill looked in the direction Erin gestured. The woman in question was leaned back with a drink, smiling. "Maybe he should be the next president."

"He is a great speaker, even if the message is a little too right wing for me." Erin said and checked over her clipboard, guiding Jill into another area of the room.

Doug Riley stood against a wall, practicing the same visual sweep that Jill had been doing.

"Any sign of anything?" Jill asked.

"No," Doug shook his head. "Walker wraps up in twenty. If I wanted to make a splash, I'd do it now in front of all these people."

"Maybe security is too tight."

Doug scoffed. "The woman behind this, if the intel is right, is way too skilled to have her plan ruined. We confirmed it, by the way."

"What's that?"

"Debi was FBI. She was instructed to take Grafton off the ship, but not kill him. The FBI claim that the toxin screen of what the guy was poisoned with doesn't match what they gave her." He paused. "I don't know if you are aware of this--but the FBI can't kill people. Other agencies have different missions and charters. Do you understand?"

"But the FBI says they gave her something other than what the man was killed with, right?"

"They claim someone tampered with the toxin, or that it simply could have been an accident. Maybe someone got to him first and she had nothing to do with killing him. Personally, I rule out the accident. Accidents like this just don't happen in the FBI." His tone made Jill study him a moment longer.

"Not an accident?"

"I have never believed in accidents. Either Debi had her own agenda, someone messed with it, or there's more going on here than even I understand."

"It makes me feel better to think that Debi might not have killed him intentionally," Jill admitted, "Even though it may not be the case." She spotted Erin's motion and excused herself from Doug. "By this point, we may never know what happened to Grafton."

Erin had a number of shots lined up. By the time they finished, Walker announced his official run for the presidency. The cameras closed down and the party began. Jill followed Erin through the now relaxed individuals, taking a number of shots. She stayed longer than she usually did, long enough to see the buffet consumed and dismantled, the band stop playing, and the majority of individuals retreat back to their rooms.

Nothing happened.

Chapter 40

Saturday Morning

Jill stared up at the ceiling after a long near sleepless night. The FBI had combed through her suite mercilessly during the gala. She expected that they had now been through every inch of Debi's territory, looking for signs of an ulterior agenda.

The invasion, while appropriate, made Jill feel a bit violated since they also looked through all of her things. She noticed the sun finally peeking its head up over the horizon, which was as good of a time as any to stop the pretense of sleep. Rolling out of bed, Jill showered and finished packing. She moved from there to her office where she finalized the master disks of the trip and wrote a general report explaining each file. She then made a set of disks of the non-campaign, non-crime photos that she wanted, and a third set of everything for Doug. She labeled each one and wrote another detailed explanation of how they were organized. When finished, she moved her small set aside and put the others in envelopes.

It didn't take her long to clean out her office and walk to the conference room. Doug was there alone, hair mussed and suit seriously wrinkled.

"You haven't slept," Jill accused.

"No. I haven't. I don't understand what happened."

"Nothing happened." Jill sighed and sat down in a chair across from Doug. "I don't get it either."

"Are people disembarking?"

"Not yet. We've been docked for hours, but we're setting up a net around the pier. I'd like your help, front and center. If anyone can spot this woman, you can."

"Okay."

"The problem is that Walker's campaign manager and his security think this whole thing was a scare tactic. The Secret Service presence is very small. Typically, they wouldn't be protecting a candidate this early. Technically, the security is still leading this effort, which is almost more of a disservice. The idea is just bullshit, excuse my language." Doug said by way of apology. "Debi is dead, and I don't think she was killed to scare Wayne Walker. On the other hand, with a murder on the ship, the killer had to figure that security would have to be extremely tight. There is a bizarre sense of ease. Everyone told Walker it would happen at the gala event. Now that it's over, I think the team has relaxed."

Doug shrugged his shoulders. "I am as much to blame as anyone. I insisted canceling the gala was the best thing to do. Walker seems to think he's invincible."

Jill laughed at that. "I am under the same impression. Did I tell you that he offered me a job?"

"What?" Doug asked, surprised.

"It's a long story, and I'm not even sure what job it would be but... it's flattering to think a presidential candidate wants me to work for him."

"Wow. Jill Traynor goes to Washington."

Jill smiled and twisted her wedding ring showing it to Doug, "I'm soon to be Jill McCord, and I'm not leaving Drummond."

"Not even for the next president?"

"I am getting married. No way," Jill said, thinking of her baby.

Doug didn't press her for details. "Are those the pictures?"

"Yes. These are for you. This other package is for the cruise. I am not totally sure who to give them to."

"Actually, Jill, I would like those as well."

"I made you copies of everything. I figured you never know what's in the background, or who is shaking hands that might be of some relevance to the case."

"Perfect."

"I am going to go drop these off..."

"No, hold up for a second. Why don't you come with me to the candidate's suite? If Walker likes you, he may trust your opinion on this. I don't think the threat is over."

"And you want me to support you?"

"Yes. Are you willing?"

"I'm not sure I can help, but I will try." Jill swallowed, trying to calm her nerves. She still felt uneasy about her talk with Walker.

"Leave the pictures here. We'll come back for them."

Jill followed Doug, waiting while he locked the

room down. It only took five minutes or so to make the journey to the aft section of the ship. Doug and Jill approached the secretary, Jill quietly standing at his side.

"Hello, I am FBI Agent Doug Riley. This is Jill Traynor. We would like a few minutes with the candidate."

The secretary shook her head. "Mr. Walker gave me specific instructions that he is not to be disturbed."

A housekeeper approached the door and smiled to the secretary. Jill recognized her. "Hello, Maria. How are you?"

She nodded to Jill and smiled, turned to the secretary. "I have the towels. Would you like me to leave them with you?"

The secretary glanced up at Doug, and waved her in. "No, take them in. I'm sorry you have to go through these checks, dear." She smiled at the housekeeper, who smiled back.

Jill watched the guard at the door looked through her towels and let her pass, while she wondered what role she was really going to have in this conversation.

"Please check, ma'am. If Walker doesn't want to hear about the threat assessment, then I'll come back when he can listen."

She picked up the phone and pressed a button. After a few minutes of conversation, she set the phone back down. "He'll meet with you in forty-five minutes, right before his party leaves the ship."

"Okay. Thanks." Doug relaxed his stance. Walker would be safe in the suite until the meeting. He was distracted for a moment as the housekeeper called goodbye over her shoulder, as she left the room. "Thanks," he repeated. He turned to Jill. "Why don't you drop off the photographs and meet me at the disembarkation gate?"

"Sure."

"I do not want to miss this woman. We need to look at everyone.

Doug checked his watch, "They will allow people to begin leaving in eight minutes. The luggage is all on the docks now."

*   *   *

The pier was sprinkled with a few of Chicago's finest in uniform, as well as the three federal agents on board and Jill. Doug explained that there had been debate about bringing in more people, but the final consensus was that more people would create more confusion and opportunity to miss the woman.

Jill was given a prime location, positioned eight feet off the gate with a new copy of the picture that was divided into four images of what the woman might look like now. She watched the first guests trickle off the ship, quickly realizing this uneventful task was going to take some time. In her mind, she was hoping that the would-be assassin would make a mad dash from the ship and immediately be surrounded by officers. She smiled to herself, found a more comfortable standing position, and kept watch.

*   *   *

An hour passed with painstaking pace. Combined with the fact that Jill barely slept the night before, she was ready to commit herself as a member of the walking dead from sheer boredom. Yawning sounded attractive but took too much energy, so she simply stood and watched. Bizarrely, the crowd hadn't acted at all like she thought it might. Instead of moving away from the ship with intention, guests lingered, sampling from the trays of finger foods that servers made rounds with. They chatted about the week's events, business arrangements, and whatnot. It almost seemed as if they dawdled intentionally, wanting to see if anything was going to happen or not. Jill couldn't help but feel annoyed. They were making the spotting process more difficult for everyone.

Doug approached her grimly. "I've been called back inside. There's been a shooting, but I don't know the details."

His words alarmed her. She had been expecting something, but... a shooting? She wanted to ask if it was Walker, but he didn't know. Instead she asked, "Do you want me to come with you?"

"No. Stay here. You need to spot this woman if she tries to exit the ship. Take my handset and keep watch. I'll be back out soon."

One of the other feds followed Doug back up the ramp and into the ship. Jill held the handset and waited.

Chapter 41

Quinn McCord paid the taxi driver and hauled his large green duffel over his shoulder. The cab was able to drop him off about eighty feet from the gate. He walked in, noticing a crowd of elegantly dressed individuals on the dock, but he spotted Jill's long dark hair rather quickly.

"Jill!"

At the sound of her name being called, Jill turned. "Ohmygod," she whispered. "Quinn!" She yelled back and waved. Her eyes welled with tears as she motioned him over, wondering what he was doing here. She turned back around, still rattled when her eyes landed on someone who looked vaguely familiar.

A woman in a crimson sweater and jeans walked down the ramp. Her hair was light in color, worn down under a baseball cap. She looked out of place, vaguely like she didn't belong. Jill studied her for a moment longer. Quinn yelled again and the woman's eyes picked up, landed on Jill's and held for a moment too long.

Recognition dawned through Jill's foggy awareness slowly. She was the housekeeper. Maria Sanchez had access to Scott Grafton's room and was just in the candidate's suite. She remembered running into her on the cliff at Pictured Rocks also, but then she had darker hair, glasses. She glanced at the pictures in her hand--Maria didn't look much like the pictures, but Jill couldn't ignore her instinct. Maria wouldn't have changed her hair to have a day off. There were too many coincidences. Jill brought the handset to her face, speaking quietly as she hurried her words. "I see a possible suspect. She's wearing a red sweater and jeans. She's five-six, light brown hair, baseball cap. She is a housekeeper on board. She's moving down the ramp." Jill moved toward her, staring intensely.

The woman looked into Jill's eyes, realizing she had been spotted. She spooked and sprinted down the ramp drawing a gun from the small of her back. A passenger spotted the gun and screamed. The housekeeper rushed past, pointing the gun at Jill but was bumped by a person trying to get down.

"I see her!" One of the agents called into the set.

"I don't have a shot," she heard.

Watching chaos unfold quickly, Quinn dropped his bag and ran the rest of the way toward the dock.

"Get down!" Jill yelled.

The woman directed her gun toward the agent and squeezed the trigger before diving behind luggage.

"Agent down!"

The woman fired at an officer who dropped, still trying to fire a shot off. The assassin leaned out from behind a small trunk and aimed at Jill.

Quinn dove into Jill, knocking her out of the gun's path, while at the same time twisting her on top of him to cushion her fall.

The housekeeper-assassin fired again, but this time an officer behind her was ready and pumped one bullet into her shoulder and another caught her center chest. The woman went down hard, lifeless.

Jill took a deep breath and rested her head on Quinn's chest, making no effort to move.

"Jill? Are you okay?"

"Mmhmm," she said, listening to the heavy beat of his heart. "Nice to see you," she whispered.

"Someone just shot at you!"

Laying there for a moment, Jill knew that Quinn's tension would balloon radically if she didn't calm him. "I know. Her name is Maria. Well, I don't know if that's her real name or not. She's a housekeeper on board. I didn't give her a big enough tip, I guess."

Quinn's panic eased with Jill's humor. He took a moment, and then thought to ask, "Is anyone else going to be shooting at you?"

"No, Babe. I didn't stiff everybody."

They laid there, laughing for a moment as the excited guests ran in all directions. When they realized they were safe, the dock took on an eerie quiet. She picked her head up and looked at him. "What are you doing here?"

"I missed you."

"Jill?!" At the sound of her name, Jill stood up, pulling Quinn up with her. Doug rushed over to her.

"Are you okay?"

"Yes. Quinn saved me. Doug, this is my fiancé, Quinn McCord. Quinn, this is Agent Doug Riley with the FBI."

The men shook hands.

Doug looked hard at Jill, not sure how to tell her. Finally, he said, "Jill, he's dead."

"The agent?"

"Walker."

"What?!"

"The woman walked into the room with towels. We were standing right there when she killed him."

"He's dead?"

"Yes, he's dead. She walked into the suite..." Doug ran his hand through his hair, utterly rattled. "She left Mrs. Walker napping on the bed, who never heard the shot because of a silencer."

"Mrs. Walker is alive?"

"Yes."

Jill's head drooped. "After all that, I couldn't save him."

"You aren't to blame, Jill," Doug offered gently. "The FBI was convinced the assassin was on board as a guest. We took our direction from them."

Jill nodded slowly.

"I have to go."

"You don't need me to photograph..."

"No. They'll bring in a team from Chicago. They will need to question you, possibly several times."

"Okay."

They said their goodbyes. Quinn held her hand gently, not saying anything until Jill was ready. She stood still, blankly staring at the ship for several minutes. "He thought I could save him," she whispered.

"The candidate did?"

Jill nodded and turned into Quinn, wrapping her arms tightly around him. Quinn enfolded her in his arms, dropping his head to rest on top of hers. After a few moments, she looked up. The tears were gone from her face and she looked calm, Quinn realized. She arched a brow at him. "What are you really doing here?"

"I thought I might be able to steal you away for a few days of vacation," he mumbled.

"Take me home. As soon as we're done here, take me home, okay?"

"You don't want to go on a road trip, or lounge in a spa for a few days? We can do anything you want."

"If you take me home, I'll marry you. Any day you want. Tomorrow, next week, next year, whenever you want."

His eyes widened.

"Well, maybe somewhere this side of seven months would be good."

"What?"

"I wouldn't want our baby to come before the wedding."

Quinn's eyes filled with tears. "Are you telling me you're pregnant?"

She grinned, the smile radiating in her large green eyes. "We're going to have a baby!"

Quinn picked her up into his arms, swinging her around while they laughed and cried together. He didn't set her down until he found a seat on a bench, and then he allowed her to merely relax on his lap. "Wow!" He breathed. "We're going to have a baby. A little Jill running around and bugging her Uncle Chase and..."

"Or perhaps a little Quinn..."

He scoffed at that. "It's going to be a girl. Some things, I just know."

"Thank you for coming to get me, Quinn. You saved my life."

"No, I didn't. Her aim seemed a bit off. I think I saved the woman behind us. She tripped and lost balance when I accidentally pushed past her. Maybe she would like to marry me also."

Jill laughed, swatted at him playfully and rested her head against his shoulder. "Did I tell you that I am officially a civilian consultant to the FBI?"

"Are you going to have to do this getting shot at thing more often?" His tone was lighthearted, but he needed an answer.

"Take me home, love. I'm all done." Jill whispered, thinking for a moment that if a person could be a home, he was hers. He had always been hers.

Chapter 42

Three and a half months had passed since the cruise. Jill stood on the deck at home, watching the construction crew haul shingles onto the roof. She smiled, rested her left hand on her ever growing belly. She now wore a wedding band to compliment the engagement ring; she had somehow survived the late September ceremony. They tried to keep the event small, but over two hundred came.

Lily kicked softly, making Jill wince even as she smiled. "Hungry, baby girl?" She wandered back into the kitchen, startled by a knock on the door. She yelled, "Come in!" She stood over the sink, scrubbing a pan from one of Chase's weekend visit baking adventures. She wiped her hands and turned, expecting to see an islander.

Agent Doug Riley stood in the breezeway connecting the garage to the main body of the house. He smiled and stepped in.

"Doug! Wow, this is unexpected." Jill hugged him and welcomed him into her home.

"Hi Jill. How are you doing?"

"Wonderfully. Lily is being good to me." She patted her growing belly.

"Lily?" Doug asked. "So, it is a girl?"

"Yes. We're actually not sure about the name.

We were too excited to wait. Come on in and sit down. Can I get you a cup of coffee or anything?"

"Sure, sounds good."

"You didn't drive here from Wisconsin, did you?" Jill asked.

"No, I flew in on a prop-jet to your local airport and then rented a car and drove here. The boat ride was really bumpy."

Jill glanced out the French doors in the living room and looked at the water and treetops. The water seemed modestly calm, but the trees told a different story. There was a decent wind coming from the northwest.

"Is it always this windy?"

"It's November," she offered as an explanation. "Sometimes we get a lot worse." A shiver ran down her spine, as she remembered the November night she was nearly beaten to death. "What brings you to my part of the world?"

"On the ship, do you remember when I told you I would help? With your mother, I mean."

Jill nodded. "Yes." She sat down on the couch, adjacent to his position on the chair. She handed him his cup and nestled back against the cushions with hers.

"Look at the magazine covers!" Doug exclaimed.

There was a selection of magazines--Newsweek, Time, and Forbes, as well as others, scattered across the coffee table. All of them featured photographs of Wayne Walker taken by Jill. "I know," Jill blushed. "My agent calls me daily with offers. Good Morning America invited me to come on air for an interview."

"No kidding?"

"Yes. I guess I might have a unique perspective, as an artist up close and personal to the candidate the week before he died. My work is getting some extra attention, because I am not a portrait photographer. Their saying I have a fresh perspective." Jill laughed softly.

"And the connection with your aunt, right?"

Jill nodded. In the time since the cruise, their link had become public knowledge. Walker had written about the connection in his notes from the week's events--now published.

"Are you taking jobs?"

"Not many of them, no. I don't feel like traveling yet. With the wedding, and the baby coming... I want to take some time off." She thought about her weekly therapy sessions, and the effort she went through to try to process and heal from the news that her parents were murdered, that she had been lied to throughout her life. Of course, she didn't mention this to Doug. He was here for another reason.

"It has taken me a long time to clear the cruise ship case. And then I got tangled up into another matter, but in my spare time, I have been looking for answers."

"About my mother?"

"Yes." Doug sipped his coffee. "Do you still want to know?"

"Please," Jill requested.

"I can confirm your suspicion that your mother

was assassinated. The FBI verified it years ago through the deposition of a witness tied to another case. It was classified, and my telling you this..."

"It's safe with me, Doug."

"Okay," he breathed deeply before continuing. "The plane was intentionally brought to the ground because of your mother's willingness to testify in the case against the shipping company she worked for." Doug continued, filling in details about the company and the plan. He explained that the nuclear material had eventually been recovered. The FBI believed they had found most of those individuals responsible for the crimes. When finished, he handed her a folder. "I don't even know if you want this, but I know that I would want it. Maybe not today, but someday, you might want to read what's in here."

"In a few months, I'm going to be a mother. No matter what is in that folder, I can't bring my parents back. And if you leave it here, I'm going to read it. I don't have the discipline not to. I'll see an angle, I'll do some research. I'll end up getting involved. But I made a promise to Lily, Doug. I have to stop living in the past. I think my parents would want me to get on with my life."

Jill accepted the folder but didn't open it. She sat in silence for a few seconds and then handed the folder back to Doug. "You keep it for me." Jill looked down at the rag rug under her feet, as if there were answers braided into the fabric. She tried again.

Doug let her sit quietly for a moment. "Okay." He tucked the folder next to him on the chair. He sipped his coffee. "I understand. And if you change your mind, the offer still stands."

"Thanks." Jill swallowed, ignored the pang in her chest that wanted so desperately to ask for the folder back. Sometimes doing the right thing doesn't always seem like the right thing, she thought.

"The Deputy Director of the FBI called me to Washington for a meeting a few weeks after the cruise. He explained that Debi was an undercover agent. He doesn't know how or why Scott Grafton died, but he doesn't believe Debi killed him intentionally. That might be a mystery we'll never solve. I do know that Grafton was on the ship to take down the candidate."

"And the housekeeper?"

"Her name is Jude Bristall. According to our sources, she was working as an independent contractor hired by a faction within Korea. We can't prove whether or not it was a government sanctioned hit. At least, I can't prove that, and I haven't been told." Doug finished his coffee.

"You know, Walker told me that he believed we were connected by fate... that somehow, I could save him. That's why he offered me the job," Jill said. She had already explained the connection between her aunt and the candidate to Doug some time ago. "I can't decide whether or not I failed fate, or if my aunt did."

"I think that everything happens for a reason. It's possible that some master plan dictates that Walker was supposed to die in the time that he did. But why were you brought onto the ship?"

"Was I supposed to die in the plane crash?" Jill questioned.

"I don't believe that for a moment. Think about the life you're carrying," Doug pointed out.

"What if I failed to save him, and thus save the world? He really believed he could do it." Jill relaxed suddenly. "You know Doug, I have no idea why my aunt saved his life, or ultimately why I was brought onto the ship. But I can tell you this..."

She perched forward, meeting his eyes. "About two years ago, I was assaulted. Before my uncle came to visit, I lived in fear. I locked down doors and windows every night, I was dependent on frequent therapy sessions--I was a mess. I was not at all the picture of an extraordinary woman, like so many women before me in my family. Since the cruise, I have realized that I don't need to be involved in all this drama to be okay. Quinn and I are going to have a baby. Whatever else has happened, from my mother's death to Walker's, I know I can trust who I am. I am going to be a good mother. I don't need to save the world."

"You sound like you're trying to convince yourself of that."

Jill leaned back, nodded slowly. "You might be right."

"You'll figure it out, Jill. And in the meantime, I have no doubt that you'll be an excellent mother."

"Thank you, Doug."

"I hate to drop all this and leave, but I need to go. I am flying from Kincheloe tonight."

Jill understood, walked him to the door. "Thank you. I appreciate you coming here."

"You're welcome. Thanks for your help on the case. I couldn't have done it without you." Doug climbed into his rental car and drove off, leaving Jill to muddle through her thoughts in silence.

Epilogue

She watched Doug's car round the curve in the road and leave her sight. No longer in the mood to wash dishes, she took a few moments to walk out to the rocky shore, camera in hand. Her body knew the way to her rock without having to think about it. She sat down, pulled the band from her hair and allowed it to blow in the wind. She recalled Uncle Dave's explanation that she came from a line of extraordinary women. A few years ago, she would have loved that history and now, the only thing she could think about was home, Quinn, and the baby. Perhaps, her grandmother had been right to keep the story from her. Knowing the truth made her want to dive under the thick down-filled duvet in the bedroom and hide, something she had been doing more or less since the assault.

She looked out at the November sky, pulled her sweater closer around her shoulders. Jill allowed herself to go back in her mind, to re-live another moment. Years before, after she had just moved to Drummond Island, she had stood on the beach with Joe. She remembered first connecting to the water, first realizing how strongly she was pulled to that place and knowing that, ultimately, everything was going to be okay.

I don't have to be afraid anymore, she thought. She wasn't going to hide from life, because it had not waited for her. Children were growing, friends were aging. She spent too much time grieving for herself, her family, and loved ones who passed along the way. It was time to move on.

There was opportunity within her, growing more quickly than she understood. Her grandmother wasn't right. I should have been allowed to know the truth, she thought. But she wasn't wrong either. Knowing the truth about her parents today was different than learning the truth years before. She might have come from extraordinary women, but her mother--both of her parents--had died for it. Jill placed her hands over her belly rubbing it gently.

Finally, she said, "Baby, you are safe in me. If I am extraordinary, if this is something passed down... then I will be this woman in my effort to give you love and peace until you are old enough to make decisions for yourself. I will tell you the stories of your ancestors, your grandmother, and those that came before us."

She looked out into the lapping waves of Huron, squinting into the distance. A tall ship, a schooner, she decided, sailed across the waves. Jill picked up her camera and zoomed in to look at the ship more closely. It looked old, haunting almost. Across the hull, the word Alice loomed large as life across the wood. The figure of a woman, barely recognizable, leaned out and waved. Alarmed, Jill lowered the camera quickly. She blinked, but the ship was gone, vanished like a ghost into the blurry horizon.

Jill breathed in the northern air and smiled wistfully when the baby kicked inside her. Without hesitation, Jill knew her daughter's name. "Rest, Angelique. You'll need your strength for this life."

Author's Notes

In August 2005, I (James) traveled to all the National Parks and other locations visited by the *New America*'s cruise. One of these locations, Miner's Castle at Picture Rock National Lake Shore is pictured on the lower right corner of the front cover. In the picture there are two turrets at the top of the rock formation. On April 13th, 2006 the turret to the right fell into Lake Superior. After some consideration, we decided to leave the cover artwork developed as it was at that time, reflecting the original look of the formation.

As in all of our novels, we again used real life to craft the story formation of this book. For example, the 1987 plane crash, including the story about the Miracle girl, was inspired by what truly happened. In the book, details have been changed for the nature of story-telling. We have been told that the original Miracle girl is alive and well.

The 1949 Noronic story is also based on the true event. We used details like the small row boat and acts of heroism that really took place to tell the story of our character's experience.

Similarly, our deep historical connection, the 1828 story about the British leaving Drummond and the Schooner Alice Hackett also closely reflect history for that time. Mrs. Francoise (Angelique) Lepine and her daughter Therise are real individuals. Relations to these two women still live in and around Penetanguishene, Ontario to this day. There are parts of this story that the authors had to fabricate for there isn't documented written history to cover many of the smaller details. The Alice Hackett, for example, did hit a shoal off of what is currently known as Fitzwilliam's Island (located off of the south east corner of the Manitoulin Island). After the men reached their state of reported drunkenness, Angelique and her daughter were somehow abandoned on the schooner. To survive a storm, they tied themselves to the mast. It is written in The Migration of Voyageurs from Drummond Island to Penetanguishene in 1828 by A.C. Osborne that when Angelique's husband woke from his drunkenness and saw his wife tied to the mast, he believed she had died.

Some historians who have studied the British history of Drummond will tell you that there is no history of the Alice Hackett. This was the same standpoint that the Ontario government took. They referred to the story of the Alice Hackett as folklore.

However, in Osborne's writings, he reflected that three different people wrote of the Alice Hackett and all three said it shoaled off of Horse Island. The Ontario government said there was no Horse Island in the area. Through research we found that at one time Fitzwilliam's Island was once called Horse Island and to many locals, it is still called by that name. They then told us that the Alice or Alice Hackett didn't exist. There was no record with the British that there ever was such a ship. We wrote to Bowling Green State University, Historical Collections of the Great Lakes, and soon discovered proof of it's existence. The Alice Hackett (a real schooner of the fifty foot class) was owned by Captain James Hackett, and built on the Detroit River. We found two dive masters in Tobermory, Ontario, one of which is Patrick Folks, author of books on Diving and shipwrecks that confirmed finding the Alice Hackett. The schooner is exactly where those in Osborne's writings say it should be.

Furthermore, in "Reports on the 1992 and 1994 Excavations at the Fort Drummond Site 20CH50 Drummond Island Michigan" by Paul A. Demers (Department of Anthropology, MSU), it states that two ships came to Fort Drummond. The brig Duke of Wellington and the schooner Cincenata were chartered to remove the garrison on or before November 14th, 1828. These two ships were the last to visit Fort Drummond under British rule and they removed the garrison. Before this date, in the fall of that same year, it is believed that several ships visited Fort Drummond and transported some of the residents and their belongings.

Mrs. Lepine's heroic story lives on thanks to Mr. Osborne recording the stories of those voyagers. Some may claim that the collection of these facts is not proof enough. In an e-mail from personnel within the Ontario government, they agreed that the story will no longer be considered folklore. Without a living eye witness or an official government document to support these findings, the truth will always be in question.

References

1,000 Places To See Before You Die by Patricia Schultz

National Geographic Guide to America's Outdoors Great Lakes

Lake Superior: The Ultimate Guide to the Region by Hugh E. Bishop

Scrapbook of Emma Johnson and her trip aboard the Noronic

Original copies of the Northern Navigator and other items put out by the Canada Steamship Lines Limited.

The Soo Locks Vistor's Guide

Drummond Island by S.F. Cook

Drummond Island, Michigan by Ray M. Belden

A Wampum Denied Procter's War of 1812 by Sandy Antal

The Visual Dictionary of Ships and Sailing

Scene of the Crime by Anne Wingate Ph.D

"Report on the 1992 and 1994 Excavations at the Fort Drummond Site (20CH50)

Drummond Island Michigan" prepared by Paul A. Demers, Department of Anthropology, Michigan State University.

Ontario Historical Society papers and Records Vol. 3, Published in Toronto in 1901 Pages 123-166.

The Migration of Voyageurs from Drummond Island to Penetanguishene in 1828 by A.C. Osborne

Newspaper Articles from Detroit Free Press and the Detroit News (August 17th, 1987 and dates immediately following)